Polito, Rick,author.
Attraction :house of illusion

2021
33305249367206
ca 01/13/22

THE ATTRACTION:
HOUSE OF ILLUSION

RICK POLITO

WISE WOLF BOOKS
An Imprint of Wolfpack Publishing
wisewolfbooks.com

THE ATTRACTION: HOUSE OF ILLUSION. Copyright © 2021
by Rick Polito
All rights reserved.
This is a work of fiction. All of the characters, organizations, publications, and events portrayed in this novel are either products of the author's imagination or are used fictitiously.

Cover design by Wise Wolf Books

ISBN 978-1-953944-16-0 (paperback)
ISBN 978-1-953944-15-3 (ebook)
LCCN: 2021943098

First Edition: November 2021

To my offspring, Gianni and Finn, especially Finn for being the best "subject matter expert" ever and helping me keep this book grounded in the 2020s.

THE ATTRACTION: HOUSE OF *ILL*USION

1

WAKING UP AND TRIPPING OVER YOUR ALREADY-PACKED suitcase that you didn't pack and that you instantly know your mom put outside your door is no way to start a Saturday—or really any day when you didn't know you were going on a trip and have basically zero idea what's going on. This is especially true if that Saturday comes not even a full week into summer break, and you were out until 2 a.m., and the only reason you know your bag is packed but you didn't know to step over it is that you got up to take a piss and the extent of your morning agenda was to go back to sleep.

And when you see your sister's suitcase also packed and also knocked over outside her door, you know something is up, and you have a strong suspicion that the something in question is going to suck because you didn't want to be up at all, not at 7:30 A-*freaking*-M when your day wasn't even supposed to start until 11:00 or so because, you know, summer.

But there I was, standing in the hall right outside the shambles of my bedroom, rubbing my eyes and looking over at Lily's suitcase, also packed and also knocked over outside her door, which suggested I was not the only one to stumble into Saturday with what I was guessing was an equal state of confusion and concern—alarm, even. That assumption was confirmed almost immediately when I heard Lily talking to Mom in the kitchen in the very urgent tone of a very upset eleven-year-old. I debated, for a few seconds, whether I really needed to join this discussion. I had an idea that lasted even less than a few seconds that I could just crawl back into bed, pull the sheets over my head, and go back to sleep and that my suitcase would be back in the garage where it belonged when I got up for real a few hours later.

If Lily hadn't sounded so upset, I might have committed myself to at least the back-in-bed part. I could have convinced myself that although my suitcase would probably still be there when I got up, I could deal with it in a more-rested and less-cranky state. Instead, I decided I would take the previously mentioned piss first and then see what was going on. I even took a moment in the bathroom to glance at my only slightly hungover face and run my fingers through my hair in the mirror before walking down the hall to the kitchen, past Mom's home office, "the supervillain's lair". We called it that because of the six —*who needs six?*—computer monitors she had splayed across one of those folding plastic tables in what should have been the dining room. Mom's job was companies paying her to find out who hacked them, but the array of monitors and servers always made me wonder if Mom was leading some hacker army of her own.

I heard at least three "but Mom!" squeals from Lily before I got to the kitchen, with "Mom" stretched into three syllables each time. Mom was on one side of the kitchen island and Lily was on the other, practically climbing over the butcher block as she pleaded to stop an impending departure I had known nothing about two minutes before.

"Mah-ahm," she said, down to two syllables now. "I had a whole summer planned out, and now what am I supposed to do?"

I was instantly awake—real awake, not the half-assed awake I'd achieved trudging down the hall. The last dreamy veil of sleep evaporated as my bleary consciousness was instantly scorched with the searing light of a thousand suns. "Whole summer" implied something more than a spontaneous weekend trip. "Whole summer" didn't have to mean the *whole* summer, but it meant some sizeable chunk. And from what I caught of Lily's tone, that chunk wasn't going to be spent anywhere remotely cool. She confirmed that panic with her next words. "We don't even know Uncle Kevin. We've seen him, like, three times since Grandma died. It's like he's not even family."

Lily was pounding on the butcher block now, both fists. "And now we're supposed to live with him?"

Okay, so those one thousand suns were just a warm-up. The words *whole summer* and *live with* stopped my heart—or at least my breathing. The summer they were talking about—the one that had barely started—was the summer between junior and senior year. The last real summer of high school. It was also the summer that I'd begged my way into a job at the Golden Gate Racquet Club and thus the summer when I was going to see both Olivia Blum and Ashley Caldwell every day—or almost every day, and maybe in swimsuits because the snack bar faced the pool. That made it the summer when at least one of them might succumb to whatever plan I came up with to convince them they were in love with me or at least liked me enough to go to the movies or something.

My life wasn't flashing before my eyes, but my summer was, all of this going through my head in what was probably five seconds but could have been even shorter because Lily was still in the first deep breath of a stare-down with Mom.

And Mom was having none of it. It's not like eleven-year-olds win arguments with their parents, especially not when said parent is the mom and, worse than that, a single mom. Single moms have superpowers of sheer will, and ours employed that will with great frequency and window-rattling volume.

"Look, Lily," she said, "I don't know where you got the idea that you're in charge because you're not. I make decisions. It's a mom thing. This is what's going to happen. And it's going to happen today."

I was still a spectator at that point, standing completely still between the refrigerator and the chalkboard like I was a wildlife photographer watching a mama bear teach her cub about the concept of whoop-ass, but then both of them turned toward me in slow motion, almost like they'd choreographed it.

And they paused for a second, allowing me to say what was the totally obvious thing to say, which was, "What's going on?"

Lily didn't wait for Mom. "We're going to Uncle Kevin's for the summer. That's what's going on. Mom is going to dump us off in the middle of nowhere, in a swamp, and we're just supposed to deal with it."

She wasn't snarling at me, but she was snarling. "This is so unfair!" she screamed, shoving on the counter so hard the floor creaked under her slippered feet, as though she was going to push this thing that was bolted to the floor into the next room.

I didn't know what to say except what I'd already said, but I said it again, this time addressed to Mom and in a kind of casual-polite tone so that I could sound like the reasonable one compared to Lily's gnashing teeth growl. I thought I'd try the good cop/bad cop routine, only it was more like *good cop/rabid badger with a flamethrower*.

"Mom," I said, "what's going on?"

Mom looked simultaneously relieved that she could turn away from Lily for a moment and also like she was tensing up because she knew she had to tell a whole new person something that she was fully aware this new person did not want to hear. "Something has come up," she said. "Grown-up stuff. I wish I could tell you more, but I can't. I just need some time to figure things out."

Two things here:

First, "grown-up stuff" sounded like bullshit to me in a different way than it probably sounded to Lily because, at sixteen, I was not all that far from being a grown-up for real. I was about to start a job that was more or less full time, and I was supposed to finally get my driver's license in the next week, if Mom could break away from defending the internet long enough to get me to the DMV. I was apparently grown-up enough to take care of Lily a lot more than I wanted to, like cooking her dinner, and getting her up for school, and basically being the live-in nanny and after-school care Mom was too cheapskate to afford.

Second, "I just need some time to figure things out" is breakup code talk, the kind of thing a girl says to you when she dumps you and doesn't want to tell you it's your fault even though she totally thinks it's your fault. I didn't think Mom was breaking up with us—because that's weird—but I did think, in that moment, that we'd done something wrong.

Except that didn't make any sense either. Lily was way too young to get in real trouble, though I knew she had incredible potential, and I hadn't gotten into any serious trouble either, at least not any that Mom knew about. I was several minutes past that tripping over a suitcase, and it still felt like I was stumbling, except I was stumbling into some gaping abyss of suck instead of the not-gray/not-brown carpeting that seemed to be standard issue in every apartment we'd ever lived in.

"What does 'grown-up stuff' mean?" I asked. I knew I was pleading a case that the judge had already ruled on, but that didn't keep me from pleading it. "Are we on the run?" I asked. "Are the cops after us? Did you double-cross the mob? Really, Mom, what the fuck?"

I'd been test-driving the *F*-word around Mom a bit in prior weeks and had gotten consistent correction, but she had bigger fish to smack me in the head with in that moment. "Listen, Nathan," she said, "I told you that it's not something I can explain to you right now. We're not on the run, but I'd feel better right if you were at your Uncle Kevin's, just for a while, just to be on the safe side."

"On the safe side of what?"

"On the safe side of me, if you don't back the hell down right now!"

Like I said, superpowers. I shut up and stepped back.

"Just a while?" I said.

"Just a while," she answered. "I promise."

I'm sure all of that sounds as dramatic as hell—and it was—but it also wasn't completely unusual around our house either. Mom lived on a crisis-to-crisis schedule, like clockwork if the clock had been dropped out of the window eight times too many. She had some overcooked X-ray vision for perceived threats, lurching from one "I've got a bad feeling about this" hunch to the next. Half of the time—way more than half—it was stuff that Lily and I could roll our eyes at as soon as Mom left the room, but we also knew we had to take some of it dead-on serious. We were California kids, raised on earthquakes and apocalyptic wildfires, programmed from early on to greet just about any calamity with something between a shrug and grim determination. It could be raining frogs and zombies—zombie frogs—and we'd find a way to deal with it.

And that was without Mom lurching us down the one-thing-after-another highway. We'd moved out of apartments in the middle of the night more than once. It's not like I'd turned my school backpack into a bug-out bag, but I kept a few things in there, like the last photo I had of me and Dad, just in case we were suddenly throwing suitcases into the car, bound for destinations unknown. It had happened before, once because some guy Mom had been dating wanted to keep seeing her past his expiration date, another time after somebody she'd worked with turned kinda scary when she called him out for sneaking around with another start-up. But other times we never really got an explanation. She played the "grown-up stuff" card.

That backpack was tucked between my knees in the front seat of the Subaru roughly one shower and four frozen waffles after I'd limped away from that kitchen showdown. Lily was in the back seat with her phone four inches from the tip of her nose. Mom was driving. I hadn't bothered to ask if I could drive, learner's permit or not. I don't think she believed I was going to U-turn us back to the apartment at the first intersection or drive somewhere other than the shithole town Uncle Kevin lived in, the town Mom had been smart enough to flee when she had finished high school, but Mom was the captain on this voyage and she wanted us to know that. There was no way I would be allowed anywhere near the helm.

Here's the thing: we were not given a choice, but Kevin wouldn't have been our first choice no matter what the circumstance. He was all the family we had here on the West Coast but still a precarious branch on the family tree. Of course, it's not like Mom had planned this trip weeks before or even hours before. My suitcase hadn't been there when I'd gone to bed. It's not like she'd been getting us excited with brochures from the Owl Harbor House of Illusion, the spooky roadside attraction that Uncle Kevin opted to keep going after Grandma, "the Mistress of Illusion" had died.

Lily had already pointed out that we knew almost nothing about him and not just because we didn't see him a whole lot. Mom almost never talked about him, and when she did, every mention came with a heavy sigh. I didn't know if it was because of something he'd done or something she'd done, but it often seemed like she felt guilty about it either way. Mom and Uncle Kevin had grown up on the Sacramento River Delta in a shithole town 50 miles up from the Golden Gate. He still lived on the other side of the fence from their high school. She couldn't get away fast enough.

And she'd been getting away ever since, one

broken lease at a time. I always got the impression that among her chief goals in life was that we wouldn't turn out like Uncle Kevin, like he was the family curse she prayed would skip a generation. Now she was going to leave us with him and all his eccentric and isolated splendor.

I waited till we were on the freeway before I attempted to reopen the discussion. I hadn't called the Racquet Club because I was still hoping that she would come to her senses and we'd be heading back to Kentfield before we even got to Owl Harbor.

"Are you sure about this, Mom?" I spoke as though Lily was too intent on her phone to pay attention to important grown-up conversations, even though I knew she was diagramming every word and phrase. "You can't just drag us out of the house like that, drag us out of our summer," I said. "You've got to tell us what's going on. I'm old enough to deal, whatever it is. You haven't even told us how long we're going to be there."

She tapped her thumbs on the steering wheel as though she wanted to impose some cadence on the conversation and slow things down. "I need to spend some time checking things out," she said. "It's complicated, but we can get through this. We always do."

I think she knew she hadn't really told us anything with that, but it's not like she had that realization and suddenly veered back in the direction of full disclosure. "I get feelings about things—things and people—and I've got a bad feeling right now," she said.

"We're going into hiding because you had a bad feeling about something?" I said. "I've got a bad feeling about your judgment if that's the way this is going down."

She tapped on the steering wheel again—but faster and more manic.

"It's called intuition, and mine is stronger than other people's. It's like a special ability. I've always had it. It's taken care of us this far."

I thought about telling her that I didn't always feel taken care of and that I'd like to spend more than one Christmas in the same apartment and spend a little less time raising my little sister. I wanted to tell her I was sick of worrying about where the next bad feeling would take us. I tried one more thing.

"Are you sure Uncle Kevin's is on the safe side of whatever it is your bad feeling is about?"

"No," she said. "But I hope he is."

She stopped tapping the steering wheel. I took it as a sign our little interview was over and that I was supposed to enjoy the scenery. I picked up my phone instead.

"I'm going to need you to leave that in the car when we get there," she said. "I don't want the whole world to know where you are."

I could feel Lily stiffen in the back seat. I didn't want to lose my phone, but I knew Lily would rather amputate a limb than give up hers.

"This just keeps getting better," I said.

"That's the plan," Mom said. "To make things get better."

I didn't want to give her the pleasure of seeing me throw a Lily-sized fit over my phone. I didn't want her to know that she'd taken another important thing from me, in addition to my summer. So I stared out the window with that obvious intention, tuning out her and the whole nightmare for a while.

2

It was two hours to Owl Harbor by car, most of a century by cultural whiplash.

This was a land of country roads and pickup trucks. Most of the billboards were for churches, and most of the bumper stickers were for country stations. A few days into a summer that I'd thought was about to ramp up to awesomeness when my job started at the Racquet Club was about to lurch into some kind of deep-south time warp on the Sacramento River Delta, the closest thing California has to a swamp. I wasn't going to be working the snack bar by the pool. I was going to be gutting catfish or whatever Huckleberry Finn shit my uncle would have us doing.

Most of the fog had burned off by the time we reached the exit that would take us to the upper Delta towns, and the sun was blazing across the last hills we'd see before the flat marsh/rice paddy *bleh* of the Delta. We were rolling into farm country—

and not the kind of farm country from postcards with red barns and smiling cows but the kind that's all rusted metal buildings and sagging fences separating weeds from more weeds. As we drove through one shitty town after another, liquor stores roughly even with churches in most of them, I could see Mom tensing up, and I knew that she was driving into a past and a childhood she didn't recall with happy thoughts. Driving across the causeway to Owl Harbor, I gazed out on a tangle of small waterways and scrubby sandbars wilting in a steamy haze.

We arrived to a rare morning of calm air, and the tatters hung limp on a billboard announcing *The House of Illusion*. The wind that carried the fog inland was incessant on the Delta, the only thing that kept the area from going full Mississippi, but there was barely a breath of it when we pulled into the gravel parking lot, stopping beneath the water tank mural of Professor Mysterio.

Mom had called from the car and gotten the House of Illusion answering machine. Yes! Some people still have answering machines! But when we got out of the car, we could see the *Closed* sign on the gift shop door. A farmhouse that backed up to the crumbling facade of Owl Harbor's most famous—really *only*—attraction was where we were likely to find Uncle Kevin, sorting either comic books or ammo for all Lily and I knew.

Mom stopped us before we could get out of the car. "Your phones," she said in this really dramatic way, and she triggered the power locks for emphasis.

She pulled a black bag out of the little compartment between the seats. "I need your phones."

Lily looked like she was going to faint, like she'd seen a ghost and the ghost had pictures of her at a Dora the Explorer party and was going to post them on the school Instagram account. "Really?" she said. "You were serious?" Her voice full-on trembled.

"This is a Faraday bag," Mom said, as if we cared what kind of bag it was, but then she explained. "It blocks all radio signals. I don't want anybody to be able to track where you are."

That kind of thing was actually pretty close to Mom's expertise. She was a cyber forensics expert. When companies got hacked, they called people like my mom to figure out how they were hacked and who did the hacking. So she knew all kinds of super-tech secret agent stuff like that.

But she should also have known this was not going to go over well with either of us. I didn't have the phone superglued to my hand 24/7 the way Lily did, but the phone still felt like a last link to civilization. I was not eager to surrender that link. "Just give us the bag, then, and we'll only take the phones out when we use them," I said, attempting to squeeze out a little more of the "I'm the reasonable one" act I'd been shooting for—and missing—all morning.

It wasn't working.

"Every time you turn on that phone it sends out a little ping, and all it takes is one ping for somebody to find you. Give me your phones. There's a landline in Uncle Kevin's house that you can use when you need something."

I held Mom's gaze as I dropped my phone into the bag. Lily's hand shook, and she wouldn't let go. Mom finally pried her fingers back. When she had both phones in the bag, she tucked it under her seat. "Don't worry," she said. "I will bring them back. I will reestablish your connection to the universe."

We got out of the car in silent protest—or at least in silent sulking.

A path in white gravel snaked past some drooping willow trees, leading from the House of Illusion to the farmhouse that Mom grew up in and where Uncle Kevin lived his lonely and, let's face it, creepy existence. Lily stayed behind Mom, more shook up than angry at that moment, though I was sure she'd be sharing the anger part at some point. Lily could be damn fearless most of the time, but this was clearly not a "most of the time" moment. The unknown was running up to slap us in the face, and we couldn't know how hard that slap was going to be. I walked a few steps ahead of them, convincing myself that it might look more normal to Lily if her big brother wasn't cowering behind his mom.

I got to the porch first. The wood on the steps felt more spongey than solid, and the doorbell wires hung out from the door frame. I knocked instead, and Uncle Kevin was at the door before the last knock faded into the tropical steam, pushing aside a curtain that had once been tie-dye but had faded into a shroud-of-doom kind of thing.

"Rachel," he said to Mom, giving Lily and me a quick up and down in that "oh my, look how you've grown" way that's pretty annoying when you're a kid, before turning back to Mom and saying, "I got your call," throwing in a smile so forced it looked like it hurt.

I noticed Mom's shoulders tighten. Mom talked about him so little that I had to think for a minute to remember that he was her older brother. Mom stiffening up might have meant she felt bad about dropping us off without notice, or it could have meant she thought he was going to slit our throats and bury us in the yard. He didn't really look like the throat-slitting type, but he didn't look like he was used to having house guests either—or, really, any guests. When he said, "I apologize I don't have the guest wing all spruced up just yet," I wasn't sure at first if he was joking. When he punctuated it with a grin that came no more naturally than the smile, it felt more cringey than funny.

And creepy too.

"I've got coffee," he said as we stepped past him. "These kids drink coffee?"

It was kind of a weird thing to say. I'd assumed Lily's prime coffee-drinking days were still ahead of her. It sure as hell wasn't the kind of question an ordinary person would ask ordinary kids, but Uncle Kevin didn't have kids, and the only thing I could think right then was that if he did, they wouldn't be ordinary. It wasn't a kid kind of house either.

The farmhouse was probably a century old, at least, and it seemed obvious it had never been a prosperous farm. The rooms were small, and it would have felt like tight quarters in the living room even before Uncle Kevin had crammed it with bookcases.

Every shelf was so thick with dust that I couldn't make out the titles, but it looked like an odd mix of science textbooks, books about the Gold Rush, and books on the history of the occult.

We had to weave our way through to get to the kitchen and a whole different kind of clutter. The windowsills and nearly all the counters were packed with small bottles, a bit bigger than the ones they use to sell liquor on airplanes, most of them made out of that blue glass I always imagined old-timey pharmacists would use. I pictured Uncle Kevin scrounging the banks of the Delta for the glint of glass and building his collection one bottle at a time, but each bottle still had a cap, which didn't make sense. Most people don't put the caps back on bottles when they throw them away, and I assumed that had been true back in whatever era these bottles had been used and discarded.

A small, folded strip of paper floated in each one, not a message in a bottle but dozens of messages in dozens of bottles, except you couldn't really read them.

By the time we'd threaded through the piles of books to discover this weird collection, Uncle Kevin had become more animated, as though his view had been reeled in from that one thousand-yard focus he'd blinked through at the door. "I apologize for the clutter," he said. "Nobody comes back here. I may play host to the mysteries of the universe at the attraction, but I'm a full-time hermit back here."

He was right. I'd never been past the front porch any of the three or four times Mom had deigned to stop by since Grandma had died. Lily and I had seen about half of the illusion house—not the good stuff—and only once before Mom had dragged us back to the car. We'd never gotten Uncle Kevin's narrated tour. We'd bugged Mom about it a bunch of times, and the best answers we'd gotten were "That stuff creeps me out" and "Maybe when you're older".

Motioning for us to sit down at the kitchen table, home to only a half dozen bottles with a half dozen messages, Uncle Kevin looked more distracted than creepy. To us, Uncle Kevin had an ageless quality: his hair the same tumble of gray and brown he'd always had, and it matched the plastic-framed glasses that he always wore. He wore the same black shirt and black pants as though he never stopped giving his illusion-house tours. Uncle Kevin was only a year or two up on Mom, but she looked a lot younger. I guess staring at a screen nine to five is easier on the skin than the brackish wind of the Delta.

But she looked more weary, more worried.

Uncle Kevin put a kettle on the stove before he sat down, and the low hush of the flame was the only noise when he looked up to Mom. "So," he said, "what's all this about?"

I gave up my good cop act for a moment and said, "That's what we want to know," which earned me a squinting glance from Mom, who set her elbows on the tabletop, toying with one of the bottles and watching the unreadable message swirl around. She let the bottle go, and it rocked on its base for a second before she spoke.

"There are people—maybe just a person—and

they're getting close," she said. "I think it's going to be bad." She stopped and gave the bottle another wobble. "I've got a sense of it," she said. "Like Mother could get."

Uncle Kevin nodded, like that made sense, instead of asking the obvious question which was "What the hell is that supposed to mean?" The nodding did slow for an instant when she mentioned Grandma, and I noticed the way he pursed his lips. I looked from Uncle Kevin to Mom and back to Uncle Kevin, trying to figure out if they were occupying the same hallucination or whether he'd decided that arguing about her magical intuition was counterproductive. Or whether they'd attended the same webinar on "Spooky Shit to Mess with Your Kid's Head".

I scooted my chair across the wood floor, and bottles all over the room rattled. I didn't plan it, but it provided some dramatic punctuation to the scene. I could tell it broke Mom and Uncle Kevin out of their secret-code mind link because they both looked at me.

"This is bullshit," I said, glaring at Mom. "You can't take away our summer based on one of your hunches. You can't dump us out here because you're all *yikes* about something or somebody."

She turned away, and then she did something that was really weird. She looked at Uncle Kevin in this helpless way, maybe even scared, like he was supposed to come to her aid or maybe referee the confrontation, call a foul or something. He didn't look eager for either role, but he leaned forward slightly in his chair as though he was steadying himself before he began.

"Nathan—and you too, Lily—you both need to listen to your mom. She sees things that we can't always comprehend, not just grown-up stuff that she can't talk about. It's more than that. It's an essential part of who she is," he said, pausing. "A gift."

He sounded solemn, like he was borrowing parts of his speech from his House of Illusion script. It seemed to be working on Lily though. Lily could be epically strong willed, but when you're eleven, there are times when you know you are beat before you even start. She was probably looking for something that would explain the situation, to make it make sense, and Uncle Kevin's spooky narration was the only option available.

It wasn't working on me.

"Gift?" I said. "More like a curse. This isn't a house of illusion. This is the real world, with real people, and two of those real people are me and Lily. We're not giving up our summer for this mumbo-jumbo nonsense."

I was standing up at this point. I noticed I was holding one of the blue bottles tight enough that my knuckles were white and the raised *10 OZ* imprint on the glass was pressing into the palm of my hand. I was ready to throw it against the wall, actually pulling my shoulder back for the shattering pitch. But I stopped when I saw the way Lily was looking up at me.

She was scared. Shaken. And I wasn't making it better.

I could keep yelling and call down some epic rage, a dramatic oratory on the injustice of the universe, but part of me knew that wasn't going to change anything. Mom may or may not have had a "gift" or some secret psychic power, but I remembered the superpower she did have. She was a single mom. She was the unstoppable force and the immovable object all in one.

We were not going to get into the car and drive home.

We were staying in Owl Harbor.

In the shadow of a House of Illusion.

3

The lead-up to goodbye was that mix of sullen grimace and averted eyes that you know you're going to remember way better than some magic holiday memory or the birthday party your mom got just right. Stuff that sucks stands out that way. That's basic human nature shit.

Mom sent us out to get our suitcases, and I carried Lily's in because I felt bad for her. It was pretty clear that Mom wanted us out of the room while she talked to Uncle Kevin, and I knew it would be impossible to sneak back in and spy on them because that rickety wood house would creak if you breathed on it.

But whatever conversation they were having seemed dead-on serious. I could see them through the window leaning toward each other across the bottles on the table and whispering even though they were the only ones in the house.

"What do you think they're talking about,

Nathan?" Lily asked me. We were just short of the porch, and I put the suitcases down in the gravel.

"Not how to ruin our summer. They've already taken care of that," I said. I knew I wasn't exactly comforting Lily, but she wasn't the only one allowed to wallow in sulking misery. "Probably some haunted illusion house voodoo bullshit."

"I know," Lily said. "Did you see them back there? It was like we were in a movie, and we were about to find out our whole family is a Satanic cult."

"And you're the daughter of Satan."

"More like the sister of Satan," she said, yanking on my arm.

"Yes," I said in the spookiest voice I could come up with. "And we will rule the Central Valley with the full might of our demon legions. Everything from here to Modesto will be ours!"

We shared the collective shrug of the doomed.

"How long do think this is going to last?" she asked. "Being out here, I mean."

"Not long but longer than we want it to is my guess."

Lily furrowed her brow, which is almost kind of cute on a kid her age, I have to admit. She said, "You know how she gets, but I wish we knew why," and then changed her voice to something approaching Uncle Kevin's Professor Mysterio voice. "Perhaps the answer lies in the House of Illusion."

"I'll buy that," I said. "The illusion part."

Uncle Kevin had seen us peering in through the window and nodded to us in a "just a minute" way that suggested it was best if Mom didn't see us trying to spy on her. I put the suitcases on the porch, and Lily sat down next to them, her elbows on her knees and her chin in her hands, like a little porcelain figurine of preteen despair. I left her there and wandered back to the parking lot.

I was kind of surprised that Uncle Kevin hadn't opened the attraction yet. It was a Saturday, coming up on noon, and summer. It would seem like prime time for the roadside attraction biz. But it's not like there was much of a road to be on the side of. We were miles from a main highway. A sign by the pull-in said we don't open until two. I'm not sure how he came up with that, but it gave me a chance to poke around a bit, with Mom inside. Seriously, I was going to have the whole summer to poke around, but it felt like I was getting away with something if I did it while Mom was still there.

From the road—or, even better, from a little ways down the road—it looked almost like the House of Illusion was a real house, like a smaller version of some theme park haunted mansion, a haunted McMansion. Closer up, it was fake-ass plywood painted in gray and black, with sheets of plastic stapled to the wood to look like windows. Some of the doors were just doorknobs and a doorway outlined in strips of wood. The whole second floor was a facade, a row of windows and gables painted on. The flowers in the pots were fake too—plastic, faded and sunbaked brittle. I guess the main "illusion" of the House of Illusion was that it seemed like a real house, when really it was just a shack, with all the structural integrity of a kid's treehouse. It was locked up, but I knew that most of what was inside was that kind of distorted-room stuff where you know you're standing upright but you feel like you're leaning to the side. Bowling balls rolling "uphill", mirrors that make it look like you're staring down a long hall when it's actually just a closet, shit like that.

It sure as hell wasn't the Golden Gate Racquet Club, but I had a feeling it was going to be my summer job after all. Uncle Kevin probably already had a black suit and a freaky top hat for me. I was going to have to learn one of those horror movie scary laughs and hope nobody from school wandered through and outed me to the gang back home as a goth—and not even real goth: country goth, swamp goth, fucking 4-H-Club goth.

I leaned my forehead against one of the plastic-sheet windows and sighed. The summer I'd been looking forward to had turned out to be the actual illusion. I was ready to scream and throw a rock through the window, but I knew the window wasn't a real window and the rock was just going to bounce off and probably hit me in the eye because that'd be the perfect way to spend my shitty summer on the Delta: one eyed. Maybe the eye patch would go with the top hat.

"I wonder if the tour guides get tips," I said aloud because talking to myself seemed appropriate to the moment, but Mom's voice cut my monologue short.

"Nathan," she said, calling out from between the real house and the fake house, which Uncle Kevin always referred to as the attraction. "I'm getting ready to go," she said, a little louder because I hadn't answered.

I walked her way, not sure what I was going to say because, like, how are you supposed to say goodbye to somebody who is more or less abandoning you. I don't imagine prisoners high five the judge on their way to death row.

I rounded the corner to face the real house and saw that Lily had not left the steps where she was sitting. Her elbows were still on her knees; her chin was still on her hands. She was not going to reward Mom with a hug, and Mom didn't look interested in arguing for a hug because, let's face it, an argued hug is not a real hug.

I wasn't offering one either.

"So," I said, "you're off. Keep in touch. Tell civilization I said hi."

I included a steely gaze with my words. I had a tinge of guilt, but only a slight tinge. There are very few moments when a teenager is capable of feeling guilty, and that sure as hell wasn't one of them. Still, I was worried for Mom. Whatever circuit in her brain kept telling her the world was going to end and triggered the bug-out response, she was going to have to find the Off switch on her own. Me making her feel guilty wasn't going to help her with that.

But it's not like she was leaving guilt free. When she told me she'd call when she had news, I wouldn't look at her. I was scared for her, but I didn't like her much right then. I wasn't sure when I would again, to be honest.

Uncle Kevin stood on the porch just behind

where Lily simmered. She was still deep in pout—an epic pout, a pout for the ages. Lily was on the small side, almost waifish in her washed-out blonde hair, a bewildering contrast to Mom and me with our dark hair and brown eyes. But with the glare in her eyes blazing like a blue flame and her nostrils flaring with each breath, she looked formidable—fierce, even. I was on the gravel path about midway between porch and parking lot. We all stood there as the Subaru backed up and then pulled onto the highway. If Mom waved, I would have missed it. I was too busy staring at the ground while Lily's eyes burned down the world.

I heard the boards on the porch creak and turned around. Uncle Kevin had stepped forward and was even with where Lily sat. "Well then," he said, as though he were about to announce something important but he had no idea what that something was going to be, "I guess we need to figure things out. Let's start with where you kids are sleeping."

Lily sat up from her pose. "I have a different idea," she said. "Let's start with what's wrong with Mom."

Uncle Kevin reached up and scratched his chin, almost like he was auditioning for the part of the old codger in some low-budget Netflix mystery. "I don't know that I can answer that—not a quick answer anyway," he said. He was staring across the parking lot again. "I think both of you have a lot to learn about your mom. I think some of that you can learn right here, in Owl Harbor. There's some of her that's still here—a lot, I think."

He exhaled with one of those inflated-cheek

sighs. "Right now, I think we need to get you two situated. Then we can start thinking about making your time here count, make it matter. Let's go inside."

GETTING "SITUATED" was no easy feat. It's not like he could say, "You take this bedroom, and you take that bedroom, and you share this bathroom." It was more like, "There's a bed in there?" Really, it was hard to believe that Grandma and Grandpa could raise two kids—Mom and Uncle Kevin—in a house that was smaller than a lot of the crappy apartments we'd lived in. The floors creaked. The windows rattled. The rooms were packed with boxes and stuff. There were two bathrooms, but one of them was just a closet with a toilet in it, not even a sink. You had to wash your hands in the kitchen. The wallpaper wasn't peeling, but it was bubbling.

Lily got the room that had been Mom's when she was a girl. It was upstairs and looked out on the back of the attraction. I got a room that had obviously been a porch before somebody had put walls on it. The floor sloped toward the outer wall, which is good for porches so the rain doesn't puddle but kind of weird if it's a bedroom and you feel like you're going to roll out of your bed.

Uncle Kevin kept alternatingly apologizing—"I know it ain't the Taj Mahal"—and getting nostalgic—"Your mom used to hide in the back of that closet when she was in trouble"—and I started to get the idea that he welcomed the company, that we were going to make his summer special. I felt sorry for him in one way and pissed about the whole situation in another. All sympathy disappeared when I asked if he had Wi-Fi and simultaneously learned that was no computer and no cable and he wasn't sure if the old TV still worked but Grandma had left behind some *Murder, She Wrote* episodes on VHS.

We spent close to two hours getting the bedrooms cleared out, and there was now a big pile of boxes and crap covered in a tarp that took up more than half of the porch. Uncle Kevin brought up our suitcases and informed us there was "sandwich stuff" in the fridge and that he had to get the illusion house ready to open.

Lily ate Miracle Whip and cheese on white bread. I found some stale crackers. We split a peach that was about a week short of ripe. We looked at each other and shook our heads a few times, and that was pretty much the extent of our conversation until I tapped my thumb on the table and said, "I've got to get out of here."

"We're walking back?" she said with appropriate sarcasm and a half eye roll. "Should we bring some of these delicious sandwiches?"

"I didn't mean that," I said. "I mean I just need to go for a walk. Check out the local scene. Maybe there's an underground railroad for unfairly abandoned kids that will take us someplace cooler."

"Like pretty much anywhere?" Lily asked, the sigh implied.

"Yeah, like pretty much anywhere. You stay here. Dig through some of this shit and see if you can figure out what Mom and Uncle Kevin were nodding and winking about. Or maybe one of these magic books could magically get us the hell out of here."

"Got it," she said. "Careful out there. There could be pirates for all we know."

I WAS a bit surprised to see two cars in the parking lot when I stepped off the gravel pathway. Uncle Kevin had customers and was probably explaining the mysteries of Owl Harbor's gravitational vortex to his first victims of the day. One Range Rover and one Prius, they were already inside, but I was guessing snobby assholes who would be having a serious discussion about the demise of roadside Americana over pricey chardonnay back in Berkeley in a few hours. I didn't really know what kind of people were attracted to the House of Illusion, but I had some idea that nobody over the age of eight really showed up expecting a gateway to another dimension. I wasn't going to poke my head in to confirm my suspicions. I needed to get off the premises for a while, get a sense of where the hell we were.

I was not surprised to see that the wind had picked up. Wind was pretty much a constant on the Delta. Most people just put up with it, but some people came looking for it. It made for a weird mix of windsurfers zipping across the water, speedboats towing wakeboarders, and guys in aluminum boats with whiny motors looking for spots to fish and drink beer—mainly drink beer.

Owl Harbor wasn't a hot spot for either of the speedier lifestyle statements though; the waterways were too narrow for windsurfing and too choked with reeds for speedboats. Owl Harbor was better suited to aluminum boats and beer. Over the next few weeks, I'd see some birdwatcher types paddling through, but there wasn't a lot of reason for tourists to go to Owl Harbor unless they were interested in gravitational vortexes and, as I would later learn and memorize, spots where "the membrane between this universe and the next is particularly thin".

I decided I'd walk past the high school, which backed up to a ditch and a rusty fence that separated a scrubby playing field from our ancestral home. I'd seen a store past the school, and I imagined there might be a magazine or some other form of entertainment that would provide a break from plotting my revenge. Really, I just wanted to see what was around.

Gulf High was one of those schools that you know was reasonably sized at some point, back when there were more families living on farms, but you could see even from the outside that a lot of the school was closed off. It looked almost as old as the farmhouse, but in that courthouse style with stone columns and tall windows that attempted to say, *This is an important building; take this shit seriously, you little morons.*

The athletic field was similarly beat up, and there were only bleachers on one side. I guess the visiting team brought their own chairs. I was putting together a mental picture of Friday nights with pudgy cheerleaders and bucktoothed guys in pickup trucks sneaking beer into the game when I saw something that pushed all of that out of my head.

I mean, how often do you see a girl in running

shorts and a sports bra, standing in front of a canvas on an easel with a paintbrush in one hand and a smartphone in the other? She kept looking at whatever she had on the phone and then turning to the canvas with her paintbrush, alternately dabbing at it and then slashing at it. I couldn't see what she was painting. I was off to the side more than behind her. And I didn't think she could see me. So I watched this dab-and-stab process for more than a minute before she looked over her shoulder and shouted, "I don't usually paint for an audience."

"Who do you usually paint for?" I called back.

"Nobody in particular," she said. "Me, I guess. Probably not some guy who's doing a pretty half-ass job of sneaking up on me."

"Not sneaking. Just walking. Kind of hard to ignore a girl attacking a canvas. What did that painting ever do to you?"

"I don't know," she said. "You tell me."

She beckoned me over. It wasn't exactly a challenge, but she saw me hesitate and waved again in this totally *get the hell over here* way that I couldn't resist. And it's not like I was really trying to resist because it was the first time all day I'd been distracted from the yawning chasm of "oh shit!" that I'd been plummeting into since I'd tripped over my suitcase just a few hours before.

Plus, she was a girl, and I'd spent some part of those eight hours convincing myself that I would not be encountering a girl, who had all her teeth, until I was back in Kentfield, and that was a distant dream only in the moments when I could convince myself that I wasn't going to be trapped in a shithole Delta school in the fall learning to fix tractors and trying out for the goat wrestling team.

I walked over to the easel and saw what the slash and dab had wrought.

The canvas was thick with paint. I mean *thick.* I knew there was no way she'd laid that much paint on the canvas that day, or even several days. It was caked on so deep it was almost sculpture, big slabs of paint in varying depths of red, and I got the idea almost instantly that it wasn't like she was shopping for particular shades of red. She was buying whatever red they had, maybe what was on sale. And lots of it.

It wasn't even abstract in my limited sense of what "abstract" meant. It was more, I don't know, physical, visceral, as if the whole idea of the art was the act of creating it. I imagined her out on the field most Saturdays, hauling her easel and canvas out of the beat-up Ford hatchback I'd seen in the parking lot, attacking the canvas and painting over whatever layers she'd slabbed on the week before.

She stood back so I could get a good look.

"Well?" she said.

I turned away from the painting slowly and faced her for the first time. She'd worked up a sweat, which wouldn't have taken much with the sun drawing the humidity out of the shallows the way it was. She had her hair pulled back, with a ponytail tight and high to keep her hair off her neck. I don't know what I expected, but I didn't expect green eyes and an olive-skinned complexion that suggested mixed ethnicity, something confirmed in the hint of a Latina accent.

Girls who paint like they're daring you to misinterpret their intention are supposed to be deathly pale and wear clunky black frames that are too big for their tiny faces. And they're supposed to wear oversized men's shirts and yoga pants. Or maybe they could have multiple piercings, a severe haircut, and never leave the house without a black tank top.

And here was this girl who looked like she'd just finished running soccer drills, holding her paintbrush like she was ready to stab an enemy with it.

"It's..." I said. I paused because it seemed like a moment to pause, not because I hadn't figured out what to say. It just needed to sound pause worthy. "It's heavy."

She dropped her chin maybe a half inch toward her left shoulder before she blinked and brought her gaze back from the canvas. "That's the truest thing you could have said," she told me. "It's many coats and many Saturdays' worth of heavy at this point. Gallons and gallons, days and days. '*Heavy.*' I like it."

"I'm glad," I said. "Are you painting something or painting over something?"

She didn't answer my question. She didn't even acknowledge it with a pause. But she did answer what was going to be my next question. "I'm Mia," she said, "Mia Romero." She took off her sunglasses and hung them off her sports bra which drew my eyes *there*. I flinched, but she dismissed it with a half smirk. "Mia Romero," she said again, almost like she was snapping her fingers to bring me back to focus.

I blinked and said, "Pleasure to meet you, Mia," in a way that I immediately regretted because I thought it sounded weirdly formal. I knew I was dealing with a girl who was pulling off a weird kind of quirk that was maybe country quirk but probably sporty quirk. It sure as hell wasn't a quirk that matched up real good with "Pleasure to meet you". So, I offered her my name in an attempt to distract her from the fact that I had just sounded like a guy about to talk to you about his church. "I'm Nathan," I said. "Or Nate."

"Ornate?" she said. "Like fancy and covered in jewels?"

Quirky and sarcastic, apparently.

"Just Nate," I said. "Nate Cortland."

"Nice to meet you too, Nate Cortland. You're not a Gulfer. I'd know you. If you're a transfer student, school ended last week. If you're a tourist, you're lost, and maybe we should fire off a flare or something to help the search party."

"I'm not a transfer student," I said. "And I'm not lost. I'm just here for the summer—or part of the summer. I'm not sure yet."

"By choice?"

"Not exactly."

"You and everybody else around here," she said. "Owl Harbor is not a place anybody moves to. It's a place you *end up*. Unless you're born here, like me."

There was a silence, one beat short of awkward, and it was probably my fault because the conversation had taken maybe two minutes to push me back into the self-pity spiral. But I stepped back from the emotional abyss and tried to recover because Mia was still the only thing that was interesting and not excruciating or infuriating since I'd woken up. "Is that the town slogan?"

"Might as well be," she said. "I could think of worse. But maybe I should let you discover that for yourself, Nate Cortland."

The way she said my name seemed like a pretty obvious "we're done here" statement, but I thought I could get one more exchange in. "Where should I start my research?"

"I work at the marina most days during the summer. Stop by," she said. "I can give you some pointers."

She turned back to her canvas, and I stood there for a few seconds before I resumed my exploration of Owl Harbor. The whole Mia thing was a lot more than I had expected from my walk. I decided to save the store for another day. I didn't want to blow through the Owl Harbor's entire excitement inventory in a single afternoon. I headed back to the farmhouse, for the first time that day not thinking how much the summer was going to suck, though I was back on that subject by the time I got to the road.

4

One of the things about walking in the country that you have to get used to is that there are no sidewalks. And most of the roads in the Delta are raised up on an embankment because the roads also serve as dikes, helping channel water here and there to avoid flooding. Drought is pretty much standard operating procedure in California, the slow-motion disaster that's like the backup singer disaster to whatever scarier and more sudden disaster will come up, but in the years when it's not a drought, they throw in a flood because it's not like any season can be normal in the Disasters"R"Us state. What all that flood-control planning means for walking is that you can't walk on the side of the road because the side of the road is basically a steep slope that ends in a ditch.

Walking down the road meant walking *on* the road and you had to be careful not to get run over, listening for cars the whole time and never just spacing out because when a car was coming you had to somehow balance on the edge of the road without falling down the slope and into the muck.

So, what I'm saying is that I didn't cover any great distance in my first Owl Harbor exploration but far enough to see that the marina wasn't all that far, and that the next town up was walkable, in a pinch—if you didn't end up sliding down the embankment into the ditch sludge because two cars came by at the same time.

I made it back to the House of Illusion to see the parking lot empty and the door to the gift shop open. Uncle Kevin sat on a folding lawn chair just inside the door with one of those plastic oscillating fans going and *A Guide to 19th Century Folk Magic* closed on his lap with a manilla bookmark sticking out.

"Find anything interesting?" he called out as I approached.

"Actually," I said, and I stopped because I was surprised that I had an affirmative answer, "I did. Not an anything, an anybody."

"Good," Uncle Kevin said. "Among the many illusions of Owl Harbor is that we're all illiterate hillbillies. That's not to say that an illiterate hillbilly wouldn't be interesting."

I nodded. "I guess."

Uncle Kevin got up from his seat and stood up, folding the chair with a quick snap. He looked my way and said, "Ready for the private tour?"

"Should I get Lily?" I asked. I imagined her still on the front step, glaring a hole through the hills between Owl Harbor and Kentfield.

"Nah, I don't think so," Uncle Kevin said. "This

might be half tour/half training. The real summer starts next week, after Memorial Day, and maybe I could use an extra tour guide or somebody who can help me build up the attraction a little bit. More space, more illusion, you know?"

I didn't know, but I nodded anyway.

"Step right up, young man, and allow me to introduce you to the realm of the unknown, magical forces that bring taut the line between science and magic," he said, "between what you see and what you fight so hard not to believe."

It was almost as though he was speaking through some voice enhancer thing set to "wizardly", as if he had an echo effect chip in his larynx, and I was reminded of his mini speech from the kitchen two hours before. It was some ridiculous crap he was saying, but he was saying that ridiculous crap with authority. "Follow me, my child," he went on, "and allow me to explain how the world really works."

I followed Uncle Kevin into the house, stopping in front a warning sign that included *The management cannot be held responsible for philosophical drift, altered cosmologies, and seeing what you've been taught not to see*. He flipped the *Tour in Progress* sign in the window and locked the door behind us. I saw Uncle Kevin's top hat on a shelf to the right of the turnstile. He didn't reach for it. I guess I wasn't getting the top hat, but I was getting the top-hat treatment because once past the turnstile, Uncle Kevin pulled a heavy curtain closed behind us and switched off the lights.

"I invite you to shed your primitive notions of how reality operates," he said. "Let go the preconceptions and allow that glance from the periphery. Let the thing you thought you saw become the thing you allow yourself to see."

What he said was ridiculous, but the way he said it made it seem almost true. I mean, I think we've all seen something out of the corner of our eye and then turned to look but it was gone. I'd had a science teacher, freshman year, who'd told us that our brain does more of the seeing than our eyes do. That didn't mean that Owl Harbor actually "teetered on a fulcrum between our universe and a different—perhaps a more powerful—universe", but a little germ of truth could keep an audience from rolling their eyes so hard they fell down.

"Do you always do this part?" I asked Uncle Kevin.

As he spoke, he turned the lights back on but dimmer. "Yes," he said. "It's important. It sets them up for the rest."

I could see "the rest" now. With the lights back on, he drew back a curtain to reveal a grid of small holes in a wall. He motioned me to take a look through one and then stepped around the wall into the room I was peering into. As he walked across to one corner, he got smaller, or the room got bigger; I couldn't tell. But when he walked to the other corner, he got large and the room got small. It was really freaky, and he kept talking while he walked toward and away from where I stood, his size seeming to shift with every step.

"What you see," he said, back in his top hat voice, "is how gravity distorts vision and vision distorts gravity. It is something the wise men spoke of, but modern science turns itself inside out to deny."

I had to ask him to stop walking. It was making me kind of dizzy. "Okay, okay," I said. "Greet speech. What's really going on?"

He beckoned me to step around the wall and join him. "It's called an Ames room," he said. As I walked around, I could see that the floor was tilted and the distance between floor and ceiling got smaller toward the corner where Uncle Kevin had looked so tall. Other visual cues, like the size of the doorway, were also distorted. "It's a trick of the eye. Your brain tries to impose what it has always seen over what it's really seeing. Pretty cool, huh?"

"Yeah," I said. "Pretty cool."

I walked to the small corner, seeing how the floor tiles changed size to match the forced perspective. I didn't feel taller, but I could see how somebody looking through one of the peepholes could think I'd grown a foot or two.

"What's next?" I asked.

"Right this way, my good man," Uncle Kevin said.

The next part was a mirror trick. We walked into what looked like a long hallway, and we could see two more people way at the other end. I started to wave at them and knew immediately that they were actually me and Uncle Kevin when the younger guy waved back. "What you're seeing is not what you think. You are seeing what we believe is your doppelganger from the other universe, in another Owl Harbor," Uncle Kevin said. I waved again, and this time I noticed a delay. I didn't know how he was doing it, but it was obviously more than a mirror.

"How do you do that? It's trippy" I said. "It can't be just a mirror."

Uncle Kevin smiled—and not forced this time. "It's not just a mirror. It's three mirrors and a video camera and a sheet of glass, really clear glass. Pretty cool, huh?"

"Yeah," I said. "Pretty cool."

"Our next stop asks something more of you," he said. We walked a little way down another hall lit by those Edison bulbs that make everything look all steampunk-y with a bit of mad scientist thrown in. He opened a door, and I stepped inside. The room was white and bright—I mean really bright, especially after the dinky bulbs in the hall. The brightness hurt my eyes, and I squinted. "Here, put these on," Uncle Kevin said, handing me a pair of blacked-out goggles.

I did, and I could see nothing.

I heard a light switch behind me, and I removed the goggles. I was standing on the edge of... basically nothing. I could see the walls as my eyes readjusted, but at my feet yawned a chasm that looked deeper than I knew was possible, dimmed pin lights on the wall of a pit dropping off into infinity, with me right on the edge. I stepped back out of reflex. "Whoa," I said, instantly feeling like a total loser because it was obviously another reflection thing. Later Uncle Kevin would later explain it as "an infinity pool" and another mirror trick, but right then he declared it to be "the Well of Worlds".

"Infinity is not a double-edged sword," he said,

back in his carnival professor voice. "It is an infinitely edged sword. One wrong step, and you could be trapped between universes, caught between existence and nonexistence."

I started to dab my foot at the edge, knowing that it was glass or plastic, but Uncle Kevin stopped me. "Hold on! That's not a mirror. It's only glass for the first three feet. That's a twenty-foot drop, and you'll be up past your neck in water and mud, almost like quicksand."

My heart skipped a beat, maybe two beats. No kid likes getting fooled by a grownup, but getting fooled and also breaking your neck offers a pretty crappy mix of being mad and being scared. But Uncle Kevin didn't seem to notice. I was sitting there with that lurch of "oh shit" still pounding in my chest, and he was gleeful. "The trick is getting the guests to think it's just another trick," he said. "When I toss a pebble and they hear the splash, that really gets 'em."

He was smiling, a little demented, if you'd asked me. "The illusion here is that it's not an illusion."

The other illusion, I was thinking, was that there was a chance Uncle Kevin was going to be even half normal.

We walked through another half dozen "mysteries of the universe", although he never told me which universe. It had me wondering whether people in an alternate universe knew they were in an alternate universe. Or did they think we're the ones in the alternate universe? And for all I knew, the alternate universe me might have been having a better go of it. Alternate me was probably at the Alternate Golden

Gate Racquet Club checking out Olivia Blum's alternate ass.

I'd seen some of the other illusions. As I'd expected, I saw a bowling ball roll uphill. I saw water flowing sideways out of a faucet. I'd already heard about the gravitational vortex and that thin membrane thing, but I hadn't heard Uncle Kevin's "mysterious and mystical history of Owl Harbor" backstory. It turns out that Owl Harbor wasn't "actually magical at all". When he said that, my first thought was, *Duh!* I mean, if there was anything special about Owl Harbor, he wouldn't need mirrors and a video camera. If there was an alternate-universe Owl Harbor, it might have been an even suckier version of Owl Harbor.

But Uncle Kevin went on. I'd already figured out that I was supposed to be learning this stuff for when I made my triumphant debut as the newest incarnation of Professor Mysterio, "Substitute Teacher Mysterio". I'm surprised he wasn't telling me to take notes.

"The Miwok people who hunted this land before the pioneers arrived knew there was a sacred power here, but the full manifestation of mystic energy did not appear until the middle of the nineteenth century," he said, back in his hushed ghost-story voice. "It was only after the Gold Rush that the full force of this spot was recognized, realized, brought to its fully embodied incarnation."

I had an image of him flipping through the thesaurus while he wrote this shit. I was having a hard time imagining—*"envisaging"*—myself actually speaking these words aloud. But he was fully committed to the role.

"The magic of Owl Harbor only came to be by chance," he went on. "High up in the Sierra a group of spiritualists devoted to the metaphysical arts discovered an ancient discipline of turning intention into creation."

I half expected a fog machine and organ music.

"This group, led by the charismatic Luther Ludlow, believed that if they wrote their aspirations on small sheets of paper and put them in small vials filled with water from a sacred spring at the headwaters of the Tuolumne—and if enough of them did it together—their wishes would become real."

He pulled one of the blue bottles out of his pocket and held it close to one of the filament bulbs. I didn't know what to make of Uncle Kevin's dramatic pause here. It's not like I was a paying customer. But he got this starry look in his eyes before he continued, "Their greatest wish was to find the mother lode, the source of all the gold trickling down the rivers and streams, but the early settlers of California then did not take well to Ludlow's teachings. They declared it a cult and came to burn his compound down."

He got more animated in this part, explaining how some torch-bearing mob descended on the hapless Ludlow and that one of his followers escaped in a boat packed with these vials. "He nearly made it too, but the boat overturned in the rapids. The bottles, however, kept going, packed in a crate that made it all the way here before it settled into the bogs, forgotten for more than a century until my family began farming this land and discovered the secret power of Owl Harbor."

I'm sure this is the part where he would have taken off his top hat during a paying-customer's tour. "Perhaps it was the power of this place that drew that crate here, or perhaps it was happenstance, but the combination of these forces—gravity, psychic energy, dimensional transference—is what made this House of Illusion more than just some carnival gag. There is no illusion in this place, only the power of Ludlow's teachings and the perch of Owl Harbor on the precipice of another dimension."

He said it so seriously, like he was a preacher or a holy man or just some guy mumbling to himself on the street, that I almost thought he believed it. I'm still not sure. It's not like he gave me any reason to doubt that with what he said next. "There is much to investigate, and I am continuing my studies. Owl Harbor will remain a mystery for only so long."

I was behind him while he was saying all this, and we were walking down another dimly lit hallway. He couldn't see me rolling my eyes and I couldn't see him winking. So I flat out asked him, "Uncle Kevin, do you really believe this shit?"

He turned to face me, kinda sudden-like, which made me think he was angry, but the way he talked didn't sound angry at all. "You know, Nathan, I'm not always sure what I believe," he said. "The only thing I know is that I want to know more."

Okay, so that was a bullshit answer. I was beginning to wonder if he ever turned the illusion host act off. I pressed him. "What do you want to know?" I said. "I mean, besides how to get more people in here paying for tours."

He offered a grin, the most natural of the few I'd seen so far. "That, my boy, is the most elusive of mysteries. Maybe you and I can figure that out this summer."

5

LILY WAS NOT IN HER SULLEN GARDEN GNOME POSE ON the porch when I walked back to the house, but just because she wasn't pulling a porch pout did not mean she was not sulking somewhere. I found her in her room, on a bed that was shoved up against a floor-to-ceiling stack of boxes. I could instantly tell that she'd heard me coming because she was sitting up in this kind of formal way that triggered my *what's she up to?* instinct. Anybody who has been in charge of a younger sibling for very long develops a sense of when that snotty little sib is hiding something. She was definitely hiding something, but the day had been such an earth-shattering shit show that I was not inclined to investigate.

I still asked, "What's up?" But it wasn't a real "What's up?" more like a "How ya doing?"

"Nothin'," she said. "Just sitting here thinking about what I'd be doing at home that I can't be doing here because there's nothing to do here."

"Got it," I said. "I took the tour. I've experienced the mystery of Owl Harbor—probably seven or eight mysteries. Uncle Kevin ran down some crazy stuff."

"Sounds fascinating. Do I get the tour too?"

"I guess," I said. "You'll probably be giving it by the end of the summer. He already told me I'll be Professor Mysterio Junior. I wonder if he's going to order me a top hat."

"You'd look like a loser in a top hat."

"Yeah, but I'd be a mysterious loser."

We both smiled, suggesting we weren't going to be at each other's throats all summer. If you've ever had a sibling, you know that's totally possible.

"Okay, I'm going to go to my room and stare at the wall for a while," I told her. "I presume Uncle Kevin is going to figure out something for us to eat tonight. See ya then."

"See ya then."

I WAS TOTALLY ready to go to my crappy little enclosed-porch room and seethe. It's not like I'd had no opportunity to seethe—and seethe I had—but alone I could snarl at the world without interruption. Except I got there and figured out pretty quick that seething without an audience feels really stupid. There was a reason Lily hadn't been glaring at the ground from the porch when I'd gotten back from the attraction and my encounter with Mia. Try a little nostril flare with nobody around sometime. It gets boring really quick—and also kind of lame.

Instead, I fell asleep until Lily knocked on my

door and told me Uncle Kevin was going to take us out to find dinner.

I took a moment to check my hair, suddenly wondering how I'd looked when I'd met Mia, and I was on the porch with Lily at what looked pretty close to 7:00. The sun was dunking behind the far-off hills, muted by a fog bank we couldn't see but knew was there. The wind was steady and smelled of salt. We heard Uncle Kevin tap the horn from his old Jeep Wagoneer, and pretty soon we were on the road, ready to make our debut into Delta society.

"Where are we going?" Lily asked. "Got any Thai around here?"

"Or perhaps some French provincial fare?" I said, elbowing Lily. The Wagoneer was old enough that it had one of those bench seats, and we were all sitting up front.

"Ah, yes," said Uncle Kevin, "you big-city foodies and your refined tastes. I will say only this: your choices tonight range from deep fried to plain old fried. And everything comes with ranch dressing around here, even the ice cream."

We groaned, but Uncle Kevin quickly added, "I'm kidding. It's not great, but we'll hit the grocery store on the way back. I'll keep you kids fed. Don't worry."

We slid through the first cluster of businesses—what I'd thought from the distance might be a "town"—without stopping. It was more or less a gas station, a church housed in one of those metal buildings highways use to store construction equipment, and a dollar store. We drove for another ten minutes and entered the metropolis of Lago Vista.

Lago Vista had *two* dollar stores.

It also had one of those grocery stores that's like the poor cousin of a big grocery store chain, but the big grocery store chain wants to pretend they're not related. It had the ridiculous name of City Market and might as well have had "Past Expiration Date but Probably Still Good" as a store slogan. There was also a liquor store, another church, and an "outdoor equipment outlet" with most of the equipment in question designed to kill stuff in the outdoors: a few fishing rods and lots of guns. My assumption was that you could combine the liquor store and the outdoor equipment place, and it'd outrank the church as the favored house of worship.

But then we saw the great mecca of Lago Vista. Paris has the Eiffel Tower. Rome has the Coliseum. Lago Vista has Los Burgerritos.

Even with half the neon burned out, Los Burgerritos was probably visible from one end of the Central Valley to the other, and it stood with its own forgotten-highway grandeur. A what-were-they-thinking? combination of '50s carhop diner and Mexican restaurant chain, this fast-food dead end was simultaneously a summation of all that was wrong with the Delta and also a little *I'll try that!*

Uncle Kevin pulled into one of the parking spaces, next to a squat stucco thing that looked like a Spanish mission ripped out of a miniature golf course, about mailbox high with a push-button speaker and a laminated menu hanging from an elastic cord. He stretched the cord and pulled the menu inside, handing it to me. I had to hold it pretty tight so it didn't go flinging back through the window, and a whole thirty seconds later, he was ordering three Burgerritos because of course.

"Should we get out of the car?" Lily asked.

"That's not how drive-ins work," Uncle Kevin said. "The whole point is you eat in the car."

I'd already figured that out, mostly from seeing drive-ins on TV. It's not like we were hanging out in restaurants with car-side service very often. The locals, however, had nowhere else to hang out, and I could see several cars' worth of teens and some up into their twenties mostly sitting on the hoods of older cars, with a few perched on folding chairs in the backs of pickups. I'd never seen this happen, but one of the lowriders had the front wheels hopped up on hydraulics at the perfect angle to create a lounge chair with the windshield as a backrest.

"Welcome to Saturday night in Lago Vista," Uncle Kevin said. "When your mom and I were your age, this place was Dad's Hots and Tots but the rest of this was more or less the same, only more crowded."

"Those were the days," Lily said, pulling off an amazingly droll tone for a kid her age.

"Did Mom hang out here too?" I asked. I had some weird picture of Mom in a poodle skirt with a boyfriend driving a hot-rod muscle car because that was most of my movie experience of drive-in joints, but I had to remind myself that Mom had been our age during the '80s. She'd have been more Madonna than Marilyn Monroe, but it still made me wonder why she never talked about this kind of thing. It was harmless and the kind of retro that was cool in its own way.

"Not a lot," Uncle Kevin said. "She'd get down here once in a while, but if she had a friend with a car she was pushing to go into the city or at least Sacto."

"Sacto" was Delta talk for Sacramento. Obviously, Sacramento was way cooler than the Delta but practically an Old West town from our snobby North Bay point of view.

Lily leaned into the Mom History 101 thread. "Did she have a boyfriend? Was she a jock, a drama geek, a country girl? I always assumed she was a brainiac."

Uncle Kevin was quiet for a few seconds. "Your mom was quiet, more 'stay at home' than anything," he said. "I don't think your mom was cut out for the Delta."

"That's probably why she never talks about it, I guess," I said, cutting in.

"There might be more to it than that, more than I want to talk with you guys about tonight at any rate."

It got quiet in the car. I could tell Lily had more questions and was deciding which to ask first, but her inquiry was interrupted by the arrival of the burgerritos. Uncle Kevin took the tray and perched it on a dashboard that had room for a buffet, but as soon as he'd paid, Lily was begging to sit on the hood. Dividing up our greasy wax-paper bundles we were soon perched on the front of Wagoneer with a view of Lago Vista's cultural scene sprawling out across the parking lot.

The burgerritos were pretty good, unexpectedly good, but they were easily outgunned on the greasy-goodness scale by the chili cheese fries. Digging through the mess of potatoes, cheese, and chili, I had a momentary thought that life on the Delta might not be all that bad after all, but I quashed that thought quickly. Looking out at the T-shirts and cutoffs congregation, I wondered how I was going to survive. My social life was at a full stop, beyond all hope of rescue or resuscitation. I might as well have been a leper living on a desert island. It wasn't like I was going to stroll up to some group of Delta kids, introduce myself, and join in their various capers, especially when I imagined most of the capers around began and ended at Los Burgerritos with the occasional field trip to the dollar store.

And then they walked up to me—or two of them did.

"New kids!" a girl in torn jeans and a red tank top shrieked to her friend as they walked away from a squad of other kids clustered around an old Nissan pickup. There were about four parking spots away so it's not like I had a bunch of time to figure out why they were coming over, but several scenarios ran through my head:

- These girls were bored, and new kids in town were about the most exciting thing that could happen at Los Burgerritos, probably the most exciting thing that would happen all summer (this was the most plausible of my thoughts).
- They thought that by cozying up to me and Lily they could convince Uncle Kevin

to score them some beer (also plausible, but probably too elaborate an enterprise).

- They found me devilishly handsome (least plausible).
- I was about to be the victim of some cruel prank, and I'd be walking home pantsless from an isolated location with something profane magic markered on my chest before the night was over (plausibility low, mainly because it was unlikely they had a Sharpie with them).

None of the scenarios turned out to be right. "Hey," red tank top said, "I'm Hannah. This is Hattie." The two of them had walked up to the front of the car and were standing there almost like they were auditioning or about to give a speech for an audience of three. "Everybody knows Professor Mysterio here," she said, pointing to Uncle Kevin. "But we never seen you two. What's your deal?"

She said "you two", but she kept her gaze completely focused on me and so did the other girl. A whole other set of scenarios ran through my head, even more outlandish.

Uncle Kevin broke what was starting to turn into an awkward silence. "These are my niece and nephew," he said, "Lilith and Nathaniel. They'll be working at the attraction this summer."

Okay, first off, "Nathaniel"? Even my mom didn't call me Nathaniel. That'd be my name if I lived in, I don't know, colonial times. Even Nathan was feeling formal. And sometimes I forgot that Lily's real name was Lilith.

Lily didn't give that formality time to hang in the air before shooting out, "Lily and Nate!"

Hannah and Hattie looked at each other and giggled, and I wondered if I was about to be introduced to the rest of Lago Vista society as "Nathaniel" and whether I'd be recruited to the Colonial Army before the summer was over. But Hannah granted me a reprieve.

"Nice to meet you, Nate and Lily," Hannah said, and it struck me that she'd never broken eye contact with me. "We're partying at Seventeen Poles tonight if you can escape the maze of illusion."

"And if you don't suffer Burgerrito's revenge," said Hattie, her first words in the encounter.

And with that, they turned and walked back to the other dozen Delta kids still grouped around the Nissan.

I leaned back against the windshield and tried to interpret the situation. I should say here that neither Hannah nor Hattie were super attractive, but I don't think anybody pulls off "super attractive" in the glaring fluorescent light of a drive-through parking lot. I guess the yellow neon probably helped, but let's just say more yellow neon would have been required. They looked a lot like I would have pictured if I'd been asked to imagine Delta high school girls that morning: cute maybe, but not city cute. That had been before I'd met Mia and my whole vision of Delta life had been thrown out of whack. With

Hannah and Hattie receding across the parking lot, my Deltavision had snapped back into focus.

Lily did not let the opportunity to tease go to waste. "They were, um, friendly," she said. "I didn't know there was a chapter of the *Nathaniel* Cortland Fan Club out here. They're having a meeting tonight at Seventeen Poles, whatever that is."

Uncle Kevin sat up from his windshield repose. "Seventeen Poles is bad news, that's what it is—way too old for you," he said, looking straight at Lily and then shifting his eyes to me before adding, "and way more trouble than you need."

I didn't need trouble, I understood that. But I didn't need any more mystery either. Uncle Kevin and Mom had been tight lipped about Mom's little *bad vibes* hunch, and that was infuriating but maybe explainable. But whatever "17 Poles" meant, I thought I deserved to know.

So I asked, "What hell is Seventeen Poles?"

"It's a party spot," he said. "Kids have always gone there, since your mom and I were in high school, probably before that. It's seventeen telephone poles past the bridge on Eighty-Four, on the right."

Another Deltavision scene snapped into focus. I could hear the twangy country station, smell the campfire, taste the cheap beer. MTV probably sent talent scouts for *16 and Pregnant*. It was nothing I needed to be warned against.

"No thanks," I said. "Just passing through, and I don't want to get mixed up in local politics."

"Smart move," Uncle Kevin said, "smart move."

It felt smart just then, but as we were leaving, I

took a glance over at the kids dispersing across the parking lot, probably headed toward their cars and getting ready to count telephone poles, and I felt a twinge of *How bad could it be?* followed quickly by *I wonder if Mia hangs with them*. But a half hour later, after ducking into the "this ain't no Whole Foods" City Market, we were back on a dark highway, and perched between rice fields and mud, I rediscovered my resolve.

I wanted a social life. But I didn't want a *Delta* social life.

6

My training was far from over. It's not like I had expected to toss Uncle Kevin's top hat onto my head and start pontificating on the cosmic specialness of Owl Harbor the day after my private tour, but I was in no way prepared for what played out for me over the next several days. What Uncle Kevin expected was a depth of knowledge that I'd associated with, I don't know, college. Uncle Kevin wasn't getting me ready for a job. He was inducting me into the order of the spooky-talk roadside prophet. Once properly ordained, I'd be able to say, "The reality of Owl Harbor is the reality of every other place on Earth, only more so," without laughing or having to offer everybody their money back.

My training started with tagging along on the real tours. On a good day, he'd have eight or ten groups come through, and if the group was anything smaller than two minivans' worth of paying consumers, I'd join the tour and listen through the whole thing.

When business was slow, which was most of the time, he'd be testing me, asking me to recite bits of the tour. The disclaimer part was easy. I could warn that the tour "may not be appropriate" for pregnant women, people taking anti-seizure medicine, and "the closed minded". The history part was harder: the part about the Gold Rush cult and the blue bottles. I couldn't tell the story of the boat overturning in the rapids and the crate of bottles floating downstream without thinking how much it sounded like a *Scooby-Doo* episode and whether I should lapse into a Shaggy impersonation and punctuate my delivery with "Zoinks!"

But I slowly cobbled together my bits, and after much coaching on timing and delivery—"Don't be afraid of the silences; use the pauses to create the mood,"—I was ready for my first victim: Lily.

Lily had taken the tour a few times with Uncle Kevin delivering the introduction to the improbable. But this was my premiere performance. I'd basically cribbed some of his spiel and substituted a bit of my own stuff that I was reasonably sure I could say with a straight face. I was surprised to feel a bit of stage fright as I began the show, flipping the *Tour in Progress* sign even though we were an hour from opening. I scanned the parking lot as I drew the curtains closed (my own added gesture of sly intrigue) and turned to my audience of two.

"Welcome to the Owl Harbor House of Illusion," I said, "a place where the unknowable and the unnatural hold court with the incredible. Please leave your preconceived notions here in this drawing room and set aside your rigid definitions of reality, for I have something entirely new to show you."

Uncle Kevin saved his history of Luther Ludlow's cult and the blue bottles for several stops into the tour, but in my version, I used it early in the introduction. "The truth of Owl Harbor is a combination of happenstance and history, of location and luck," I said, my voice especially low for this part. "Currents brought the cargo of cultism to the banks and shores of Owl Harbor, but it was the gravitational vortex that warped the currents to this end. One could not happen without the other; both tugging in different directions on the same threadbare fabric of reality."

I was feeling pretty pumped about what I'd put together, and I didn't let Lily's eye-rolling slow me down. Uncle Kevin wasn't stopping me. "Follow me, friends," I said, "and witness the bizarre and the bewildering, the infinite and the inscrutable."

The layout of the attraction imposed a sequence, and I stuck to it. "Gravity is now what you have been taught," I said when I let loose a set of pool balls to wander across the floor and roll to what appeared to be the highest corner in the room. "Size and proportion mean little when the framework of the universe is tilted from its center," I told them when I walked across the forced-perspective room and seemed to grow taller.

In the hallway where we saw our delayed reflections, I explained that "time need not be linear" and when we got to the Well of Worlds room, I let Lily stand with the blacked-out goggles another thirty seconds or so while I drew out my explanation of "the depth of an infinity without edge" and told her to "tread carefully at the slippery slope of a dissolving reality".

I wrapped up the tour with what was basically improv. I hadn't rehearsed this part, but I warned Lily, "Do not ignore the uncanny; do not let the instinctual hold sway over the perceptional." I took Uncle Kevin's advice on using the silence and let the last phrase hang in the air before adding, "Please explore our gift shop for more teachings on the invisible and the inscrutable."

And then Lily let me have it. "I had no idea you were such a geek. Who were you supposed to be? Dr. Strange? Or just strange? I couldn't tell."

We shared a smirk. I'd totally been asking for it with all the absurd crap I'd just thrown down. I was surprised she'd held it in that long.

But then she surprised me. "You got the Luther Ludlow stuff all wrong," she said.

"What?" I said. Uncle Kevin looked uncomfortable, as if he had not expected this exchange.

"Luther Ludlow, the cult guy. There are, like, five books up in the house about the Ludlovians. You're hardly telling any of the real story."

Uncle Kevin shuffled like he was looking for a way to end the conversation and hadn't settled on one that wouldn't just keep it going.

"I didn't even know it was a real thing," I said. "I was just copying off what Uncle Kevin says on his tour."

"Well," she said, "there's more to it, more you should know—maybe not for the tour, but just because you should."

I'd just laid down my Professor Mysterio Jr. crap about the imponderable and the unknowable, and along came Lily to inject some actual mystery into the affairs. I didn't know what she was talking about, but I also didn't know what she'd been doing in the week or so while I'd been studying at the feet of our preposterous prophet uncle.

That prophet, in the moment, looked positively ruffled. "Hey, hey, hey," he said, practically stuttering he was so knocked out of his composure. "We can talk about all that later up at the house. Right now, we've got to get the attraction open for business."

That last part was pure crap. It took all of two minutes to open the doors and turn on the lights in the gift shop. We had at least thirty to spare, and I was having trouble seeing how a brief history of the now apparently real Luther Ludlow was going to use up all of that. But Uncle Kevin's manic discomfort and the tone of his pronouncement made it completely clear that such a history lecture was unlikely to take place until he'd had some time to think about what he'd say.

Lily seemed to understand that too because she said, "Okay," and followed that with an oddly peppy "Later!" to make it clear she was resigned to the postponement of all things Ludlovian.

My first afternoon at the helm of Owl Harbor's most famous and only attraction was minutes away.

. . .

I DIDN'T GET A HAT. Uncle Kevin's fit me—I knew because I'd tried it on when he hadn't been looking—but it felt a bit presumptuous to ask if I could wear it, as though I were a pretender to the crown. The more I hung around the attraction, the more I felt like Uncle Kevin was on a solemn quest and that I'd be pulling a sword out of a stone before I'd be privileged to put on his sacred top hat in front of customers. But he did give me a black leather vest to go with the black khaki pants and the black T-shirt he'd already picked out. I felt like I was a barista in some dystopian Starbucks or maybe the bouncer at a Chuck E. Cheese on the wrong side of the apocalypse.

And my first guests were definitely in need of some bouncing. You have not been heckled until you've been heckled by twelve-year-old, fat, freckled twins from Modesto. Later in my career as a curator of the cosmic, I would know to say, "All children must be accompanied by a parent" and I'd know that when a mom on a road trip says, "I'll meet you at the car when you're done," it's code for: "If I don't spend fifteen consecutive minutes away from these brats I'm going to drive this minivan right off a cliff!"

For starters, the twins were unclear on the concept of "illusion". Gus and Pete, the genius twins from Modesto, had to explain that everything was "just an optical illusion", and I had to bite my tongue and not remind them that they were paying customers in a house of illusion, and it said so on the sign outside. Then they had to tell me, both of them, one after the other, that illusions were "not real", and I had to nod and say, "Yes, you're right," and stop myself from smacking them in their fat little faces. When they heard the story of Luther Ludlow and his Gold Rush cult, they chastised me for promoting cults and told me all about a school assembly where they learned all about how bad cults are. I learned that their dad was a minister and "wait till he hears about this!" and I was never more happy to see that their mother had not bought them season passes.

Gus and Pete were followed by a trio of stoner dudes—and not just stoners but middle-aged stoners, the lamest kind of stoners. They were actually a great audience, my every word greeted with that hushed reverence rarely experienced outside megachurches and Phish concerts.

After the stoners came the great wait. I guess Uncle Kevin had chosen a midweek day for my debut because there wouldn't be many guests and I wouldn't have to work very hard, but the hardest part of the job was wondering when the next group would show up. Later on, I started bringing books, but the only book in the gift shop that wasn't a coloring book or a hokey occult book was from the Delta Historical Society, and it was a little too focused on the miracle of rice cultivation to hold my interest.

And so, I waited, with the clouds burning off and the glare of the sun shrinking the patch of shade on the porch until I was up against the wall and about to retreat inside when I heard a car pull into the gravel parking lot. It was a station wagon and old enough that whatever model it was hadn't started to evolve into an SUV. The passenger-side mirror was taped on and not well because you could see it wiggle against the door frame on the rough gravel. I wouldn't say the driver skidded to a stop, but I wouldn't say she glided gracefully to a stop either.

It was Hannah, the girl from Los Burgerritos, and neither she nor Hattie, who was along for the ride, brought the word *graceful* to mind, then or ever.

They got out of the car as though they'd choreographed their dismount and came walking toward where I was sitting. It provided me a good look at them that the mix of neon and parking lot lights had not allowed. Hannah was medium height, and her hair was less red than I remembered, another trick of the light. Her face was wider though. She didn't have high cheekbones; she had heavy cheekbones. She was wearing what could have been the same red tank top, but she'd traded the torn jeans for frayed cutoffs.

Denim took a beating around this girl.

They'd climbed out of the car in that weirdly timed way, but Hannah was in front of Hattie most of the way across the parking lot. Hattie looked like Hannah's understudy, as though she were watching the way Hannah walked and what she wore and tried to recreate it on her shorter and less "chest-forward" frame.

"So," Hannah said when was about ten feet away, which put Hattie roughly two feet beyond that, "this is where you been hiding?"

Okay, so what are you supposed to say to that? It

was sort of like she was setting me up to say something flirty, but when the only thing a girl knows about you is that you're connected to one particular place and then she sees you at that one particular place it's not a great setup for a clever comeback when she asks if it's where you been hiding.

But I made an attempt at it.

"Drat," I said, "foiled again."

Now, I should have been at least marginally intrigued. I'd been more or less marooned on the premises for most of a week studying the wizardly ways of Uncle Kevin, and I had before me a pair of girls my age, who'd come, apparently, to see me. But all I could think of was what kind of trouble they had in mind.

"Professor Mysterio puttin' you to work?" Hannah asked me. "Are you the guide to the alternate universe now?"

"I've studied his teachings," I said, aiming for deadpan but possibly overshooting it. "I have become wise in the ways of the vortex. The mysteries of the universe are less mysterious to me than to most people."

"You're funny," Hannah said, turning to Hattie to add, "Ain't he funny?"

"Can I interest you in some tickets?" I asked, hoping to steer the conversation away from the awkwardly flirty to something I could drone through and at least postpone whatever agenda they'd clearly talked through on the way over. "I'm sure I could offer a locals' discount."

Even Hattie rolled her eyes at the notion, carefully waiting to see Hannah roll her eyes first, of course. “Nah,” Hannah said. “We were just wondering if you were free later after you’re done teaching tourists about gravity and shit.”

“Maybe,” I said, which was pretty lame if you think about it. Nobody had a packed social calendar on the Delta, and I knew they knew that. But I asked, “What do you have in mind?”

“Some friends are getting together,” Hannah said.

“Just some friends,” Hattie echoed. I swear I saw Hannah nod to her as though she approved the qualification.

“Well, maybe more than just friends,” Hannah said. “We got a boat, and we got beer. We thought we’d rescue you from the mysteries of the universe.”

“Sounds interesting,” I said, which was true but implied more enthusiasm than I actually felt. “Where and when will this voyage embark?”

They both looked confused. I think it was “embark”.

“When and where?” I said.

“Owl Harbor Marina, around nine,” Hannah said. “See ya then.”

That must have been about all they’d rehearsed because they were backing up as she said it. The whole thing had this weird, slow-motion dance number feel to it, with their eyes not exactly locked on me but still mostly on me. Super eerie, like *Children-of-the-Corn* eerie if the Children of the Corn were a little slutty.

That left me on the porch and grateful that the big water tank with the mural on it was blocking the sun. The parking lot stayed empty for the next two hours, and I flipped the sign to *Closed* before heading back to the farmhouse.

7

Uncle Kevin and Lily were sitting at opposite ends of the couch when I walked in. Lily didn't look up. She had her nose a few inches from a book, and I was instantly reminded of her near-constant pose with her phone. It struck me that she hadn't really complained about not having it. I was expecting a twitchy withdrawal setting in, but I had yet to see it. Uncle Kevin did look up and said, "Well, how was life at the attraction today? Lose any children to the Well of Worlds?"

"No," I answered, "but there were a couple nobody would have missed."

"Yeah, you get those. Teaches you patience."

I cleared a stack of books off a dusty armchair across from the couch and sat down. Lily brought the book down just below her nose and said, "Don't lose those. They're important," which gave me a reason to look at her reading materials.

It was not light reading. At home, she'd transitioned out of her annoying *Twilight* phase and had been picking up the occasional mystery, but she really wasn't reading much at all lately, a previous pastime surrendered to lure of the small screen. On Owl Harbor, there was not a lot else to do, but that didn't explain why a kid her age would be reading *Pioneer Evangelicals of the Central Valley* or *19th Century American Mystics: A Review*.

I was puzzled and a little worried. "What the hell are you reading?" I asked. "You're kinda freaking me out."

Uncle Kevin had put down his book. I got a sense of the same nod-and-glance communication I'd seen between Uncle Kevin and Mom. And I was not going to let it pass, no way.

"Hey, both of you," I said, raising my voice. "What is this? What are you guys not telling me? Are you rebooting the Ludlow cult? Should we be ordering little blue bottles in bulk? Should I add speaking in tongues and snake-handling to my tour guide act?"

Lily turned in this jerky swift way and stared me in the eye. "We've been talking about a job for me in the attraction," she said, "and I've been studying old stuff to get ready."

I didn't have a better response than "Huh?"

"You see, Nathan," Uncle Kevin began, "part of the story of Owl Harbor is Luther Ludlow's belief that women could develop psychic powers when they were exposed to the waters of the spring, up in the mountains, and we thought that with Lily here, we could offer fortune-telling in addition to the tours."

I knew what he was going to say next, even

though I am clearly a guy and thus obviously not psychic. And I was right. What he said was, "Your mom used to do it before she moved away."

"So Mom's hunches and bad vibes and the rest of that crap got Lily and me here, and now Lily's going to join the franchise?" I said. "If it's just an act, that's one thing. But if it was just an act for Mom, that act went on way too long."

"Your mother formed her own beliefs," Uncle Kevin said. "I'm not asking that of Lily."

I turned to my sister. "Lily, is that true? Is this school play, or is this the sacred sisterhood of Owl Harbor?"

"School play!" she said, a little too perky. I don't think she needed psychic powers at that moment to figure out what I wanted her to say, and she'd said it. I was still a little amped up, and I could tell Uncle Kevin was trying to put me at ease.

"Lily and I are merely reading up on the history so that we can make sure it all fits and works with the rest of the Owl Harbor legend that we already talk about on the tour."

I was only slightly reassured. "What?" I said. "She doesn't need a history lesson to throw on a scarf and some earrings and start telling the future. To be honest—no offense here, Lily—I don't see too many people lining up to pay a kid to tell their fortune."

"That's why we need to get it just right," Uncle Kevin said. "That's why your sister is doing the research."

"The research is to make it authentic," Lily added.

Okay, so the words *research* and *authentic* do not fit

into an eleven-year-old's vocabulary without implying a whole *Village of the Damned* vibe, but it was starting to lean away from the "this requires an intervention" to "harmless but I'm gonna keep an eye on it". I laid it out pretty much like that, saying, "Okay, but if this starts to turn into some weird voodoo *the chosen one* thing, I'm putting Lily in the Wagoneer and we're driving to the nearest Child Protection Services office. Summer in Owl Harbor is bad enough without having to worry about my sister starting her own cult."

Lily surprised me with a mischievous grin. "The spirits tell me your future holds great promise if you promise to lighten up," she said, smiling semi-sarcastically.

It's not like I was totally cool with the situation, but I'd stepped back from the edge. In some ways, I'd let my guard down on keeping Lily out of trouble because Uncle Kevin was actually around a lot more than Mom had been at home. I guess there were different kinds of trouble I needed to look out for though.

Uncle Kevin sensed an opportunity to change the subject. "Everybody okay with pizza?" he asked. It was a rhetorical question—all kids are up for pizza at all times—but he still scanned us for a reaction. I knew he wasn't really expecting either of us to say no, but he was obviously gauging whether we were ready to end the discussion of Lily's new career.

The answer was obvious. We were done, at least for the night.

. . .

THE "RULES OF THE HOUSE" talk had been pretty quick. Basically, it began with, "Don't make a lot of noise," and ended with "Stay out of Uncle Kevin's room," without a lot in the middle. I definitely hadn't asked about what time I should be home at night because we were home every single night, which would've made a curfew like throwing salt in the wound, although a wound might actually have been a break in the monotony and perhaps too much to ask for.

So when I told Uncle Kevin I was going "out", he didn't have a "Look here, buddy, we talked about this" card to play. No rule had been established, so there was no way I could have broken it. I might even have made it out the door without any interrogation at all if Lily hadn't asked the obvious question:

"Where ya goin'?"

I could have lied, but that would have required dreaming up an alternative activity in an area where no alternatives exist. So I just told the truth, which sounded even lamer when I said it out loud than it had running through my head for the past several hours. "Those girls from Los Bugerritos invited me to hang out at the marina. I thought I'd check it out."

This got Uncle Kevin's attention. "Stay off the water at night. That's trouble. Beer and boats don't mix."

I noted the lack of lecture on beer *without* boats and shrugged *okay* as I headed for the door. But, of course, Lily wouldn't shut up.

"I've got a bad feeling about this," she said. "I see trouble."

"Whatever, Madam Lilith," I replied, my hand already turning the knob on the front door. "Save the psychic schtick for the customers."

THE WHOLE THING with walking on the narrow roads without slipping down the slope into the muck is even tricker at night, but there was zero traffic. So I stuck closer to the middle of the road. Walking past the high school and a cluster of houses, I noticed everything was a lot spookier at night. It wasn't full-on dark yet but dark enough that the Delta looked even more like some swampy Old South nightmare. The high school could've been the haunted plantation. The smaller houses could've been home to some redneck zombie army.

Of course, none of that was what gave me the jitters. I'd tried really hard to coax up an idea of how the evening would not suck. With Mom moving us around so much, I'd been "the new kid" in a few schools, but I'd never been the new kid in a swamp. Compared to the string of Bay Area zip codes I'd grown up in, the Delta could have been nineteenth century Alabama. The fact that I was willingly swan-diving into the social swirl of cropped-sleeve T-shirts and cheap beer was a sign of how desperately bored I was.

It was about a twenty-minute walk to the marina, which gave me plenty of time to concoct a series of nightmare scenarios, and by the time I got there, I'd already been left stranded on a sandbar, injured in a freak cow-tipping accident, and been "I never'd" into admitting that I'd had a favorite Jonas Brother when I was five. So when I got there, it seemed a lot less threatening than it had been.

Hannah and Hattie were actually watching for me, which was both a bit stalker-y and also a relief that I wouldn't have to bumble around the marina looking for them. "Hi, Nate," Hannah said. "We're so glad you're here." I could sense Hattie wanting to say it with her, in chorus, like demonic twins in an '80s horror movie.

"Thanks," I said. "What's up?"

Hannah didn't answer. She just waved her arm for me to follow her, and we started walking down the dock. About halfway down, I saw what looked like a porch pried off a mobile home bobbing in the water with Christmas lights wired to the railings. I found out later that it was something called a pontoon boat, but that night it was introduced to me as "the party barge" and then *el barge de la fiesta* after Hannah's third beer. There was a motor at one end, and at the other end, two guys sat on lawn chairs. They were both wearing T-shirts and shorts, but the shorts were corduroy and both blue, and I instantly knew they were brothers. And that if they didn't already hate their mom, they should start. Corduroy? Blue?

"This is Brett Dugan," Hannah said.

"And this is Luke Dugan," Hattie said, matching Hannah's inflection.

"They're brothers," Hannah added, as though that weren't obvious even without the same last name.

Brett, who was a little taller and also maybe a little slower, kicked at an ice chest squeezed into an inner tube and said: "Help yourself," adding, "dude," enough microseconds later to make it awkward. Luke didn't say anything but followed me with his eyes as I leaned over to grab a beer.

I'm not a big beer drinker, but I know cheap beer when I taste it. This was beer in a can, the kind of can that would look at home empty and rattling around the back of a pickup truck. I leaned my head back and plainly exaggerated the first big gulps as though it were an initiation and I needed to prove to the party-barge clan that I was worthy.

When Luke said, "Awesome," I took it as a sign that I'd been accepted. I wasn't sure how I felt about that, but pride and belonging were not among my immediate reactions. They were all still looking at me.

"When do we push off, and where do we push off to?" I asked. "Is this a 'second star to the right and straight on till morning' thing, or do we kind of float around?"

"We're waitin' to see who else shows up," Brett said. "Unless that 'who else' is the cops, we're goin' to stay tied up for a while. That all right with you?"

There was a little bit of tough-guy challenge in his tone. I wondered for a minute if Luke and Brett had their eyes on Hannah and Hattie and if I was the unexpected obstacle in their carefully laid plans for romantic conquest. Thinking strategically, I asked, "How long you all been taking these little cruises?" trying to imply that I understood they were a quartet.

"Ever since Hannah here got her fake ID," Luke said, reaching over to high-five Brett.

I felt like the banjos were coming out any minute.

We stood there for a half hour or so, talking about nothing, mostly music and funny YouTube videos. I recommended a search for "treadmill" and "mishap". They preferred "stuff that blowed up good". I was wondering how many beers it would take for me to start enjoying their company and whether lead chips were included in the school lunch program when I heard a voice I recognized.

"You guys need anything from the snack bar? I'm closin' up."

I was sitting on a different and larger ice chest with my back to the dock, but I instantly knew it was Mia, even though I'd only talked to her for a few minutes. The truth was I was kind of hoping I might see her there and it was part of my decision to take a chance on the nautical nightlife with Hannah and Hattie.

I looked over my shoulder and was greeted with, "I see you've made your entrance to Delta social swirl; didn't take long," from Mia and a weird little squint from Hannah, echoed in a more exaggerated way by Hattie.

"Me?" I said, even though it was obvious she was talking about me. "I have accepted the invitation of these fine young ladies to partake of the local environs and culture."

"How nice," Mia said. It was a short little "How nice", and I instantly felt like I'd stepped off a narrow sliver of roadside and was sliding into the muck. It had taken me exactly one evening out to figure out that even on the Delta there was a social hierarchy and that I'd probably bumbled into a seat at the dork table. I told myself that it didn't matter, that I'd be gone in a matter of days, but it still felt pretty shitty with Mia standing there as the one interesting person on the Delta and me as the fifth wheel on the party barge.

"Careful out there, kids," she announced and started back up the dock.

Hannah pretended to wait for Mia to be out of earshot and then announced in a stage whisper loud enough to be heard across the water, "No need to wait for the cops to show up when we've got the buzz kill patrol running the marina."

"Yeah," Hattie said, offering no further observation.

Luke seemed anxious to change the subject and stood up suddenly. "How about some music?"

It was the first intelligent thing he or really anybody had said, but I made the "Is there a bathroom around here?" excuse to get back on the dock, ignoring Luke's "Over the side, dude", suggestion.

The need to pee wasn't urgent. What I really hoped was that Mia hadn't left.

I made it just in time.

Owl Harbor was the kind of place where the vending machines need cages over them, and that cage needs to be locked at night. That's where I found her, a fist full of keys in one hand and shoving the cage door with the other to line up the hole where the lock went through. I said, "Excuse me," and pushed on the door, freeing up a hand for her to slip the padlock through.

"Thanks," she said. "I see the booze cruise has yet to embark."

"They're waiting to see if anybody else shows up," I said. "I'm getting the idea this is a regularly scheduled voyage."

"Yeah, but they'll be waiting a while if they're expecting additional passengers. It's usually just the four of them."

"I was getting that idea," I said. "They were on me pretty quick at Los Burgerritos last week. Scouting new recruits, I guess."

"You really *are* making the rounds, aren't you?"

I shrugged and offered a half eye roll.

Mia reached up with another little key that turned off the lights over the dock and gestured for me to follow her. We walked along as she checked the locks on the gates to where the bigger boats were tied up, and she pulled a trash bag out of a can at the end of one of the dock and handed it to me while she replaced it with a fresh bag. Finally, she stopped and turned to me.

"Listen," she said, "I know you're bored and probably lonely out there. But you can be bored and lonely even with people around you too, especially if you're not from around here. Keep in mind that the water can get pretty deep, but socially, every end is the shallow end."

"I know," I said. I got the feeling that she knew what lonely meant, but I had a harder time imagining her bored. "Maybe you could show me the best spots."

"Come round tomorrow. I'm on day shift, off at

six," she said. "I've got to check on some stuff at home tonight. Now, back to your excursion. Don't keep Hann-attie waiting."

I STUCK around the boat for another beer and a half, probably forty minutes. Mia had been right. No additional adventurers arrived. No cops arrived either. I was guessing that underage drinking was a traditional pastime on the Delta, and they didn't need to go out of their way to find it. I left the second time the Chainsmokers' "Closer" came up and I surmised Luke had chosen a "songs best left unplayed" mix.

Walking back to Uncle Kevin's, I thought a lot about Mia and a little about whether Lily was going to tell me she'd been right with her "bad feeling about this" prophecy. Back home, cheap beer and a pair of oafs on folding chairs might have been a social disaster, but out on the Delta, it was practically an Oscars afterparty. And certainly not proof of Lily's psychic powers.

Still, by the time I got home, I was pretty sure I was going to hear about it.

8

I WAS NOT WRONG ABOUT HAVING SUPPLIED PROOF OF Lily's psychic powers. An exchange that started with "How was your big night on the town?" the next morning progressed quickly to "See!" on its way to "I knew it!" I didn't go to the trouble of calling bullshit on her extrasensory prowess, mainly because I didn't want to give her any more chances to talk about it. But let's face it, predicting that a teenage night out on the Delta was going to be a less-than-stellar affair doesn't require a very large crystal ball.

So, after a bowl of the kind of sugary cereal Mom never would have let us have at home (one of the very few and very slight benefits of life on the Delta), I was out at the attraction with Uncle Kevin. "Having another hand around here" was all the excuse Uncle Kevin needed to expand the operation. We were still a few hours away from opening, and I didn't have an excuse not to lend that hand. Pretty soon, I was holding boards and two-by-fours in place while Uncle Kevin hammered and nailed a new wall on wheels into place. The gag was that guests would have to figure out how to get out of a room with no doors and would eventually learn that twisting a candlestick would unlatch a wall that opened to the outside, without a way back in. Uncle Kevin had an idea that eventually there'd be a set of illusions that wouldn't require a guide and the doorless room would be the last one. When they were done with that, they were done with the whole attraction and couldn't hang around crowding the place.

"I call it the Room of No Return," he said. "It moves 'em through."

I nodded and said, "Cool," even though I was having a hard time imagining the attraction so busy that we'd have to worry about moving anybody through. I think the biggest illusion about the House of Illusion was Uncle Kevin's belief that it was just a few tweaks away from becoming a major tourist draw. But I had to admit the wall thing was pretty cool.

I also had to admit there might have been more to Uncle Kevin than my early assumptions because of something he said while we tested the moving wall over again and again (it had to work every time, or else you could have a room full of angry tourists trapped without an exit). What he said was, "You're worried about your sister, aren't you?"

I didn't answer right away. It was the first sense I'd gotten of Uncle Kevin as somebody who had feelings and thoughts, and it took me a second to adjust to that idea. "I guess," I said. "Right now, I think she's just bored and looking for anything that would be a break from that."

"Welcome to the Delta," he said. "And you guys have been here less than two weeks. Your mom and I? This was all we ever knew."

We found a spot where the moving wall rubbed against the ceiling, and he was sanding down the rough edges with a long file to even it out. I waited till he was done and asked, "What happened with Mom anyway? Why doesn't she talk about growing up here? Why was she so eager to get out?"

Uncle Kevin turned away from me and I worried that he was going to close down again, but he was just moving on to another spot with the file. It felt like he wanted to talk but he didn't want the pressure of eye contact while he did it.

"Your mom was different," he said. "You can question whether or not she has powers, but you can't question whether or not she believes she does. She was raised with the idea. She got it from your grandma."

"And where did Grandma get it from?"

"I think she made it up out of necessity," he said, running his fingers along the wood of the door frame to find the rough spots. "She didn't invent the whole story of Owl Harbor. I mean there really was a Luther Ludlow—and we sometimes get some wackos poking around who believe the whole thing, but your grandma invented parts of it. The bottles, I think. The powers, for sure. She needed a story that would draw in customers."

"So it was just stories, stories to tell the tourists?"

"That's most of it, but I think she started to believe it too. Tell a story enough times, and you start to remember like it was something that really happened."

The wall was moving freely now, and Uncle Kevin was messing with the latch/candlestick mechanism. The idea was that the guests would be checking every book on the bookcase and every doodad and design in the wall but that the actual answer had to be pretty obvious.

"What about Mom?" I asked. "Did she believe it?"

"I don't think she had a choice. It wasn't just an idea for her. It was something she was told, not something she made up."

"Okay. So she had hunches and bad vibes, but something else had to happen too for her to want to get away so bad. What was it?"

Uncle Kevin was futzing with where the cable pulled through behind the candlestick. "She had a bad feeling about something, and it turned out to be right. Doesn't mean she has special powers; she was just right about something. The fact that she was right about her best friend dying is what made it different."

"Wow, that's rough," came my eloquent reply.

"There were some kids driving to Sacto, for a concert," Uncle Kevin said. "Your mom got one of her bad feelings and didn't go. The guy driving went off the road, and the car ended up upside down in a canal. Your mom thought she should have put up a bigger fuss. She blamed herself."

The mechanism clicked and the latch unlocked.

Uncle Kevin looked up at me for the first time since he'd started the conversation. "It was senior year, and she counted days until she could leave."

"Didn't Grandma tell her the truth?"

"I'm not sure Grandma knew the truth anymore. I know she didn't know how to tell her daughter she'd been raised with a lie. And maybe she still wanted it to be true, for her and her daughter, that they could be something special and not just Delta kid, both of 'em."

It was my turn to look away. I guess I wanted to know the truth about Mom and her feelings and whatever her history was on the Delta. But it still wasn't easy to hear. I mean, for a long time, I wanted to believe my mom's hunches and feelings were true too, but I'd begun to figure out that it wasn't a power; it was something else.

"But what about Lily now?" I said. "Why are you letting her get mixed up in the same thing?"

"I don't know," he said. "Maybe I think it could be different this time. Maybe she can get to feel special without thinking she's *that kind* of special. Maybe I can help her get it right, in a way I didn't for your mom."

"And maybe you believe in it too."

"Maybe," he said. "Maybe part of me."

I shoved past him and left, false wall swinging and banging against the toolbox he'd left on the floor. "Great," I said, as I left the doorless room. "Just great. I'm going to go open the attraction. Maybe I can find my way to an alternate universe where this family isn't so full of shit."

. . .

It took me a long time to settle down. I couldn't decide if it was a good thing or a bad thing that Uncle Kevin didn't come around and try to explain himself to me. But sitting in the doorway of a crazy house of illusions roadside attraction waiting for suckers isn't the quickest path to peace. The afternoon crept by with little distraction.

A family from Santa Rosa on their way to Tahoe had heard about the attraction from a friend and wanted a tour from "the old guy who runs the place". That obviously wasn't me, but I laid on the embellishments and they liked it enough to give me a tip. Two men from Half Moon Bay peppered me with questions about how long the attraction had been there and where we got ideas. One of them said he'd taken the tour when he was a kid. He was older than my mom or Uncle Kevin.

Three other groups trickled through, not a bad day and really a sign that the summer had arrived, but the afternoon still felt like a generous slice of forever. Lily wandered up a couple of times, and I avoided all talk of psychic ability. The second time, around 4:30, I told her to go find Uncle Kevin and tell him I needed to hand over tour guide duties.

When he showed up, we stepped around each other in the doorway without saying anything. It was a bit awkward, and I waited till he was in and behind the gift shop counter before telling him I was going "out". He asked, "Where?" and I answered, "Out, that's where."

He didn't react, and a quick shower and a sandwich later, I was walking toward the marina again, fourteen dollars' worth of tips in my pocket, ready to quit thinking about Uncle Kevin, Lily, Mom, and what I was supposed to do about any of it.

9

WITH ALL THAT ON MY MIND, THE WALK FELT A BIT shorter than it had the night before. It could also have been that I knew where I was going better, or maybe I was just better at walking on the lip of the road. I could easily see how a car could end up upside down in the water.

I got to the marina about twenty minutes before Mia said she got off, and I waved to her when I saw her walking down one of the docks with three life preservers hanging off each arm. She smiled. I sat under a tree halfway between the parking lot and the snack bar/office and watched the day winding down. It was a Wednesday—not too busy, but Mia seemed to have plenty to do: checking in rentals, coiling rope, stuff like that. I figured out that the Owl Harbor Marina was a family-run business. The blonde woman with the keys on her belt was obviously Mia's mom, and I was sure it was her little brother who was tending to a small earthworm plantation to sell as bait. It was such a different experience from my apartment-to-apartment home life that I was shocked to find myself a teensy bit jealous of life on the Delta. I snapped out of it when I saw a sputtering aluminum boat cough its way up to the dock by the gas pumps and watched Mia run down to manage the transaction.

It's not like the guy had a confederate flag flapping from the bow, but there is a kind of guy who buys a T-shirt and then tears off the sleeves instead of just buying a tank top. And, of course, it had to be a Kid Rock T-shirt because the Venn diagram that encompasses Kid Rock fan and T-shirt-sleeve-ripping bass-boat owner is basically one circle, a circle also inhabited by middle-aged men conspicuously checking out high school girls when they reach down to put the nozzle in a covered-in-bird-shit gas tank.

I couldn't hear what he was saying, but I could see by the way she held her jaw tight that she was trying to ignore most of it. Mia rolling her eyes at me as she walked up the dock confirmed my suspicions. "I've just got to check one more thing," she said and trotted back to the snack bar.

I was reminded that I was supposed to be working a snack bar at that same moment and how different the Racquet Club would've been from the Owl Harbor Marina. Instead of Kid Rock in the beat-up bass boat, it'd be Pilates Mom with a Tesla asking whether the frozen tofu bars were gluten free. Both were clearly obnoxious in their own way, but I'm sure the Pilates mom tips better.

Mia plopped down onto the bench next to me.

"Life's rich pageant," she said, as though she knew what I was thinking. "And me a witness to it all."

"Yeah" I said. "I presume you get all kinds here, all kinds of guys who gargle spitting tobacco and who are saving up for a Harley."

"That was a little harsh," she said, but she grinned. "And also a little accurate. I'd say wait till you experience the nightlife, but you already have. How long did you hang with the Hann-attie and the brothers Dugan?"

"Not long," I said. "I was intimidated by their intellectualism and embarrassed by my lack of Ultimate Fighting trivia knowledge. Did you know Conor McGregor collects Amish needlepoint?"

"Is that true?"

"I don't know," I said. "I left before it got that deep."

We both laughed, and it felt infinitely more natural than anything that had happened on "el barge de la fiesta" the night before.

"Well, I guess I can't say I warned you but only because you were already here when I saw you last night. Otherwise, I totally would have warned you. I was thinking we could actually leave the dock this evening."

"Is that a euphemism?"

"Shut up," she said, and she punched me in the arm, pretty hard too; she was wiry. "Let me show you the best part of the Delta."

"What's that?"

"The actual delta."

. . .

I SHOULD SAY HERE that I'm not really a boat person. Growing up in the Bay Area, the ocean and the Bay itself is something you look at, something you drive past or drive over. It's too cold to swim in without a wet suit, and unless you're into surfing, you're not dipping so much as a toe in it.

Hence my skepticism when Mia tossed me a paddle and told me we were going canoeing. I must not have hidden my skepticism well because she said, "You'll love it; you'll see." And she didn't even ask if I'd ever been in a canoe before, which saved me the embarrassment of asking, "Does the Pioneer Adventure at Six Flags count?"

But here's the thing: not knowing how to canoe meant I was going to be in the front of the canoe because the whole steering of the canoe is done by the person in the back of the canoe and that person was clearly going to be Mia. That meant I'd be sitting in front of Mia, and it'd be really hard to flirt. She could be sitting behind me making faces like she was gagging and basically writing me off as the dork I was beginning to feel I was, and I wouldn't even know.

To be honest, I didn't even know if I should be attempting to flirt or whether flirting would be involved at all or if she'd just invited me out to stage a social intervention and save me from the loser sand trap of Hann-attie and the Dugans. It didn't even occur to me that I could experience both flirting and the intervention or that Mia wasn't sure what she wanted either.

For the first ten minutes of our adventure, it seemed like what she was after was to quiet my mile-a-minute brain because we paddled away from the little bit of open water where the bass-boat flotilla was polishing off their last beers of the day. She guided us into a little area that was tucked back behind a sandbar and some trees. I could still hear the bass boat stereo systems, but it got fairly quiet, and the trees blocked the wind some too. I started to ask her if we were going anywhere because I guess the silence and not knowing what she was doing behind me was making me nervous, but she said, "Just listen, just be quiet.

"And breathe," she added.

Being told to be quiet is generally not a way to get me to settle down, and usually anybody shushing me is going to get some profanity in reply. But we were on a still-water stretch late in the day when the light was turning soft, and I understood that being quiet was actually what I needed to be doing. The way the canoe rocked just slightly and the way I could feel the wind pushing us made taking deep breaths feel like a natural thing to do.

Whether I'd planned to or not I was listening and being quiet and breathing.

A bird was singing, or whatever you call it when a bird is making noise. It would make these three little quacking "caws" and then pause before doing it again. It wasn't a super spectacular bird noise, not particularly pretty, but it felt insistent, urgent, like this bird had something important to say.

And then I saw the bird swoop low over the grass on the sandbar and stop to peck at something, and my first thought was, *Nice paint job*. It was black and white with a blue racing stripe and a bright-yellow beak. "That's the yellow-billed magpie," Mia said from behind me. She dipped her paddle into the water to keep us pointed at where the magpie seemed to be hunting bugs. "In the winter, a ton of different birds come through the Delta, but the magpie sticks it out the whole year," she said. "I think that's kind of cool."

"It's pretty cool looking too," I said. "Nice design."

"Yeah, but the really interesting thing about the magpie is something it does. The magpies are social; they live together and hunt together. If you look up in the trees, you'll see a few more. We're near where they nest."

"That's interesting, but don't lots of birds live together, *flocks* and all?"

"Yeah, but it's different for the magpie. They're social. They're cooperative. They pair up for years," she said. "And they know their mortality. They mourn their dead."

"Get out of here," I said.

"It's true. When a magpie dies, the other magpies stand around the body and sing. I think they're the only animal that does that."

The magpie in the grass flew back up into the trees. I wanted to turn around and look at Mia, but every time I looked over my shoulder the canoe wobbled. I couldn't believe she'd brought me out here to talk about bird funerals, but it seemed to have a significance for her. All I could really go by was her voice.

"I think about that sometimes," she said. "They

live their whole lives on the Delta not thinking about someplace else, not thinking about someone else, something else."

"Did you bring me out here to tell me that?" I asked. "Because that sounds kind of heavy."

She laughed. "I know," she said. "It does. I didn't plan it. And I didn't mean it like you're supposed to be happy you're here, satisfied with everything that's changed for you. I guess I just wanted to show you the Delta. It's not just rednecks, meth heads, and bass boats. It's sort of all those things, but it's also nature and quiet and just being in a place."

"I get that," I said. "But is it enough?"

"Not all the time, but some of the time. What's back in the world you left before you got dumped out here? Is that enough?"

"Not always, hardly ever. It's just faster."

"I bet," she said. We were drifting under some tree branches that arched out over the water. I could have reached up and grabbed one, and I felt Mia's paddle keeping us with the current away from where the canoe could have been caught in the brush. "See what happens when you slow down?"

"Yeah, you learn about bird funerals."

"And you learn to think."

She dug the paddle into the water, and we picked up a bit of speed, more than the drifting current propelling us. We paddled a good five minutes without saying anything. Even one minute can feel like a long time when nobody's talking, and I was glad Mia couldn't see my face because I am sure there were times when I looked a little twitchy. But when we did start talking, she mainly wanted to know about me, and I had to keep steering the conversation back to find out more about her. I think we both understood the little dance of interrogation and were getting more comfortable with it as it went on.

I found out that she was from the Delta, but she'd lived in Mexico for a while when her dad had been getting his master's degree. When I asked what had brought the family back to the Delta, she got quiet, and I understood, even though I couldn't see her, that the subject was not to be discussed.

She was more ready to talk about learning to spend a lot of time alone and "focusing on the natural world more than the social world". She talked about college a little bit, but it didn't sound like she was ready to rush off to some big-city school. "There's a lot of stuff I don't like about the Delta, but it's not the Delta itself," she said. "I guess you've already figured this out because I was pretty obvious about it, but I like quiet."

"I'm quite fond of quiet," I said, and I could tell she was smiling even without turning around.

Her questions for me were a lot more direct.

She asked me about Kentfield and school, and I had to explain that we moved a lot. She'd clammed up on her move back to the Delta, but I was ready to talk to just about anybody about my current predicament. Mia got a heaping plate of "poor, poor me". I told her about the job at the Racquet Club I'd missed out on, the suddenness of our departure, and my indoctrination as Adjunct Professor Mysterio, and she told me to watch out for "weirdos who like weird places".

"It's all fun and games and spooky bullshit, until somebody starts believing in it," she said, "and there are people who believe that Ludlow stuff." But she was most interested in what had happened before all that: the moves, Mom's hunches. She was pretty frank about it too.

"Do you worry about your mom?" she asked. "I mean, like, really worry."

"I guess," I said. "When I'm not angry at her, I keep trying to think of ways I could help her."

"What do you think she'd do if you just told her that?"

"I don't know," I said. "I never tried."

"Are you worried about what she'd say or what she'd do? I mean, do you think about what's coming or what's going on right now?"

"Probably what's coming," I said. We'd stopped paddling, and the canoe was gliding across water that was clear enough I could look down into it and see small fish darting under the shadow of the canoe. "We never know what's coming. So there's lots to worry about."

"Maybe you just *be* once in a while," she said. "Listen, be quiet, breathe."

"You sound like you're going to tell me the membrane between this universe and the next is particularly thin."

"No. But this universe might be a whole lot clearer if you took the time to look at what's here without being scared about what's next."

10

WHEN LILY WAS READY FOR HER PSYCHIC DEBUT, IT turned out to be a debut perfectly suited to the Delta. Uncle Kevin had set up one of those awning things that people put up at the farmers' market when they're selling tomatoes and strawberries, and with the addition of some folding chairs and a piece of plywood propped up on sawhorses and draped in a paisley bedspread, Madam Lilith was open for business. Uncle Kevin found a girl's pirate costume at the thrift store, and with some old costume jewelry Grandma left behind, Lily was able to pull off something vaguely resembling a ren-faire mystic.

She didn't need a crystal ball or tarot cards. Instead, she kept a dozen or so of the little blue vials in a velvet-lined box. She'd pick one up, hold it to the light, and speak in this old-timey way about what the spirits of the water told her.

Her character was fairly ambitious for an eleven-year-old, but it still looked an awful lot like a kid's lemonade stand.

And about as financially lucrative as a lemonade stand that first day.

Nobody, it turns out, goes way out of their way to get psychic readings from an eleven-year-old. The few people who stopped—people driving by—actually thought they were stopping at a lemonade stand. But Lily did persuade some of the people who'd paid for the illusion tour to stop at her psychic lemonade stand to get their fortunes told. She said one person pulled over to get directions and decided those directions could benefit from a psychic component.

She worked for tips and was making maybe five or six bucks a day for the first week, and then the fortune teller's fortunes suddenly improved.

A video blogger from the East Bay visited the attraction looking for corny stuff to make fun of and thought the story of an eleven-year-old psychic was both adorable and hysterical. That put her sideshow on the radar for a TV news station in Sacramento that focused on the "adorable" part with an implied "ain't the Delta the corniest place on Earth?" All of a sudden, she was getting customers. I'm not saying she was getting mobbed, but people were diverting from the freeway to visit the world's youngest psychic. Uncle Kevin added walls (more bedspreads) to the awning to make it look like a carnival tent. Lily was eating it up too, knowing she was the cutest selfie on Instagram as almost everybody who visited her leaned in for a shot with Madam Lilith, the youngest person in history ever referred to as "Madam".

The attraction was benefiting from the traffic too. Uncle Kevin could never have afforded a commercial on Sacramento TV, but the House of Illusion was in the background of every shot. I guess the segment ran in syndication or something because I heard that people all over the country were talking about the #SweetestLittlePsychic.

I never would have thought it possible—and I'm sure Mom's child psychic schtick never got this much attention during the pre-viral era—but the attraction was busy. Lily was making money. I was getting my own share of tips. I went almost an entire afternoon without thinking about how much the Delta sucked.

One of the things that made it not suck was Mia, of course. We started hanging out most nights, even the nights when she was working at the marina. I'd stop by, sometimes watching the snack bar while she ran off to check boats in or lock up gates. But mainly it was pretty slow, and we could just hang out.

And talk.

I'd rant about the stupidest customers, like the bushy-mustache guy who kept asking questions about the Ludlows like I was some kind of historian, providing probably the creepiest moment in my tour guide career. She had a few of her own, mostly of the drunk and leering type. But mainly we just talked about whatever was on our minds. It wasn't like we were dating, but we were getting, I don't know, "close".

And she was getting more attractive every time I saw her.

Most evenings she declared a "topic", which was

really just an outlandish question, and we'd spend sometimes as much as an hour discussing or even debating our answers. One night, I asked her what book she'd want if she were trapped on a desert island, and she said, "*Getting Off a Desert Island for Dummies.*" So I asked her what album she'd bring, and she told me, "The audiobook version of *Getting off a Desert Island for Dummies.*" Another night she asked me what person from history I'd have dinner with, and I said Albert Einstein so he could help me with my homework. She said Amelia Earhart so she could "solve the mystery and be famous".

It was the Monday of the last week of June when she asked me what decade I'd live in if I had a time machine. I said the '90s so I could buy Google stock, but that answer was deemed "unacceptable", and when she pressed me, I said "the twenties, because flappers". That earned me a playful glare before she told me, "I guess I'm supposed to have a Jane Austen fixation and want frilly dresses and formal dances, but I'm really thinking the 2030s might be best because they'll let girls do even more stuff. All they did back then was fuss about getting married. That's the last thing I want to do."

"Good," I said, "because I don't want to rush things."

She punched me in the arm, and we both laughed. We'd sort of avoided the "I like you" stuff, but I did notice the punch was softer than the last time. I grabbed her hand and said, "Stop punching me," still laughing. She didn't pull away.

"Stop saying goofy shit, then."

"Deal," I said and then, with faked some formality, added, "Let's talk about serious stuff."

It got quiet. I mean, it was already in the getting-dark part of sunset and a slow night at the marina, but it was quiet between the two of us, maybe for the first time since the day we'd taken the canoe out.

She went first. "Have you heard from your mom?"

"Once," I said. "It was a week or so ago. She sounded kind of weird, like quiet weird. I only talked to her for a minute. I was still pissed."

"Does that mean you're not pissed now?"

"I'm less pissed."

"Why's that?"

"I'm making money," I said, smiling and knowing it wasn't exactly what she expected or wanted to hear. I wasn't going to make her work for it, but I was going to make her wait for it, all of two seconds. "I also made a friend."

"So did I," she said, and she smiled in the cutest way ever. "Your turn."

Okay, so I was working my way up to a kind-of-obvious question. I'd told her my dad had moved to the East Coast about five moves into Mom's bad-vibes-and-hunches odyssey. We hardly heard from him. Mom said he'd "moved on" in a way that felt so icky I didn't like to talk about it. But Mia only talked about her dad in past tense, which was, in a way, worse. "Serious stuff" was an opening, but I still didn't know how to ask it. So I just asked it.

"You never talk about your dad," I said. "What happened to him?"

This time the silence felt more like a presence,

like it wasn't just the two of us anymore, a presence broken only by the bugs flying into one of those zapper things at the end of the dock. Finally, she looked up at me. "He was killed," she said.

"An accident?"

"No," she said. "Not at all."

The silence closed in even tighter before she went on. "We were living in Guadalajara, and Dad was getting his Master's at the university there. He was doing his thesis on the political influence of the drug cartels."

There are times in life when you know to just sit back and listen. I've always sucked at that. It's a guy thing, I think. But in that moment, I didn't know what to say. I just hoped me looking scared came off as me looking concerned, which I was, but really, I was more scared than anything.

But then the silence between us seemed to crumble as she spoke because she brought her eyes to mine. "He asked the wrong questions in the wrong places," she said. "They shot him on a street corner in broad daylight."

We were sitting cross-legged on top of the snack bar's plywood countertop under the fluorescent lights. I reached out to her, my hands on her shoulders. "And nobody saw a thing," she said, dropping her chin to her chest as I pulled her close.

"I'm sorry."

"Don't be," she said. "I don't like to talk about it, which means I don't talk about it very well. Sometimes I can't understand why he needed to take those risks. Sometimes I'm mad."

"You sound sad too."

"I am."

She moved her hands to my waist. I wasn't just holding her. We were holding each other.

"Sometimes serious stuff sucks," she said, her lips almost touching my ear.

MIA'S MOTHER ran the marina with Mia's uncle. She'd retreated there with her kids after her husband had been murdered. The whole extended family lived there too, on a houseboat. But the one that Mia's mom and brother lived on was small, and Mia's bedroom was actually a smaller boat tied up next to the bigger boat. It was the kind of boat I think they used to call a "cabin cruiser", but it was pretty clear there hadn't been any cruising in its recent history. You could see where the fiberglass was starting to unravel and other places where it was patched over, which made the whole thing look a bit like a model somebody had made out of tape and popsicle sticks.

Of course, I'd never been invited aboard. On the nights when I came by, we'd usually say goodbye at a gate that locked off the docks. On the night she told me about her dad, she followed me out to the parking lot, and I got the idea there was going to be kissing—away from family eyes and all—but it wasn't so much kissing as one quick kiss.

But still enough that it was about all I thought of on the walk home.

By the time I got home it was probably close to 11:00, and I was expecting to creep into my creaky porch room and fall asleep. Uncle Kevin's light was out, but from the yard I could see a flicker in Lily's room that was unmistakable.

It wasn't a flashlight or a candle. It was a screen. I'm sure there are naturalists who can see a wing flapping from a half mile away and name what kind of bird it is and whether it was a male or a female. There are probably sailors who can look at the wind on the water and know when a storm is coming.

But the American teenager can practically smell pixels. Lily didn't have a TV in her room.

Lily had a phone.

The obvious thing to do would have been to storm up there and snatch it out of her sneaky little fingers. Such would be the role of the big brother in any circumstance where the big brother stood to benefit from his courageous fight for fairness and order. But there was a small wrinkle in that big-brotherly action.

If Lily had a phone, that meant I had a phone or at least the use of a phone. If Lily had a phone, it meant I could see what people back in Kentfield were up to. It meant I had access to Olivia Blum's Instagram feed, Ashley Caldwell's TikTok dance moves. Lily had in her sneaky little hands a pixelated passport out of the Delta, a digital express train back to civilization, or at least a virtual slice of civilization.

She had to let me use it. She couldn't play the "IT'S MINE!" card because she wasn't supposed to have it. I figured out that part instantly, but I still stood in the yard looking up at the blue glow in her window for probably close to a minute thinking about what I was going to do with the holy tool of tools when I got it from there.

Of course, by the time I'd come into the house and crept up the stairs, the blue light was shut off. It was not the kind of house that allows you to sneak up on anybody. It was the kind of house that creaked if you turned over in bed, the kind of house where slamming a door threatened structural damage.

So by the time I got to her room, she was curled up peacefully with her head on the pillow, like one of those kids you see in a commercial for burglar alarms sleeping peacefully while the robber prowls outside. Lily was like a sleep mime overplaying her game —hard.

I turned on the light with my finger already to my lips in the international signal for *hush the fuck up*. Her eyes were open instantly. She wasn't even pretending to be groggy.

"Where have you been keeping it?" I whispered.

"Keeping what?"

"Don't bullshit me. Your phone."

I couldn't believe she was sticking to her guns, but it was almost admirable when she said, "What phone?"

"The phone I could see lighting up your window. Either you dug up a magic elf stone or you're using a phone up here. But I guess your psychic energies could have been lighting up one of those blue bottles. Yeah, that must have been it. Sorry for the inconvenience."

I gave her the kind of look Mom had given me a thousand times, the kind of look that says, *The gig is up, buster. If you're lucky I'll let you walk out of here with a limp*. Lily knew it. She was screwed.

"Okay," she hissed, as though a bit of righteous indignation could salvage the evening. She knew she couldn't throw a full fit without waking up Uncle Kevin, but she glared a beam of pure tween venom. She reached into the space where the mattress shoved up against the boxes and pulled out her phone.

"Here."

I knew it was going to be her phone, but it was kind of a relief to see the purple case and the anime stickers. I didn't want to think she'd stolen a phone or arranged some black-market delivery deal. But I had to ask how she'd gotten it.

"It was easy," she said. "Mom put our phones in that bag, and I just snuck back into the car before she left. I guess she never checked. That special bag blocks the signal, but it didn't block me from unzipping it and grabbing my phone."

Suddenly the world began to make sense. I had expected Lily to be the whining snarl-faced harpy of the Delta, scowling at every shadow. But she'd actually been pretty easy. Even before she became Madam Lilith. I should have figured it all out in the first twenty-four hours when screen-withdrawal symptoms didn't have her chewing through telephone poles.

I guess Mom threw the bag in the back of the car and forgot about it because she clearly hadn't figured it out either.

I felt the weight of the phone in my hand, a weird

sensation like a lost limb suddenly reattached. I made her unlock it for me, carefully watching her tap in the code, and prepared to reacquaint myself with the world.

Except it was more complicated of course. All the apps were signed in as Lily. So when I opened Instagram, I was swiping through pictures of her annoying little friends and the even more annoying Instagram stars she followed. When I did sign back in with my username, that lack of interest carried over. It was hard to unsee Lily's friend Maddy showing off her new go-go boots when I saw two of my friends showing off their new shoes. I wasn't at all impressed that Chris Cameron could fit his fist in his mouth. And there it was, reflected in Olivia Blum's Ray-Bans, the goddamn Racquet Club pool.

The phone wasn't a passport to civilization. It was my nose smashed up against the glass looking into a life I was cut off from, and one that didn't look as attractive from afar.

I did check my email, and that was only a bit less depressing than watching only the grand parade go by without me in it. Only three friends had emailed to check what had happened to me. I had sent out a handful of texts the morning of our abduction. I could only hope a stack of texts were waiting for me if I was ever reunited with my own digital companion. But I was surprisingly unexcited by the prospect of such a reunion.

And then TikTok showed me a guy who could wiggle his belly fat to the beat of "Wrecking Ball", and that became another thing I couldn't unsee.

I'm not saying I picked up the phone and it burned my fingers like kryptonite, forcing me to cast it aside in a gleaming moment of Zen. I was glued to the thing for a good twenty minutes, Lily staring at me the whole time the way a dog stares at you when you eat fried chicken.

But I wasn't sure I liked how it felt. It was kind of like I'd woken up and the lights were too bright, and things were moving too fast, and I just wanted to go back to sleep. But I also wanted to see what happened next, and it was only one screen swipe away.

I gave it back to her—sort of tossed it on the bed, really—and said, "I don't need to tell you not to let Uncle Kevin see this because you've done a damn good job of that. I'm not going to try to take it and hide it from you either because I don't want to spend all my time playing *Spy Kids* with it. I'm not going to snitch on you either. But if I need to use that phone—for anything—you will hand it over the second I ask, you got it?"

She looked up at me and nodded in this solemn way that was equal parts cute and creepy but also designed to distract me while she snaked her hand across the bedspread to grab it back.

"And I think you've used it enough tonight. Lights out," I said. "You've got a busy day of foretelling the future tomorrow."

She nodded again, but I was onto her.

"Actually, hand it over. I'll give it back in the morning. It's bedtime." She glared at me, but she knew she'd gotten a good deal. I could have told Uncle Kevin about it. I could have called Mom. I could see her little head tabulating the cost/benefit analysis of staging a confrontation when a grown-up was sleeping a few thin walls away.

She handed me the phone, notching up the glare only slightly.

I didn't even turn the phone back on. I slipped it between two boxes in my porch room and went to sleep.

11

Hann-attie could not be easily discouraged. I was hanging at the marina most nights, and the two of them had seen me there at least three times. Each of those times I was quite clearly with Mia, in whatever they took that to mean (and I hoped they took it to mean we were dating because that's what I hoped it meant). But the two of them, Hannah of course always in the lead, would sometimes spontaneously materialize whenever Mia was off at the other end of the marina, checking in a boat or hosing down the docks, and I was by myself.

It was usually just "Hi, Nathan" always in that vaguely sinister chorus and often with a reminder that they'd be hanging at the barge later if I wanted to stop by. I actually considered it a couple of times in the way an anthropologist might consider living with headhunters to study their rituals. But I'd usually feel bad about my snobbish curiosity as soon as Mia got back, and I was reminded that the Delta was inhabited by actual people with hopes and dreams and disappointments. It wasn't a freak show or a *National Geographic* special. It was just people.

Still, when they stopped by the attraction and once again invited me to witness the wonder of 17 Poles, I was actually tempted to put on my safari suit and delve into the darker corners of the jungle and witness the primitive ceremonies of the natives, or whatever it was they did at 17 Poles.

I should say that this sudden urge to document the social hierarchy of the Delta clan was not entirely driven by curiosity. Mia had some family thing with cousins in Sacramento, which left me facing another night in the farmhouse with Madam Lilith and Uncle Kevin. Even the possible excitement of a Los Burgerritos run did little to inspire my interest.

This 17 Poles thing could be amusing, I told myself.

I said yes, and Hannah said they'd pick me up around 9:00. It all happened pretty quickly. Hannattie had not rehearsed any small talk, I guess.

Lily heard all of this, of course. It was Friday, and demand for the services of a child psychic was not so high that there was not the occasional lull. She was sitting in her bedspread-walled fortune teller's grotto, stealing glances at her phone which she had kept under the box with the glass bottles.

She waited a whole ten seconds after Hannah's station wagon disappeared down the road before she popped up from her folding chair and marched over to me, announcing, in her Madam Lilith voice, that she had "a bad feeling about this".

"Of course you do," I said. "I'd be worried if you had a good feeling about it. It's drinking beer with Delta kids. How good of a feeling could you get?"

"No, Nathan," she said, folding her hands in front of her and stomping her foot in the gravel. "Something bad's going to happen."

"I'm sure it will," I said. "I can see it now: They'll run out of beer right when I get there. I'll get mud on my shoes. I'll lose the country-music trivia contest. I will embarrass myself with my lack of proper etiquette."

"Shut up," she said. "I mean it. Somebody's going to get hurt, and it's going to be bad."

I could tell she was legitimately upset. If I actually were an anthropologist, my doctoral thesis would be on Stress-Validity Markers in Preteen Californians. It didn't really matter right then if she had true psychic abilities. She wasn't pulling a ruse on customers anymore. She'd pulled it on herself.

"Nathan, I don't want you to go. It's something bad."

To be honest, it was starting to sound like a convenient excuse. Saying yes to Hannah and her shadow had been an impulsive decision, a moment of morbid curiosity, but that moment had not passed without some severe second thoughts. Almost any other time, I would have used my sister asking me not to go as an excuse not to go.

But doing that would have meant acknowledging Lily's psychic abilities, which was really the last thing I wanted to do. I'd told myself I wasn't going to let it go too far, and it had already gone too far. I could only imagine how impossible Lily and Mom were going to be when they combined their psychic powers.

"Lily," I said, pointing to the attraction and then to her little fortune-teller stand and then back again. "Do you know what these two things have in common? Do you know what ties them together? I will give you a hint: it's not Luther Ludlow's magical spring water."

I didn't wait for an answer. Her glare was enough. I kept going.

"It's not the Owl Harbor House of *Reality*. It's the Owl Harbor House of *Illusion*. And that," I said, pointing to her fortune-teller stand, "is the *tent* of illusion. Don't forget that this is an act, an act our grandmother came up with. She didn't pass down her psychic ability. She passed down a scam. That's all it is."

Lily clenched her jaws so tight her cheeks turned red to match the plastic beads on the gaudy necklace she wore. She started kicking the ground, but it turned out she was just warming up to kick me. I was very glad nobody, especially not Mia, was there to see me getting chased around the parking lot by an eleven-year-old. "You don't understand," she said, scrambling after me. "You'll never understand. You'll never know what it's like for me and Mom. I told these guys' fortunes today, and I knew they were bad men. They're up to something, and I just know it. That's what it's like."

There was a wooden picnic table under a tree across the parking lot from the attraction. People sometimes had to wait for the next tour, or one parent would watch a toddler while another parent took the older sibling through the attraction. The table was a place to sit. When I got there, I did my best to stay on the safe side from the kicking, spitting demon I had provoked. She'd surrendered words to growling and actually bared her teeth at me several times.

Five laps around the table later a bit of the steam had subsided, and I contemplated attempting to reason with her. But I decided another three laps were in order before I spoke.

"Listen, Lily," I said, "I know it feels real, and maybe part of it is. But Mom's made-up psychic powers are the reason we're out here. Did you think about that?"

"And maybe Mom was right," she said. She was breathing pretty heavy from the chase. "Did you think of that?"

I was glad we were done with the chase part, but I was still keeping the bench between us. I leaned on the tabletop, my palms on the weathered wood. "No," I said. "I didn't. And you know what? It wouldn't matter. I'm tired of our lives being ruled by her psychic bullshit."

"You couldn't call it bullshit if you were experiencing it."

Okay, so an eleven-year-old saying "bullshit" is always hilarious, but what struck me in that moment was that all the years of shared eye rolls at Mom's "gift" didn't seem to count anymore. Lily was all-in on the psychic thing, and really the only thing I could do was hope that it would be over when the summer ended, that Madam Lilith would be a phase she was going through and even something we could laugh about in a few years. All I had to do was not let it get her into trouble, and out in Owl Harbor, where there was not a lot of trouble to get into, maybe that wasn't going to be so hard.

"Okay, okay," I said. "I'm not going to argue with you about it. I won't question your power to see the future through the vortex, or whatever Ludlow line you're using now, but I will not let that power make decisions for me either. I'm going out tonight."

"You'll be sorry," she said.

"Hell, I'm sorry now. And I haven't even gotten to the first pole yet."

I DIDN'T TELL Uncle Kevin where I was going. He'd gotten used to me walking over to hang with Mia, and I decided not to tell him Mia was out of town. I waited for Hann-attie out by the road so that they wouldn't have to pull into the parking lot and arouse enough of Uncle Kevin's suspicions that I'd need to explain myself. I was only out there for about five minutes when they pulled up. I was ready to get into the back seat when I saw that Hattie was already there. Maybe I was the "guest" and it was the local custom that I got to ride shotgun, but they could have made that offer when they showed up instead of basically staging the whole thing so that I had to sit up front next to Hannah.

So yeah, awkward before I was even in the car.

I said, "Good evening, ladies," as I settled in, and Hattie immediately giggled. I saw Hannah look up quickly at the rearview mirror with a half squint I interpreted as *Did I say that you could do that?* But then Hannah went ahead with her own laugh. The delay was only maybe a second, a second and a half but long enough that I felt like I was watching a play and one of them was about to whip out a script and point to the part that the other got wrong.

"Nathan," Hannah said after another of her sharp glances at the rearview mirror, "Parties at Seventeen Poles are always a blast, and it's going to be awesome tonight because this is your first time."

"Yeah," I said. "Are you sure I'm ready for my debut in Delta society?"

"Oh, it's not a society," Hannah answered, and it was immediately clear that she didn't know I was joking. "It's just a party—anybody can come." Did she think that I thought 17 Poles was a club or something?

I gulped. I didn't want to spend the evening carefully weighing every half snarky remark to make sure it suited the audience.

"That's great," I said. "I'm glad I don't have to apply for membership." I was about to say, "I didn't bring any references," but I caught myself. Instead, I asked, "Who all comes to Seventeen Poles?"

I think I'd hit on a question they'd rehearsed because Hannah nodded at the rearview mirror again and Hattie said more words in a row than I'd heard from her yet. "Luke and Brett will be there. You know them. Some friends from school will be there. You'll like Tom Boland. He's really funny. Tony Llewellyn too—both of them. A lot of kids who used to go to Gulf High but stayed in the area. But not a lot of girls, mainly just me and Hannah."

"Yeah," Hannah said. "It's not the kind of thing that appeals to Mia and her crowd."

I was pretty sure Mia didn't have "a crowd" and what I was actually hearing was easy to translate as "Mia is not one of us but play your cards right and you'll be hanging with the party gods of the Delta".

She didn't actually say that directly. What she said was, "We're the kids who like to have fun, like *real* fun."

"Well, I guess I'm in the right car, then," I said, knowing as I said it that the sarcasm wasn't going to register with either of them. "Do we need to score beer or something?"

"Nah," Hannah answered. "Raymond Eggert has a cousin who works at City Market and leaves a couple of cases on the loading dock for Seventeen Poles. I already pitched in on that. Tonight, you're our guest."

"Thank you," I said. "You girls really know how to show a guy a good time."

I said that, and the exchange of glances in the rearview mirror became instantly excruciating. I felt like I was the mouse being dropped into a tank with two snakes and those snakes had been eyeing me from across the pet shop all day. I had no idea what was going on, but I was a sixteen-year-old boy. I had a whole set of ludicrous, porn-inspired ideas. I checked to see if my door was locked.

Hannah jarred me out of my twisted little reverie.

"What's a good time where you're from?" she asked. She was driving below the speed limit, as though she were trying to stretch out the trip.

"I don't know," I said. "We usually just hang at somebody's house, but it's only really a party if their parents are out of town. Sometimes, we go up in the redwoods or the beach if it's not too cold. But it's usually too cold."

"Doesn't sound that different from here," Hattie said, leaning forward between the seats.

I hadn't really thought of it that way, and I wasn't sure that I was ready to believe it. I had this idea I was on my way to some kind of rodeo, and I was sure I'd be betting on pig races between sips of crap-ass beer. "Doesn't sound that different" reminded me of how many parties I've been to that were mainly guys talking about video games on one side of the room and girls on the other side of the room whispering about how lame the guys were, and me standing there feeling awkward in a house with a rec room bigger than whatever apartment Mom had us living in at the time.

For all I really knew, pig racing would be an improvement.

I was relieved to see we were coming into Lago Vista because it changed the subject, at least in my head. The jewel of the Delta was in full Friday night form. The liquor store lot looked like a "beat-up Camaros!" dealership. The Elk's Club had a neon *BINGO!* sign in the window.

We didn't really stop at Los Burgerritos, but we slowed down as we pulled through the lot with Hattie hanging out the window shouting "Seventeen!" to a chorus of affirmations generally falling into the category of "Woo-hoo!"

Friday night in the Delta. I'd arrived.

A minute later, we were across the bridge, and Hannah yelled back to Hattie, "Countdown!" As we passed the first telephone pole, Hattie and Hannah shouted, in chorus as always, "Seventeen." Then she'd lay on the horn until the next pole, stopping long enough for the pair to shout, "Sixteen!" And so on. The poles were about five seconds apart, which doesn't seem like a long time until you're in a car and the driver is leaning into the horn for those five seconds. And then doing it again, seventeen times. When we got to the seventeenth pole, they shouted, "BLAST OFF," and Hannah slowed the car, jerking the steering wheel to the right and skidding into a dirt road, as though she'd suddenly decided to change course, never mind that she'd been counting down to the turn for nearly two minutes.

"Lights off!" Hattie said. That sounded like a really stupid idea, but Hannah didn't hesitate. Suddenly we were bumping along on a dirt road in the dark. If that sounds dangerous, it's because it is, but the road was white sand that stood out from the scrubby weeds, which made it doable, if barely.

"Is this really safe?" I asked, trying not to sound like somebody's grandmother but accepting that I sounded dead-on like somebody's grandmother. "I mean, why not lights?"

Hannah didn't switch on the lights, but she did slow down, in sympathy or because the road got harder to follow, I did not know. “A Seventeen-Poles virgin!” she said gleefully and held her hand up over her shoulder for a high five from Hattie. She slowed to a stop and turned to me. “Nathan,” she said. “At Seventeen Poles, there are seventeen rules. The first one is that you got to kill the lights as soon as you turn off the highway. We don’t want the cops figuring out we’re out here.”

Uncle Kevin had told us that kids had been partying at 17 Poles since before he’d been in high school. My suspicion was that the cops had already figured it out. Maybe not using the headlights made it less obvious that a bunch of kids had driven out into the middle of nowhere to drink beer underage, but it was also Friday night. Cops have calendars too. I’m guessing most of the Delta’s law enforcement personnel had also grown up on the Delta and had been introduced to the not-so-secret hideout the same way I was being introduced: in a car, with the headlights off, digging their fingernails into the armrest.

“What are the other sixteen rules?” I asked, “and how many have I violated?”

“Well,” Hannah said. She didn’t have to do the rearview mirror thing. She just turned around in her seat to look at Hattie. “Should we tell him?”

Hattie nodded, and the two of them announced, “The second rule of Seventeen Poles is that there are no other rules!” And they both laughed. I got the idea that although they’d been “Seventeen Poles virgins” at some point, they had never had the honor of depriving some other innocent of their honor.

Two minutes later, we were there.

WITH ALL THE BUILDUP, I'd expected something more than what greeted us. There were few cars and a couple of pickups already there, parked like spokes in a wheel with a piece of plywood on top of some milk crates in the middle, almost like a stage. A dozen or so people stood around a flat stretch of gravel and that kind of grass that makes you itch just looking at it.

Hannah had her door open before she'd even shifted into Park. I took my time. There's something sinister about a bunch of people standing around in the dark in the middle of nowhere. I half imagined I had a shallow grave in my future, right after whatever Redneck Satan ceremony awaited me on that plywood stage. I took a deep breath and got out of the car.

"Hey, bitches," Hannah exclaimed to the gathering. "We brought the new guy."

It concerned me that I wasn't merely *a* new guy, but not for long because what happened next made it clear that I was also the new character in some imagined soap opera. "Ladies and gentlemen," she announced in a theatrical voice I was sure she'd cleared with Hannah, "Professor Mysterio's junior assistant of illusion."

"And the boyfriend of that stuck-up bitch Mia," came a shout from the gang. It was a girl's voice. I couldn't see who said it. Hannah didn't let it lie.

"I wouldn't be so sure about that," Hannah called

out. "The boyfriend part, not the stuck-up part, 'cause we all know that part's true." She got a high five from Hattie and a laugh from the group, though a few looked uncomfortable with the whole thing.

All I could think, in that moment, was, *Maybe Lily is psychic,* but all I could say was, "Nice to meet you, I guess."

"Ah c'mon. We're just ridin' you," said a guy who was wearing a T-shirt with a glow-in-the-dark flying saucer on it that I immediately assumed was his special 17 Poles shirt. "We ain't got nothin' against Mia."

"He's right; we got no hard feelin's against Mia," said a blonde who was standing close enough to Saucer Dude that I figured she was his girlfriend. "And you ain't gonna get no hard feeling from her either, if you know what I mean."

It was a pretty stupid joke that got way more than laughter from the group than it deserved, especially from Saucer Dude. I shrugged and asked them where they were keeping the beer, more interested in getting away from them than actually having a beer. Saucer Girl pointed with her elbow at a pickup with a cooler on the tailgate. Hannah and Hattie had made the rounds and walked over to the cooler with me. "Sorry about that," Hannah said. "We didn't mean all that."

"You mean you don't think Mia's a stuck-up bitch?" I asked. My tone was sharp but modulated by the fact that I had no way home except in the Hannattie wagon.

"Well, maybe not a bitch," Hattie said, and

Hannah reached over and punched her in the arm—pretty hard too.

"Shut up—let's be good hosts," Hannah said, glaring at Hattie before she turned back to me. "Mia is just a little different. For kids around here, she's kinda hard to *get,* you know?"

"I get it," I said. "She ever come to these things?"

"Once," Hannah said. "But that's enough about Mia. We gotta get ready for the contest!"

"What contest?"

"You'll see."

Hannah and Hattie each grabbed me by an elbow and moved me through the crowd. There were three other girls there, not counting Saucer Dude's apparent girlfriend, and I had a pretty good idea which one of them had declared Mia stuck up. But I met none of them. Instead, they introduced me to every guy there. Everybody wanted to know where I was from, and I couldn't tell if they were envious or suspicious when I said, "Kentfield." You don't have to venture very far outside the Bay Area to understand that the rest of the state is both ready to call you a snob and ready to switch places with you in an instant. One guy, Rob, seemed nice enough, but I was basing that mainly on the fact that he seemed quieter than the others, most of whom couldn't go more than a minute without offering a throaty affirmation to the universe, usually in the form of "woo-hoo" but sometimes with "motherfuckers!" tagged on for reasons I did not attempt to understand.

I began calculating how long it would take for me to walk home.

And then I heard the drumming. One of the guys had grabbed a plastic bucket and was standing on the plywood with the bucket under one arm while he slapped on it with his free hand.

"Hear ye, hear ye, let the Court of the Seventeenth Pole come to order," he called out. I walked over because of course I did. It was Saucer Dude: "We gather again in the shadow of the holy pole to judge the unworthy."

His proclamation was greeted with a collective "Woot! Woot! Woot!"

Part of me thought, *Oh, this must be part of the ritual. I should write this in my anthropologists' notebook,* but a louder part of me thought, *Oh shit, who wants to guess I'm unworthy?*

By the time Saucer Dude climbed up onto the plywood stage and began stamping his foot, the group had formed something like a smaller circle inside the larger circle of cars, like some kind of hillbilly Stonehenge. I was hoping human sacrifice was not part of the evening's entertainment, but I had already recognized the signs of what was really going on. This was going to be a drinking game.

And I hate drinking games.

From what I could tell, pretty much everybody my age did not need a game to get drunk. From beer pong to the cringier moments of Never Have I Ever, the drinking game is usually the point where the evening slips into "we shall never speak of this" territory. It wasn't drinking to drink. It was drinking to show off.

And I knew there was pretty much no way of

getting out of it. I didn't count, but I knew I was a lot farther than seventeen poles from Owl Harbor.

Saucer Dude stopped stomping when he was satisfied he had the congregation's attention. "It is time, my friends, for the counting. Who'll stand first before the pole?" he said, scanning the crowd.

Everything went quiet for a moment, but then a girl on the opposite side of the circle from us stepped forward, half pushed by her friend, and announced, "I swear allegiance to the pole."

She clambered onto the plywood and bowed.

The whole anthropologist thing seemed less and less like a joke.

"Sister Chloe has volunteered," Saucer Dude said. "Do we have a challenge?"

"Cereals!" yelled a guy on the other side of the stage.

"And so it is," Saucer Dude bellowed. "You heard him. Name seventeen cereals. Pause, and you drink."

She looked confident. She started strong. "Cheerios, Rice Chex, Lucky Charms, Cap'n Crunch, Fruity Pebbles." Her rhythm slowed. "Raisin Bran, Golden Grahams, Apple Jacks." She stuttered over the *F* in "Froot Loops", recovered with "Cocoa Puffs", and then stalled out.

"Drink! Drink! Drink!" came the chant. She shrugged and chugged whatever was left in her beer. Drawing applause from the crowd, she bowed again and returned to the circle.

"Who's next?" Saucer Dude yelled, stretching out the "who's" part game-show-host style.

A guy just to our left jumped up on stage, got

introduced as "Brother Bill", and was assigned "cars," which—if you think about it—is a pretty easy category. But still, he ran out of steam around thirteen, finally sputtering out "Hyundai" before pausing long enough to earn the "Drink!" chart. He made a pretty big show out of gulping it down and received a less spirited ovation than Chloe.

One more guy volunteered. He breezed through seventeen video game characters—revealing that the Mario family is far larger than I had imagined—but he still chugged his beer.

I could sense my time was running out. At some point, they'd run out of volunteers and people would start getting called. I knew I might not be the first to get called, but I was going to get called.

I wasn't wrong. Hattie made a valiant attempt at Nickelodeon shows, and then, after making a dramatic entreaty to the "Great Pole in the Sky", Saucer Dude turned his eyes to me.

"New guy!" he yelled. "Approach the stage and face the test of the pole."

I hesitated. It's not like I was eager to be accepted into their drinking cult, but it's not like I wanted to wimp out either. I had this weird feeling that I shouldn't let Hannah and Hattie down, at least not until I'd gotten a ride home.

I stepped onto the plywood, but I didn't perform the bow. I could tell Saucer Dude was bothered a bit, but he went on with the ceremony. "Do I hear a challenge?"

The crowd was quiet. I got the idea they'd all known

one another since preschool, and I was the new guy who needed to be put in his place. It's not like they were going to throw "hog breeds" or "tractor tools" at me, but they might have been thinking about "country stars".

A guy standing off the nearest corner of the stage waved his arm. I'd seen him earlier watching me with Hannah and Hattie and wondered what his deal was. It wasn't until that moment that it clicked that Hannah, probably not Hattie, could have brought me because she knew it would bug some guy. And this was the guy.

The way Hannah was looking from him to me and back to him supported my theory.

Saucer Dude turned to him. "Logan," he said, "bring ye a challenge?"

"I do," my apparent rival said. "Let's hear seventeen chain restaurants, but they have to be chains we've all heard of. He can't just make shit up."

It sounded easy enough, but I had a feeling it could get tough up in the teens.

I started with the obvious. "McDonald's, Pizza Hut, Burger King, Subway, Taco Bell, In-N-Out." I slowed down, trying to give myself time to think and not machine-gun through restaurant names and then end up having to stop to think of more. "Olive Garden, Jack in the Box, Applebee's, Chili's, Little Caesars, Waffle House." I imagined myself driving down a street and what restaurants I'd see. "Wendy's, KFC." I'd sort of lost count, but I knew I was close. I wanted to push past seventeen just to be sure. I was pretty caught up in it. I'd also slowed my speech way down, to give me time to think. I could see Saucer Dude getting antsy.

I'd already figured out that the aim of the game for most people wasn't to make it through seventeen. It was to be seen chugging a beer on a little plywood stage. I don't think anybody had thought of talking really slow. "Red Lobster," I said, only it was more like "Red Laaaaaabsteerr".

Logan was looking pissed.

"Chi-pot-laaay." I was getting kind of panicky. I was pretty sure I was close to seventeen, but I was starting to blank out. Then I blurted out, "Pasta Henry's."

Okay, so Pasta Henry's is not a coast-to-coat operation. There are, like three, of them in the world and all three within fifteen miles of our apartment in Kentfield. I was pretty sure I was going to called on it, but I knew that I could win on a technicality. Three is a chain.

Logan was having none of it.

"Bullshit," he said. "Pasta Henry's is some made-up bullshit."

"I beg to differ," I told him. I couldn't believe it, but I was in a moonlit standoff with some stranger who fancied himself a romantic rival based on nothing and the whole thing was about whether three restaurants qualify as "a chain."

"Look," I said. "There are three Pasta Henry's. That makes it a chain."

"But I said chains we all heard of," Logan snarled back. "I don't know no Pasta Henry's. Any of you guys eat at Pasta Henry's?" He looked around the group but didn't wait for any acknowledgment before saying, "I didn't *think* so."

He had me. I guess. Caught on a technicality. I should have just chugged a beer, but that's not what I did. "You should leave the Delta some time. America's dining experience doesn't begin and end at Los Burgerritos."

I knew, even before I finished saying it, that I'd really stepped off the narrow road and was sliding into the Delta muck. I'd insulted their homeland and, by extension, them—and not only that, I had questioned the temple of all things Delta: Los Burgerritos.

He didn't bother with the typical feints and in-your-face threats that preceded every fight or near-fight I had ever witnessed in my high school existence. He tackled me head-on, and I suddenly was on my back in the gravel, covering up for the expected blows. I only took three, and mostly on my forearms, before he got hauled off by Saucer Dude and two others, one of them Hannah.

I brushed the grass and twigs out of my hair as I sat up. I could taste the blood and ran my tongue up along my upper lip where I could feel a cut—nothing big, but enough that I'd be looking snarly for the next day or so. I didn't bother to look at Logan before I asked, "I guess I should have said Domino's."

My suggestion didn't do a lot to quell Logan's rage, but he didn't need a lot of quelling. He was already cooking up an "I kicked his ass" story and made only a half-hearted attempt at struggling free from Saucer Dude and the other guy. Hannah was off to one side, glaring at me. I was getting similar looks from the rest of the group.

"Hey," I said, getting up and dusting myself off. "I'm sorry that I pissed everybody off. I thought it was a game."

The glaring continued. "Can somebody give me a ride home?" I asked.

Hannah looked like she was debating the matter but finally shrugged. We were in the car two minutes later, and the crowd had gravitated to the other side of the stage from where we were parked.

The entirety of the conversation on the way back was Hannah saying, "That sucked," and Hattie answering, "Yeah it did."

They dropped me off, and I went inside, looking for something to clean off the blood and glad that nobody was awake for interrogation.

12

There's really no good way to hide a busted lip. It didn't swell all hamburger-y, but it wasn't like I could go around with my hand over my mouth, as though I were contemplating some profound thought and about to say, "Hmmm...I never thought of it that way."

So I just came downstairs, ready for the declaration from Lily. I found her in the kitchen. It took less than two seconds. "I knew it!" she said, dropping her spoon back into a bowl of store-brand frosted Cheerios. "See! I knew something bad was going to happen!"

I sighed. It wasn't like I was going to be able to reason with her. I couldn't explain that "something bad" could cover pretty much anything that was going to happen at a high school beer party.

"Just a scuffle," I said. "I think it might be a tradition, the Delta initiation. I've been inducted into the clan."

"But you have to admit I was right!"

"I don't have to admit anything," I said, turning to the refrigerator to review my breakfast options. She answered with what had become her catchphrase.

"You'll never understand," she said, going from gleeful to resentful almost instantaneously.

I sat down across from her with another of the few advantages of life at Uncle Kevin's—a cookie dough Pop-Tart that Mom would have confiscated and burned if she'd seen it. "So, Madam Lilith," I said, "what's on the agenda today? Am I going to be struck by lightning? Gored by a bull? Or am I going to win the lottery and run off with my dream girl?"

"You mean Mia," she said in a dreamy mocking tone that was part cartoon princess and part sitcom smartass. And before I could say, "She's not my girlfriend," she said, "She's *NOT* my girlfriend," in a way that pegged the sarcasm meter.

I didn't answer. I just glared.

"What's really going to happen today," she said, "is that I'm going to make a ton of money telling fortunes and Uncle Kevin is going to make you pull weeds or something, 'cause there is no way he's going to let you give tours with your lip all bloody. It's like a sausage mustache."

She was obviously right about the "no tours" part. I was surprised she didn't claim it as another psychic prediction.

IN THE WAR between man and weeds on the Delta, the weeds are winning. They were certainly kicking my ass that day. I would have done just about any other job around the attraction, but it was a Saturday and three weeks into summer, which meant Uncle Kevin opened early and he didn't want me hammering nails or doing the meticulous glass cleaning that made the mirror illusions work.

For most of three hours, kneeling down and trying to keep the itchier parts off my leg, I did battle with the demon flora. It was hot, sweaty work, and I must have looked like a heat stroke victim when I was pushing the wheelbarrow through the parking lot, because Uncle Kevin showed mercy. He gave me the rest of the day off and promised me half the day's tips.

I collapsed on the porch, my back against the mound of boxes, with two glasses of ice water: one to drink and one to pour over my head.

I probably dozed a bit because Mia was halfway up the gravel path from the parking lot when I blinked back into consciousness. "Hey, coma boy," she said. "You look like shit, or at least you look very Delta."

"Are either of those a compliment?"

She scrunched her face and tilted her head to one side. "Nah, I don't think so, but I heard you were a hit out at Seventeen Poles, and now I can see how big that hit was."

She pointed to her lip.

"How'd you hear that? Did I make the newspaper? Local Boy Defends Delta's Honor?"

"Not the paper, but you made the Gulf High yearbook club Twitter feed. Congratulations!"

"I really have gone native, haven't I?"

Mia smiled and sat down next to me on the porch, our backs leaning up against the tarp that covered the pile of boxes. "Well," she said. "You've certainly been inducted into something, maybe the Seventeen Poles Hall of Fame."

"You're no fan favorite out there either, you know?"

"Of course I know." She put her hand over mine. "I'm obviously back from Sacto. Wanna do something? I see the real Professor Mysterio is running the show. And Madam Lilith looks busy."

"What? And tear myself away from my passion for weed pulling?"

"Take a shower, loser," she said, and she gave my hand a squeeze.

I THINK PRETTY MUCH every Delta teen gets a car when they turn sixteen. It may not be much of a car, but parents probably looked forward to a kid's sixteenth birthday as much as the kid did because they wouldn't have to haul them all over the crappy roads. Mia had a Ford Aspire, which I imagined aspired to avoid the junkyard for another year and a half, two years with clever application of duct tape. But it moved, and for that I was thankful. I didn't even ask where we were going until we'd left the parking lot.

"So," I said, "what's on the program? I don't suppose there is an eighteenth pole where the artists and intellectuals hang out?"

Mia smiled but only with the corners of her mouth. "I've got an idea," she said. "I think you need to check out your competition."

"What, there's a Dugan I didn't know about? Is he dreamy?"

"First, shut up, and second, *no*. The House of Illusion didn't used to be the only attraction in town. There used to be a water park south of Lago Vista. It was never a big deal, and when Slide Zone opened in Fairfield, this place shut down. It's still there though, kinda, and sometimes I sneak in. Half of it is collapsed but there's a beach, and it's sort of fun in an end-of-the-world kind of way."

"Is it haunted?"

"Not since they sealed up the septic tank."

I shrugged, and she smiled. It was maybe a twenty-minute drive, and half the time I just stared out the window. Mia was one of the few girls, really one of the few people, that I felt okay being quiet with. I'd gotten used to it just hanging out at the snack bar while she'd been selling candy and sodas to snotty Delta Kids, but it wasn't until I was in the car that I really noticed it.

We made it all the way through Lago Vista and south on Suisun Highway before anybody said anything. She went first.

"How's Owl Harbor's baby psychic doing these days? Has the fame needle ticked past her yet? Or is she still getting business?"

"She's still getting customers," I said. "But she's giving me the business. She made a startling prediction last night—uncanny, really."

"Tell me, what did the great prophet see?"

"She predicted something bad would happen at Seventeen Poles."

"Really? I could have told you that."

"Yeah, it's pretty stupid. I can only hope she drops it when we get back to Kentfield."

I looked over at Mia when I said that, and I could see her tighten her grip on the steering wheel; not a lot, but enough that I noticed. It was over quick, but her voice sounded different when she spoke again.

"Hath the great seer foretold such a journey?"

"Not yet. Her fortune-telling has thus far been more useless than that. I'm hoping it stays that way. I don't want her coming up with anything that could get her in trouble. At least in Owl Harbor, there's not that much trouble to get in, I suppose."

Mia was quiet. She kept her eyes on the road, but it felt like she was looking at something one hundred miles away. She held her breath for a second before she said, "You'd be surprised."

As she said that, I looked up and saw we were approaching the sagging remains of what had been Splash Town USA jutting out of the utterly flat expanse of the Delta, where anything taller than a mobile home stands out like a monument, and this one a monument to decay. Facing a patch of open water, there had been three slides at some point, one big and two sorta mediums, but the giant yellow-and-blue tubes now hung at disastrous angles from the rusting framework, the plastic baked to brittle by the sun. I always had this vision of an abandoned amusement park as being spooky—or at least creepy, and this place was just sad. It looked like a public service announcement for tetanus shots.

Mia pulled her car around to a side where she could park behind a mostly collapsed metal building that must have held the giant pumps that fed water through the slides and the vats of chlorine it took to offset the many gallons of kid pee. It also hid the car from the road, but I had an idea that the cops only came by at night when they thought they could catch skinny-dippers. I was suddenly glad I was wearing shorts—Mia hadn't told me there would be swimming until we'd been in the car.

"Is it everything I said it would be?" Mia asked, rolling down all the windows.

I was peering up through the rusted metalwork and wondering which way it would fall. "I love it," I said. "It's kind of like *Road Warrior* at the beach. Is there a warlord of the wasteland I need to know about?"

"If there is, he's probably out at Seventeen Poles listing seventeen weapons you can make out of scrap metal."

"Yeah," I said. "I think I met him last night."

We walked around a gaping hole in the fence about ten feet from a sign wired to the chain link that said *DANGER*, as though anyone sneaking into a verge-of-collapse water park might think it was safe. Still, it made sense that Mia told me to be careful as I ducked through the gap right behind her.

We picked our way through some giant barrels

that were bristling with scrap metal and a set of picnic tables so thick with bird shit they looked like sculpture. I was beginning to wonder what part of this seemed like a good idea to Mia when I saw the beach. It wasn't some sprawling Malibu beach, but it was a beach. A fifty-yard strip of sand bracketed on each side with thick tangles of reeds. It was, I had to say, "nice". And a lot warmer than the "Bring your parka!" fogbound beaches I was used to.

"This doesn't suck," I remarked, as much to the universe as to Mia who had brought a canvas bag and was pulling out water bottles and a pair of beach towels.

"Right?" she said. "A private beach just a few steps past the apocalypse."

"Is that on the brochure?"

"They didn't have room. It was mostly a liability waiver for all the things that could kill you."

She smiled up at me. The last of the fog had burned away. She reached into her bag and threw me a pair of sunglasses. "Dollar store specials!" she said. "Delta fashion!"

"Livin' large," I said, settling down next to her. The beach towels looked pretty dollar store too. "Shall I have the cabana boy mix us some drinks?"

Mia layed down on her towel and lifted her hips to pull her shorts down. She'd done the smart thing and worn a bathing suit under her clothes, a one-piece like you see swimmers wear.

"I don't suppose the dollar store had swim trunks?"

"Nope," Mia answered. "But shorts is shorts. You'll be fine."

And I was. We were flat on our backs, eyes closed, watching the sun glow through our eyelids and chatting mostly about nothing. I learned that she was thinking about colleges "but nothing too far" because she didn't think her mom could handle it. She learned that when I had been a kid, I'd thought I'd join the Coast Guard, and she laughed and said, "I hope there's not a canoe test to get in."

The cabana boy failed to show up, but she'd brought ice water, which was a good thing because it was getting hot. I held the bottle to my forehead and felt the cool condensation on my skin. "Are we going swimming, or what?"

"I'm leaning toward 'or what' if 'or what' means lying here for the next half of forever, but I could be talked into a dip," Mia said, sitting up and reaching for the water bottle in mock impatience. I pretended I was going to pour it on her and then handed it to her as though I were a waiter presenting a bottle of wine.

"Anything I should know about Delta swimming? Leaches, unexploded munitions, venomous creatures?"

"I think you met most of the venomous creatures last night—I think you got a ride from two of them, one and a half at least."

"Hattie's only half venomous?"

"Nah, she's full-on venomous, but I'm not sure she's a full person. I've long suspected that she's Hannah's ventriloquist dummy."

"Could be," I said, and I started to say something about Hattie being a robot and an example of "artificial intelligence without the intelligence part", but I got cut off by the distinct sound of a cell phone ringing followed immediately by a guy's voice hissing, "Shut that off."

Mia and I were on our feet in an instant. Standing no more than thirty feet away on the reedy end of the beach—and looking conspicuously like they'd been sneaking up on us—were two teens, one of them the girl who'd botched her cereal soliloquy at 17 Poles. Her name was Chloe, though I was thinking of her as Sister Chloe because of Saucer Dude's reverential theatrics. I didn't recognize the guy—no lights, remember—but I was ready to bet he'd been there.

For a few seconds, everybody was quiet. Standoff silence, like in a movie when two guys have guns, but they decide to warm up to the actual fighting with a staring contest. Mia didn't need much of a warm-up. "Chloe, Evan, funny we should run into each other out here!" She turned to me, sarcasm set on *death ray*. "Nate, have you met Chloe and Evan?"

It was then that I saw the water balloons. Evan had a plastic shopping packed with them, and Chloe had her phone ready. We'd been a few seconds from being a TikTok sensation before Chloe's phone had betrayed her. I watched Mia connect the very few dots in Chloe and Evan's not-so-elaborate plot. "What the fuck, Chloe? What the fuck, Evan?"

"We were just messin' around," Chloe said.

"Yeah, sure," Mia said. "You just happened to be out here at Splash-pocalypse and you just happened to be here on the same day we were and you just happened to have a whole bag of water balloons with you."

The whole time, I was watching Evan. He was looking antsy, like he knew that letting the girls have it out was probably the safest bet, with him and me both on the sidelines while Mia focused her rage on Chloe, but he also didn't want Chloe to think he was a wuss. So he was plotting something that could end up in a little face-off with me—not a real fight, just him acting like he wanted to fight.

Suddenly the cut on my lip throbbed, as if to say, *Remember me? Remember last night? Let's not do that again.* I'd sort of forgotten that had even happened, but I knew the legend of my fighting prowess was not going to intimidate my potential adversary. I was relieved when he turned away from me to watch Chloe get taken down.

"Let me guess," Mia shouted. She'd veered away from the sarcasm thing and was on full attack. "Half the Gulf High student body is wearing their thumbs down to nubs texting 'bout Mia Romero's 'new guy'."

Okay, so part of me wanted to puff out my chest a bit when I heard "Mia Romero's new guy", but the rest of me knew that she was talking about everybody else assuming it, which didn't mean I got to assume it too.

"Were you staking out the marina? The illusion house? Did you have a network of spotters tracking our every movement? Did you hack into the Homeland Security satellite system?"

Chloe was alternating between kicking at the sand and occasionally looking back up to Mia, but mainly she was kicking at the sand. I didn't think she'd thought through what was going to happen after the water balloon assault because she couldn't really handle the merely angry Mia, much less a soaking-wet-and-furious Mia. But when Mia finally ended her screed with, "Well?" followed a heavy sigh and another, "Well?" she knew she had to respond.

"Hannah thought you might come out here. She said you and her would come here when it was still a thing, when you were little kids, with your dad. She said you liked the beach. So we drove by and saw your car. Got the water balloons at the dollar store. That's about it."

"Was there a prize for who could take Mia Romero down? Because I know y'all think I need taking down."

"Well..." Chloe started.

"Well, what?" Mia snarled back. "My mom married a college guy—a *Mexican* college guy—and left, and we got what we had coming 'cause of that? And now I've got more coming? 'Mia thinks she's so smart and Mia thinks she's so this and Mia thinks she's so that.' Listen up, Chloe—you too, Evan. I'm just another kid, and because I don't want to go out to Seventeen Poles and name seventeen different words for puking doesn't mean I think I'm better than you. It just means I *feel* different than you."

Listening to that and seeing how Chloe flinched at parts and wrinkled her brow at others made me wonder how much of it Chloe was really following because I wasn't going to assume she could follow all of it. The girl couldn't name seventeen cereals. But some of it undoubtedly rang true because it sounded pretty goddamn true. A lot of what I wondered about Mia was starting to make sense all of a sudden.

"I don't need a lecture from Mia Romero," Chloe barked, but her head was turned to the side while Mia's eyes bore right through her. Chloe turned to Evan. "See, I told you so. Mia Romero can't take a joke. Never could, never will."

There were enough consecutive seconds of silence that I decided it was my turn to say something. "Maybe you guys should just get out of here," I said. "Take your water balloons over to Los Burgerritos and have a rumble, or whatever it is you guys do."

Evan took this as a cue, as though there was a "Now it's the guys' turn" decree. "Oh great," he announced. "Now we got two people thinking they're better than us. You want a black eye to go with your busted lip?"

"I don't know," I said. "You don't have your Seventeen Poles posse, do you?"

"And I don't need 'em," he growled.

This was the part I always wanted to fast forward through whenever I saw guys act like they were going to have a fight and you knew nobody was actually going to have a fight. It's almost like square dancing: a series of steps that end with everybody shuffling off the dance floor, wondering if the girls noticed their awesome do-si-do.

I pretend to look at my watch, even though I wasn't wearing a watch. Then I pretended to yawn. "Are we done yet?"

Evan looked frustrated because I was obviously not participating in his dominance ritual. I glanced over at Mia, and she was smiling. I got the idea I was scoring a shit-ton more points than I would have gained by crushing Evan's skulls between the gates to the trash-filled kiddie pool.

"You're lucky I don't kick your ass," he growled.

"I guess I am," I said. I could have said any number of smartass follow-ups—"I'm also lucky I don't have your unibrow or your future in the fast-food industrial complex"—but I felt like I was hitting the right notes with Mia by not engaging in Evan's face-off fantasy.

The encounter ended with the same uncomfortable silence it opened with but more like a collective shrug of *I guess we're done here.*

Eventually, Choe did this snitty little shake of her shoulders and Evan followed her haughty trudge through the weeds back to wherever they had parked their car.

I turned to Mia. "Was that another initiation? Have I been inducted into another sacred order? Club? Tribe? Cult?"

She pointed to the towels. "Where were we?"

"I think we'd settled on 'or what'."

"'Or what' sucked," she said. "Let's hit rewind. And forget that shit ever happened."

"Sounds good."

WE DIDN'T TALK for a while. I heard Mia take some deep breaths and then exhale really slowly, and I fell into rhythm with her. It was relaxing, which I guess is the whole point of going to the beach. I imagined I was at a real beach, like an ocean beach, and our breaths were the waves breaking and receding. I also listened to the real water going by and thought about that day on the canoe with Mia and her lesson in "not everything about the Delta sucks". I felt ready to doze off in just a few minutes, which is pretty amazing, given the Evan and Chloe intrusion. Even when she put her hand on mine, I didn't have that sudden rush of wondering what it meant and if I should make a move on her and how soon we were going to be making out and all of that.

We were just being in a place, settling into the quiet.

That's what made the whirring noise so suddenly jarring.

We both stood up. It was electric. That's all I could tell. The whine reminded me of a dentist drill. "What the hell is that?" Mia asked.

A shadow passed over us.

I looked up and saw a drone, bigger than a toy drone but not like some scary death-ray drone. It zipped across overhead, and it was obvious whoever was running it had a camera because I could see it change course when it became obvious that we saw it. It zipped around the back of what had been the biggest water slide and hovered there for a moment, just out of sight.

Then it came flying right at us, and I flinched into a half crouch before it banked wide and zipped back, past a row of dead palm tree trunks lining what had been the front gate and snack bar area.

I wasn't sure what to do, but Mia grabbed my arm and pulled me with her toward the front gate. When we got closer and could look through the metal bars and the sun-ravaged remains of a canvas tarp, I saw a mammoth gray SUV and two guys standing next to it. One of them was piloting the drone. The other one was talking on a phone. They wore black jeans and black polo shirts, less like they'd just gotten off their shifts at a fast-food restaurant. They were older than us but not by a lot.

"Who the hell is that?" Mia asked.

"I don't know, but they don't look like they came out here by accident. They sure as hell don't look like security guards either."

"I don't like it."

"Neither do I."

The drone pilot landed his craft on the hood of the SUV and started packing it into a big plastic case, stopping to unclip what looked like a thumb drive and shoving it into his pocket. The guy with the phone nodded when the drone guy said something I couldn't hear. The phone guy never took his eyes off us, even as he opened the door of the SUV and got in.

They sat there in the car for maybe a minute, hidden behind the tinted windows, before they pulled away and spit gravel pulling onto the road. It was a generic SUV, but the heavily tinted windows made it look vaguely clandestine. I would have figured it for a rental until I saw the license plate: *LUDLOW*.

Mia grabbed my arm. “Did you see that?” I didn’t say anything right away, and she swung around in front of me. “Nate? That license plate...what the hell is going on?”

“I don’t know,” I said. “But I think we’d better get home.”

13

Anybody who grew up on the Delta—and especially anybody who grew up in or near Owl Harbor—knows something about the Ludlow cult. I don't think it's something they taught in school. The California curriculum is more focused on Spanish missions and prospectors. They barely teach the shitty way the indigenous tribes were treated, much less some bizarro gold-fever spiritual cult that ended in violence. I sure as hell hadn't heard about it until Uncle Kevin's little history lesson and what I'd gleaned from that stack of books. It was some obscure crap to most people.

Unless you'd grown up on the Delta, and then it was stuff you heard the adults talking about, and you'd shared whispered shreds of the legend on the playground, all of it more or less linking back to the attraction. On the way back to Owl Harbor, Mia told me that everybody knows about the Ludlovians, and pretty much everything she ran down matched what

Uncle Kevin said, except for the psychic bullshit. All the kids heard that part too, but everybody chalked it off as crap made up for the attraction.

She'd also heard that there were still people obsessing on the Ludlow stuff, like those people who think flying saucers abducted Bigfoot, only these people think that Ludlow really did find the mother lode and that he left clues behind.

"You mean people believe this shit?" I asked.

"Yeah," Mia answered. "They still believe this shit. Ludlow's been dead for one hundred fifty-plus years, and he has, like, followers."

That was something Uncle Kevin had left out of his history lesson.

I was already anxious to get home just seeing the drone operation. I didn't want to find out that the drone guys had already been there and spooked Lily and Uncle Kevin or something worse. I could tell Mia was anxious too because she drove a lot faster on the way home than she had on the way to the water park. I don't think she even noticed the water balloon fight in the dollar store parking lot.

We got to the attraction around 4:00 p.m. The sun was blazing, and everything looked normal, except Madam Lilith had clothes-pinned the bedspread doors closed early on a Saturday afternoon when business was usually pretty good. There were two cars in the parking lot and a woman was rocking a baby on her shoulder over by the picnic table.

I was out of the car as soon as Mia put it into Park. I'd already seen the *Tour in Progress* sign, and I headed to the farmhouse without stopping to check for Uncle Kevin. I was on the front porch a few seconds later with Mia right behind me. "Lily!" I called for the third time as I opened the front door.

The house was not large. I didn't take long to verify that she wasn't there. I ran to the tent to check. It was possible, I figured, that she'd closed up shop but was still communing with the spirit world in private. Except she wasn't.

"Where is she?" I asked, turning around to Mia, who looked only slightly less upset than I did. I'm sure she could tell I was feeling panicky because she spoke really softly when she said, "Maybe she walked to the store, for candy or something."

I wanted to believe that. But it didn't make sense. She hated walking on the narrow road without a shoulder. She'd actually pay me to go get stuff because it freaked her out that much. She pretty much only left the house if Uncle Kevin was driving us somewhere.

I was about to go interrupt the tour, which was a big NO in the roadside-attraction biz, when the woman with the baby came walking over. "You looking for the girl? The fortune-teller girl?"

"Yeah," I said. "You seen her?"

"Yeah, she left about twenty minutes ago," the woman said. "I wanted to get my fortune after my family gets done in there, but she got on one of those airport shuttles. She didn't have a suitcase, just a backpack, but she hopped right on."

I probably looked like a mannequin or a mime cutout because I'm sure I went white in the face and I know I stood there, frozen in place, for a few seconds.

The first words I said probably didn't sound like somebody ready to take charge of the situation either. What I said was, "Oh shit!"

"Where would she have gone?" Mia asked. "Home?"

"Probably. I don't know. She's a pain in the ass, but she's never pulled shit like this before."

I heard a noise behind me, and the people who'd just done the tour came walking out of the secret door room at the end. I heard adults laughing and the voice of a boy exclaiming, "Glad we figured that out! We could have been stuck in there forever!"

I looked past them and saw Uncle Kevin flipping the *Tour in Progress* sign back to *Open*. I guess I looked pretty upset because he came out and his first words were, "What's wrong?"

"It's Lily," I said. "She took off. We don't know where. The woman with the baby said she got on an airport shuttle. Do you know what's going on?"

"No," Uncle Kevin said. "She's been in her tent all day. She had some customers on and off. She didn't tell me anything was wrong."

"Can we call the airport shuttle? They couldn't have made it the whole way?"

I could see Uncle Kevin's expression change. Mia put her hand on my shoulder. "They don't all go the whole way," she said. "She could have just taken it to the end of the BART line and gotten on a train. It's cheaper than riding all the way to the airport, and most people just do that. If you don't have a car, it's really the only way to get to BART. Cabs don't come all the way out here."

She looked at me like she didn't want to say the next part. "And they'd already be there by now. If she left twenty minutes ago, she's at the station."

Uncle Kevin tightened his brows. "How'd she figure all that out?" he asked.

I looked up at him, feeling pretty stupid for having kept a secret that had suddenly turned into a big deal. "She had her phone," I said. "She snagged it out of Mom's car before she left."

He didn't look as upset as he would have if there wasn't so much else going on, but I'm sure he was filing it aside for later discussion. "Have you tried calling her?" Uncle Kevin asked.

I felt stupid again. Mia took over. "We'll call her from the car," she said. She stepped into the gift shop and came out with her number written on a piece of paper. She handed it to Uncle Kevin and said, "This is my number. Call the airport shuttle first. Then call us."

She turned to me. "Let's go."

"Wait," I said. "I want to check something."

I ran to Lily's fortune-teller tent. Folded under the box where she kept the blue bottles was a piece of paper, a blank page pulled out of the back of a book. She'd left a note.

Mia was behind me, and I read it aloud.

Dear Nate,

Mom is in trouble. I KNOW it. I got a feeling about it and tried to call her, but she didn't answer. Something bad is going to happen, and she needs help. I knew you wouldn't believe me so I'm just going to go. I will call when I know something. I've got money. I will be okay.

Lily

I'd already guessed most of that before I even saw the note. It wasn't like she was going to bolt out of Owl Harbor because she was homesick. The Madam Lilith deal was too good to give up just for that. She was constantly telling me all the stuff she was going to buy when we got back home. If she'd had a credit card, there would have been Amazon trucks pulling up every hour.

But her idea that Mom was in trouble reminded me of the guys with the drone. Maybe Mom *was* in trouble.

I turned around to Uncle Kevin, who was just outside the tent. "Some guys were watching us out at Splash Town, creepy guys. They had a drone, and the plates on their big-ass SUV said *LUDLOW*," I said. "You seen anything like that?"

He looked at me and then blinked his eyes closed for a second before he spoke. "It happens sometimes, the Ludlow people," he said. "It's been happening a bit more lately. Get going, and I can tell you more later. I'll stay by the phone."

We were on the road a minute later.

We didn't have a plan that went past getting to the station before Lily got on a train, and I'd given up on that. The trains don't run as much on Saturdays, but after that brief "Ludlow people" conversation with Uncle Kevin and running back into the house to grab the two hundred dollars I'd put aside from a month's worth of tips, Lily had probably been at the train station for at least ten minutes, and we were still twenty minutes away.

I'd already tried her phone three times. She didn't answer texts either. She'd probably turned it off to save the charge. Nobody watched phone battery life more closely than Lily. She got twitchy if it dropped under thirty percent. I tried Mom and got a "This customer cannot be reached". Texts bounced back.

I leaned forward with my elbows on my knees and my head in my hands, my hair brushing the Aspire's dashboard. "Fuck," was enough to sum up the situation, but I added two "fuck"s for emphasis.

Mia reached over and put her hand on my back. "We'll find her," she said. "She's got to answer those texts sooner or later."

"You obviously don't know Lily. She's a stubborn little shit. My mom bought her a pair of shoes she didn't like, and she went barefoot for a week. In the winter. She wouldn't have taken off like this if she wanted to be followed."

"Doesn't mean we can't follow her," Mia said.

"What do you mean?"

There'd been a few times that summer when I had to remind myself that technology didn't leapfrog whole counties just because the residents listened to country music. It shouldn't have surprised me that a teen on the Delta had figured out how to track somebody else's phone. Mia told me she had SPYGYR on her phone and had used it to track people who were running late getting their rentals back to the marina. I guess it was the kind of thing that nobody had gotten around to making illegal yet. "If she's not at the

BART station, we'll run SPYGYR," Mia said. "It will tell us where she was the last time she had the phone on."

I leaned back against the seat and made a fist with my right hand, squeezing it with my left. Mia elbowed me softly. "Remember to breathe," she said.

14

The Antioch BART station on a Saturday is one of those reminders that there are a lot of parking spaces in the world and most of them are empty most of the time. People probably had to park a few hundred yards to get to the platform on a weekday, and we pulled into a spot right across from the ticket machines. I jumped the turnstile, and Mia did the same with a little coaxing. "It will take us longer to buy a ticket than it will to check if she's here," I told her.

The station was as empty as I'd feared. The train that Lily was probably on had left not long after we'd pulled out of the parking lot in Owl Harbor. I looked around, as though there were going to be some sign of her, like she was going to leave notes everywhere she stopped. "I know it's kind of what we expected, but it still sucks," I said as we walked back through the deserted station. "I hope she turned her phone on, at least for a minute."

"Let's check," Mia said.

We hopped back over the turnstiles in case some random transit cop popped out from behind a trash can, and we sat on a bench near the pickup zone. Mia pulled out her phone and opened the SPYGYR app. It was a simple app with alarming capabilities. Mia entered Lily's phone number, and it loaded a map with her last location. Not surprisingly, the dot was right on top of where we were sitting. If she'd turned on her phone, she probably saw my texts. I'd hoped maybe she'd get scared about being out on her own, but Lily liked to think of herself as super mature. She even used that word, *mature*, which sounds really annoying coming from an eleven-year-old. Turning on her phone, seeing my texts, and then continuing with her trip meant she wasn't having second thoughts.

Mia drew my face away from the screen with two fingers on my chin. It's not like I was going to make the little Lily dot move by staring at it. "Where do you think she's headed?" she asked.

"The city," I said, "San Francisco. Then she'll get on the bus up to Kentfield or take the Ferry. If she got this far, she can figure that out too. The only other thing I can think of is an office where Mom sometimes goes that's in the city. Check Mom's phone."

I read Mia the number, and she held out the screen. Mom's phone hadn't been turned on for more than a month. The last place she'd used it was back in the North Bay, a half mile from our apartment.

"Yeah," I said. "But there's no way Lily would know that."

"Still," Mia said. "Maybe we should check. She left ten minutes ago. If traffic doesn't suck, we might get there about the same time."

"Let's hit it."

DRIVING across the far East Bay is a bit like driving back in time. Far enough out, all the houses are new and kind of obnoxious: big houses that are trying to look bigger. As you get closer to the Bay, you're driving through suburbs that aren't as old because there was still room to build stuff closer in. So you start with the new houses trying to look old, with gables and stuff, and then you're driving through neighborhoods that were built when it was cool to look modern. When you finally bust through the hills and you can see the Bay, the houses look old because they *are* old.

Crossing the Bay Bridge into the city, however, is like parachuting into a crazy mix of old, new, and a lot of weird stuff in between. The bridge is super high, and it's almost like you're landing a plane when you come in. Mia looked kind of nervous. She'd only had her license for like three months and driving around the Delta is a lot different than driving into a city.

"You okay?" I asked.

"Yeah. What about you? Are you ready for this? We don't know what we're heading into."

She was right. Between the BART station and the bridge, we'd had time for a phone call with Uncle Kevin, and nothing he'd said made anything very clear. He'd said that when he was growing up there had been a few books about the Ludlow cult, but nobody had paid much attention except for a few guys with metal detectors that Grandma'd had to shoo off the property once or twice. Then the internet had come along, and the real weirdos had started popping up. According to Uncle Kevin, there were a half dozen groups that were mostly chat rooms about how much gold the Ludlovians had found and where it might be. One group had started rooting around up in the Gold Country looking for the site. They'd bought into Ludlow's voodoo bullshit and then connected it to Grandma's made-up psychic crap. Like, they'd bought into the whole "women of Owl Harbor have special powers" stuff.

Why they didn't just ask and thought they needed to creep around with drones wasn't clear but was probably pretty common practice for people who believe in crazy conspiracy theories. If you think the Kiwanis Club is a front for an ancient Druid zombie clan, you're probably not going to do anything the normal way.

Whether I was ready to deal with them was a good question. "I don't know," I said to Mia. "I guess we'll find out. There's a whole lot more we don't know than we do. Let's find Lily first and then figure that shit out later."

We took the first exit as we came off the bridge, and it spit us out pretty close to the bay and not far off Mission Boulevard, where Mom's sometimes office was. I hadn't been there a lot of times, and it took us a couple of wrong turns to get there (I was used to walking from the transit station, and one-way streets don't matter on sidewalks). By the time we found a parking spot close enough to the office, I was guessing Lily wasn't much more than five minutes ahead of us.

If she'd gone to the office and not just gotten on a bus to Kentfield.

We had to walk around a homeless couple—two shopping carts, one tarp, and two dogs—to get to the alley entrance, and I saw Mia tense up at the sight. I reached out and took her hand, and she walked closer to me until we got to the office door, which was hanging half open, a clear sign that something was wrong. Nobody leaves an alley door open in San Francisco, especially not south of Market in the shadow of the Bay Bridge.

A door hanging open was the kind of thing that a smart person would back away from as fast as they could. Unless that smart person was worried his little sister might be inside. I looked at Mia. "Wait here," I said. "I'll duck in real quick and make sure Lily's not in there."

Mia wasn't buying it.

"No way!" she said, nodding her head dramatically toward the shopping cart encampment twenty feet away. "I'm not hanging out here on my own."

I fought the urge to roll my eyes. Bay Area kids grow up with the homeless as the backdrop to every street scene, like extras in a movie. It was easy to forget that people from someplace like the Delta might not be as comfortable with that backdrop. "Okay," I told her. "But be ready to run."

"Got it," she said.

I pushed the door the rest of the way in and saw plaster chips on the carpet and some deep gouges in the door frame where somebody had pried the latch. It was a pretty serious door but not as serious as whoever wanted to get in. Mia followed so close I could practically feel her breath on the back of my neck.

It wasn't much of an office. Mom rented a space on the third floor that wasn't a lot more than a cubicle, but it allowed her to use a small conference room when she was trying to get some company to pay her to figure out who'd hacked them. It's not like she could invite them to our apartment and tell Lily to keep her music down. We were somewhere between the second and third floor when Mia's phone vibrated. She grabbed me by the arm, and I spun around on the spot. The text was from Lily.

You in SF yet? I'm following two guys I saw coming out of Mom's office

I took the phone from Mia to text back:

Yes, where are you? Stay away from the guys. They're dangerous

The reply took long enough that I was getting uncomfortable.

I'm at the bubble tea place. I recognize one guy—told his fortune

I texted back, *Stay there*

"Let's go," I said to Mia. "It's close."

I bounded down the stairs two steps at a time, and we didn't even try to shove the wrenched door back into place. The guys Lily was following would definitely recognize her, and if they were the guys from the drone flyby, they'd probably recognize Mia and me too. The place Lily was talking about was called Boba the Hut, and it was right around the corner. We got there quickly enough, but I motioned for Mia to stop before we crossed the street. Peering through the gap between a pickup truck and a beat-up delivery van that somebody was obviously living in, we could see the front of the tea shop and a pair of plastic chairs set at a chrome table. My heart stopped when I saw what was under the table.

Lily would not have left her backpack. We'd taken transit all over the Bay Area with Mom since we were kids. She nagged both of us to keep our backpack straps looped around an arm or a leg every time we were out. I figured out later that it was mainly to keep us from spacing out and leaving it someplace, but the whole backpack-snatchers storyline made keeping track of our stuff instinctual. There was no way Lily was going to leave it sitting on a chair, right off Folsom Street. Especially not when she was on a mission to save Mom.

It's not like Mia was ready to bolt across the street, but I still held my hand out to stop her. "They got her," I said. "That's her backpack. She wouldn't have left it out there. They must have grabbed her."

"The Ludlow guys?"

"Maybe," I said, and then I darted across the street, scooping up Lily's backpack and heading into the tea shop, Mia right behind me.

There are a lot of tiny tea shops in the city, but Boba the Hut was smaller than most. The fact that the owner had decided to layer rattan over everything to give it a tiki vibe made it particularly cramped. Mia and I had to duck to get through the door and then stay ducked once we got inside. "You see a little girl here, a few minutes ago?" I said.

The guy, who looked old in that shrunken kind of way, was playing solitaire on his phone. He didn't look up when I asked. So I asked again. "A little girl, a few minutes ago, did you see her?"

He still didn't look up. "She ordered peach flavor," he said.

"Did you see who she left with?"

"She ordered peach flavor," he said again, though he said it in a lighter tone because he must have gotten a card he needed.

We stepped outside, and I started unzipping pockets on the backpack. There was enough candy in there to pay for some dentist's spring break and a half-empty bag of Cheetos, which gave me the idea we could just look for orange footprints, but I couldn't find the phone.

"Do you think they took it from her?" I said.

"Doesn't matter," Mia said, pulling out her phone. "If it's turned on, we can still see where she is. But wait." She handed the phone to me. There was a message from Lily.

Don't text back

I didn't have time to figure out what that meant because right then I looked up and saw a gray SUV coming up the street. I put my arm around Mia's shoulder and spun her around so that both of us were looking into the window of a barbershop. The

SUV rolled by. I could see the plates reflected in the window.

LUDLOW

"Shit!" I said. "They got her."

"Got who?" came a voice I didn't expect.

Lily was crouched down between a trash can and a newspaper box. There was no way she'd been there when we'd gone into the tea place. "What the hell?" I said. "What are you doing?"

"I was keeping down so those morons didn't see us," she said. "Unlike you guys who were parading down the street."

"Yeah, a street we wouldn't be on at all if you hadn't taken off without telling anyone," I said. My voice was rising, and I saw Mia standing back like she didn't want to get caught in the sibling crossfire. "Lily, do you know how worried I was?" I said, immediately recognizing how much I sounded like our mom. "What made you think this was okay? What made you think Mom wanted you running all over the Bay Area? What made you think any of this was going to work out for anybody?"

Lily looked impatient. Part of it was an act she was putting on for Mia because if it had just been the two of us, she would have been fussing and crying about how I never listened to her and I was so unfair. But with Mia there, she got to tap her foot and look "mature" while I ranted. "Are you done yet?" she said.

"No," I said. "I'm not. And you'll hear more about

it, plenty more, on the drive back to Uncle Kevin's. We've got Mia's car. Let's go."

"We can't do that; not yet," Lily said. "We're following the Ludlow dudes. They're after Mom, and we have to save her!"

"How are we going to do that? Those guys are gone!"

Lily was pretty good at sounding smug, but she'd never sounded more pleased with herself than she did when she explained her genius spycraft. "I knew you guys were tracking my phone," she said. "And I knew where those guys parked because, duh, *LUDLOW*. They left the door unlocked, and I put my phone under my seat. That's why I said not to text me back. Now we can track them and know exactly where they are the whole time."

I had to admit, it was a pretty ingenious plan for an eleven-year-old to come up with right on the spot. It was also a plan I had no intention of following through with. "Listen, Detective Lily. This is not a game. We don't know who these people are, and we're not going to go chasing them across the city and get in more trouble. We're going to go back to Owl Harbor, and Mom will come get us when she's figured everything out. That's why she took us there."

"What if they're after Mom?" Lily shot back. "They broke into her office. Do we want to wait until they break into our apartment or kidnap Mom? Or maybe they already did."

"You don't know that," I said. I noticed Mia moving into my peripheral vision and got the sense she was ready to referee, but Lily wasn't waiting for her.

"I knew something was going down," she said. "I had a feeling, and I followed it. I got here, and two creepy dudes that have been watching us at Owl Harbor were breaking into Mom's office. I know stuff. You have to admit it."

"I don't have to admit anything," I said. "Now, let's go."

Mia had moved between us. "Look," she said. "Neither one of you is completely wrong. But now that we're down here and we have a way to follow these guys, let's see what they're up to. Maybe Lily's right and your mom needs our help. If we find something out, we can call the police. But if we go home right now, we're kind of leaving your Mom out there on her own."

I'm not sure how it happened, but I'd just been outmaneuvered by an eleven-year-old. It's not like it was the first time. Lily was clever that way. But it was the first time she'd managed to loop in an accomplice who I was beginning to think of as a girlfriend. Suddenly, arguing about it had more consequence than Lily complaining to Mom or glaring at me from the couch.

Suddenly, I was saying, "Okay."

15

By the time we got back to the car, we'd agreed that I'd follow the SPYGYR app and navigate while Mia drove, and Mia had gleefully declared it her "first car chase".

"You're a real city girl now," I'd told her. But it wasn't really a car chase like a movie car chase. It was more like a really slow drivers' ed video. The Ludlow guys had a good head start on us, but I don't think they knew their way around the city because we were able to catch up with them pretty quickly. The fact that we could track them on the phone meant we could stay back far enough that they never figured out we were following them.

They were obviously headed for the Golden Gate Bridge, which meant Mom's office was not the only location they'd traced her to. Our apartment was about twenty minutes north of the bridge.

"Do you think your mom is home?" Mia asked.

I thought about it for a few seconds before I

spoke. "I hope not," I said. "And not just because I don't want them to find her but also because what the fuck? She scoots us off to the Delta for the summer and then just hangs out in the house?"

"The Delta hasn't been so bad for you," Mia said.

"Actually, parts of it have been quite nice," I said, and I leaned forward in my seat to give her an exaggerated sly glance. "I found Seventeen Poles to be absolutely enchanting."

"Aw, you're so sweet."

Lily made gagging noises from the back seat. "You guys are gross," she said.

We were coming up to the bridge just after the sun had gone down, and it was a wet summer fog. Mia was leaning forward as if that were going to help her see better. "Just stay in this lane," I said. "Everybody drives slow in the fog. We're not that far behind them."

People who live near famous places are supposed to be all ho-hum about them like it's no big deal. Mom had jumped us around from one apartment to the next all over the area, but we'd never lived much more than twenty or thirty minutes from the Golden Gate Bridge. Still, every time I crossed the bridge it was kind of exciting. On that night, driving through thick fog and chasing the Ludlovian drone dudes, the bridge felt different. It loomed as this dark, foreboding shape.

I opened up the SPYGYR app and saw the SUV nearing the north end of the bridge. I watched the dot on the map take the first exit and loop around into the parking lot where the tourists stop to take pictures. It was kind of a weird place to stop on a night when the fog was that thick. It wasn't like they were going to be able to see anything. "Hey," I said. "They're stopping on the other side of the bridge, at Vista Point."

"Why would they do that?" Lily asked. The Aspire was so small that she could pretty much lean through the gap between the seats, like she was in the front seat with us—or at least her head.

"I don't know, but we can park at the other end of the lot," I said. "They won't be able to see us in the fog."

It wasn't like I needed to tell Mia to slow down for the turn. We were already going really slow. When we stopped, she let out an exaggerated sigh and slumped in her seat, her hands sliding off the steering wheel. We could see the gray SUV at the other end of the lot, but only because they still had the headlights on. When the headlights switched off, it became a darker gray shape in a sea of gray. I wasn't sure what to do except wait.

"What do you think they're doing?" Mia asked. She hadn't spoken since the other side of the bridge, and it was nice to hear her relaxing from her white-knuckle trance.

"I have no idea," I said. "Crappy night for a drone flight."

"Yeah," Mia said.

I was about to get out of the car and sneak closer as if they were going to stand outside and give a press conference on whatever stupid plan they had when another car pulled in. The dome lights in the SUV came on, and I could see both guys get out to approach the other car.

Suddenly, my sneak-and-spy plan didn't seem so stupid. Unless they were all going to get into the new car, a little conspiracy carpool, I might actually hear something about what was going on. "You guys stay here," I said.

If there was no fog and there'd been enough light to see, I would have been a full-on spectacle, crouching and scurrying across the lot looking more like a squirrel chasing a bread crumb than the *Call of Duty* commando I was trying to be.

The other car was a generic sedan, but I saw a rental decal on the back when I got close, which told me that the SUV guys had met somebody from out of state on their wack-job conspiracy chat room. The fog allowed me to get right up behind the back bumper to listen when the driver got out and stood with the drone dudes in front of the SUV.

The new guy sounded older. I'd heard that voice before. I couldn't remember where, but I was imagining him with a stupid big mustache for some reason. "What do you have to report?" he asked. "Where is she?"

There was a bit of silence, and I imagined the drone dudes shuffling with their hands in their pockets before one of them said, "We identified the younger asset and established her location at the Owl Harbor site. We attempted to reconnoiter the mother at her San Francisco office but failed to procure evidence of her presence."

This was some serious nerd speak, the way

people talk if they've spent too much time playing in some dorky RPG universe. But it made it pretty easy to figure out what they were up to. Drone Guy kept going. "The younger asset presents with abilities as predicted," he said. "We are attempting to verify the veracity of her predictions."

I couldn't even see the older guy and I knew he was getting impatient. Hell, *I* was getting impatient. He tore into them pretty good. "Look, boys, let's talk like real people, in the real world, where real shit happens. Say all that again, but just talk normal like."

A different Drone Guy talked this time. "We saw the girl at the House of Illusion in Owl Harbor. She told my fortune. She said I would find what I was looking for but I needed to watch my step. I asked her where I should look, and she said, 'Where the waters meet.' The boy is working at the attraction. We have no awareness of heightened abilities."

"You're doing it again," the new guy said.

"Okay, sorry," the second drone bro said. "We didn't see anything interesting about the boy. No abilities were observed."

"What did you find in the city?" the older guy asked.

"We went to the mother's office. She wasn't there. We didn't see any sign she'd been working there recently."

The older guy waited for a truck to pass before he went on. "Okay, she seems to have disappeared," he said. "I checked out the mother's apartment. She hasn't been there in weeks. The mail's all stacked up."

"She hasn't appeared online since before the girl-psychic stuff pinged up," the other drone bro said, the first time he'd spoken since the new guy had shut him down for the geek speak. "She probably knows we're after her."

"Of course she does," the older guy said. "She has the gift. That's why we need her. We need to find her before she goes to get the girl and the boy. If we can't locate her, we'll go back to Owl Harbor for the girl. We need at least one of them if we're going to find the lode."

"We will await further instruction," the geekier drone dude said.

"How about you just wait for me to call you?" the older guy said. "But keep it simple on the phone. The others might be tracking us."

I heard the door open on the rental, and I took off in my crumb-chasing squirrel crouch. "Turn on your lights," I said when I was back in the car. We were facing them, and I knew the fog glare would keep them from seeing what us well enough to recognize the car. They'd definitely seen it at Splash Town and probably some other spots too, given all their "reconnoitering". Their headlights swept across us as both cars looped around to leave the parking lot. The SUV didn't stop, which meant the headlights trick worked.

"Well?" Mia and Lily said simultaneously, Lily's head practically on my shoulder.

"What did you find out?" Mia asked.

I took a deep breath and turned in my seat to face them. "They're after Mom and Lily," I said. "They think they have psychic abilities, and they think it's going to lead them to Ludlow's gold—the 'lode' they called it."

"Seriously?" Mia said. "They said all that?"

"Yeah, I know. They didn't go into it a lot, but I think they've been talking for a while. It sounds like Lily going all viral pushed them to actually do something. I'm not sure they were after either Mom or Lily before all that."

Lily was quiet and leaned back from her between-the-seats perch.

"The guys with the drone were looking for Mom in the city," I said. "The other guy's been looking up in the North Bay. They haven't found her. They're probably heading back to Owl Harbor tomorrow. We need to call Uncle Kevin and let him know, but it sounds like they're just after Lily and Mom."

"What are we going to do?" Lily asked, kind of mumbling from the back seat.

"We need to get into the apartment, but maybe not tonight. We need to be careful about it, even though it sounds like they don't think Mom has been there. Maybe if we go in the morning, they'll be on their way to Owl Harbor. It just sounds safer in the morning."

"What are we supposed to do until then?" Mia asked. "Drive around all night?"

"We can crash at my friend Johnny Kim's house. His parents have a massive basement, and they're never home."

Mia looked doubtful—I didn't really blame her—but then she said, "I'll come up with something for my mom. My Sacto cousins can say I stayed another night, but we have another problem," she said, smiling. "I'm hungry too."

Lily leaned forward through the seats again. "I've got food."

"Since when are Cheetos and Red Vines food?" I asked.

"Since right goddamn now," Mia exclaimed, pivoting in her seat to hold the backpack while Lily dug through it.

It's not that I have anything against Red Vines or Cheetos, but the two together sounded more messy than good. I imagined all three of us with Cheeto mustaches and red goop between our teeth, like zombies with bad makeup. But that was only part of the problem. I guess I knew it was good that Mia and Lily were bonding, whether it was over carbs and artificial coloring or not, but I knew it also meant I was going to outvoted and outmaneuvered for the rest of this trip.

And probably the rest of my summer.

"Wow," I said, as they tore open the plastic bags. "It's like somebody threw a pizza into a hyena pen."

Mia looked up at me, a Red Vine hanging from her lip like a cigarette and handed me her phone. "Did you make reservations at the Hotel Johnny's Basement?"

I held the phone without unlocking it. "My phone knows his number, but I don't know his number," I said. "We're just going to have to show up and hope he's home."

. . .

JOHNNY'S PARENTS lived on one of those streets north of the city where you're in a cute little neighborhood and then you turn right and, suddenly, you're in the redwoods, big giant trees towering over everything like you're in *the Lord of the Rings* and you expect to see orcs and dragons. I mean, everything's expensive in the North Bay, but when you're up in the redwoods, you're talking old money or tech money or old tech money.

And like everybody else up there, it wasn't enough, or it didn't seem like it was ever enough because Johnny's parents were always off chasing more of it. His half-sister was supposedly half in charge when they were gone. I remember nothing about multiplying fractions, but I think half times half in the Kim family equaled zero, maybe less than zero. Johnny could have held a raging kegger every night and gotten away with it.

But that's not who Johnny was.

Johnny could afford flash, but he didn't like flash. I think he got it from his father, who'd grown up poor in South Korea and wanted his son to be rich without acting rich. Johnny's mom wanted a big-ass house and she got one, but Johnny still walked to school. It seemed to fit him too. Most nights at Johnny's, even when his parents were out of town, were maybe three or four people and only people who were cool with not having to be cool. Maybe that's why we were friends. When you grow up in the crappiest apartments in the highest-end zip codes because your mom wanted you to go to good schools, you surrender all right to cool before you even step on campus. Johnny was too laid back to care that I wore Walmart jeans.

Walking up the super long driveway, I was banking on laid back. You don't ask just anybody for a no-warning overnighter for three. That's why I was surprised at all the cars, nice cars, like the lot at a Lexus-Tesla dealership. At first, I was worried that his parents were throwing a party, which would suck for our lodging scheme, but when I started seeing *Student Lot* parking stickers from our high school, I guessed our lodging ideas would suck in an entirely different way.

The basement had a separate entrance—I'm not sure I'd ever actually gone in through the front door—and it was wide open with light and music pouring out. There were kids on the lawn outside the door, and I saw a couple of vape clouds puff into the sky. The whole thing looked like a commercial for Apple Watches and fake tans. On the Delta, I'd kind of forgotten that "distressed" jeans were something you paid for and not just something that happened after you'd owned them for a while. I stopped, and Mia took my hand, tugging gently to get me walking again. I felt for a moment like I was walking through deep mud in flip-flops. I saw people I knew, and most of them looked back like they didn't recognize me. I'd been gone six weeks.

Tammy Simms recognized me though. Tammy was one of those kids who knew everybody because she wanted everybody to know her. She didn't bother running for class president because that would have been redundant. The center of the universe doesn't need a button that says *Center of the Universe*.

"Hey, Nate Cortland," she said. "I didn't know you were coming. You, like, disappeared this whole summer."

It occurred to me as she noted my absence that we pretty much never talked. The fact that she hadn't seen me didn't exactly say she was stalking me, but it did mean she'd kept me on her radar when I didn't bother to think of her the moment she left my field of vision. Keeping everybody on her radar at some level must have been important to her.

"Yeah, I've been staying," I said, pausing, "with family for the summer while my mom has this big job."

I didn't have to look to see Mia stiffen. I could easily have said I'd been staying on the Delta, and I'd stopped myself because I didn't want somebody I didn't even care about looking down on me. I'd been back in my old world exactly two minutes, and I was already acting like the Delta was a mobile-home park from one end to the other, a place for *those* people. I was snobbing it up with the snobs like it was an instinct.

Tammy nodded to Mia, saying, "Who's your friend?" with enough of a space between "your and "friend" to make we knew she was being judgy.

"This is Mia Romero," I said, suddenly becoming the one who sounded stiff because I wanted to say "my girlfriend", but we hadn't had the girlfriend/boyfriend talk even though I was reasonably confident that's what both of us were thinking.

But hey, what's better for an awkward conversation than another whole layer of awkward.

I also saw Tammy's eyes flick at "Romero". I'd forgotten that as liberal as North Bay tends to be, the Delta isn't just mobile homes to them, it's migrant workers too. I suspected there were more than a few Marin kids who would march for immigrant rights in the morning and cross the street to avoid a Latino family that same afternoon.

"How nice to meet you," Tammy said, scrunching her face into the fakest smile ever. "Have a great time."

As Tammy floated away to continue her census, I felt relieved to escape the spotlight but even more relieved to see Mia smiling at me when she asked, "Is it always this weird?"

"Yeah," I said. "Pretty much."

"It must be exhausting."

"Tell me about it."

Tammy was not the only "Tammy type" we saw. I saw two of "the Camerons". I'm sure the third was studying theater in Vancouver. Austin Hearst was there, which meant sailing camp in Costa Rica was over because he'd talked about that at every chance for the last half of spring semester.

These were not Johnny Kim people, not at all. They were the kind of kids who made fun of his dad's accent, the kind of kids who honked and laughed at him from their Audis when they saw him walking to school.

For a second, I thought maybe Johnny had moved away or been replaced by some alternate Johnny

Kim. Maybe Owl Harbor wasn't the only place where the membrane between universes was stretched thin.

And then I saw two opposing universes collide.

Olivia Blum was tall. Even in Kentfield, where it sometimes seemed like there was a breeding program to raise a race of superwomen, she stood out as especially tall and especially blonde. She was also on the flashy side, further to that side than I'd ever realized before that moment. With Johnny Kim neither flashy nor tall, the pairing would be pretty "Huh? What? Seriously?" even if you were expecting it.

And I totally wasn't expecting it.

I probably stood at the doorway for at least thirty seconds, Mia right next to me and Lily glaze eyed at all the booze and vaping she probably knew existed but was several (I hoped) years away from experiencing firsthand. I didn't really think that blinking would reset the program and things would shift back to a more normal kind of normal, but I kept blinking anyway. Mia nudged me. "Are we going in?"

I turned to say something, even though I had no idea what to say, but at that point, Johnny must have seen me because what I heard from across the room was "NAAAATE COORRRTLANNND" in a throaty voice I had no idea Johnny Kim possessed.

It wasn't like there was some sea of bodies between us—it was a real party, not a Netflix teen movie party—but the few people in the room did actually move out of the way for Johnny and Olivia to cross the room. Somehow, the quiet and shy Johnny Kim had become the kind of guy people got out of the way for, the kind of guy who threw parties, the kind of guy who, I don't know, "held court".

"Nate," he said as he got closer, pulling Olivia with him. "Where the hell have you been? You disappeared. You poofed out of existence. *Poofed,* I say. I texted you at least twenty times back in June, back before Olivia and I got together."

I swear his voice boomed by ten decibels at "got together", as though the whole party wasn't already Exhibit *A* in Johnny Kim's campaign for official recognition of his conquest. I willed myself to stop blinking and finally spoke. "I've been staying with my uncle for the summer," I said. "My mom had to deal with some stuff. I've been offline."

"I'll say," Olivia declared, leaning on Johnny's shoulder in a way that wasn't at all gropey but suggested gropeyness.

I felt Mia's elbow on my ribs and snapped out of the shock for a moment. "This is my friend, Mia," I said, painfully aware I'd once again paused three too many microseconds between "my" and "friend". "We've been hanging out."

"On the Delta! I know!" Johnny boomed. "Not everybody's been offline," he added leaning around me to wave at Lily.

I'm sure I slumped at that, even though I was trying not to slump because I didn't have any slump left when Olivia said "Oh, the Delta" exactly the way somebody would say it if that somebody was tall and beautiful and dating a guy who's six inches shorter than her because his father is eight figures richer than just about anybody else in town.

Mia's elbow was sharper this time.

I turned around, and she was already leading Lily out of the room. I looked at Johnny and Olivia and shook my head before saying, "Thanks. Nice party," and turning toward the door.

"I miss ya, buddy," Johnny called out. "Don't be a stranger!"

Lily and Mia were two Range Rovers and three BMWs down the driveway when I caught up with them. "I'm sorry," I said, and it must have been a pretty good apology because Mia didn't look mad when she turned around.

"I know," she said. "I can tell." She leaned down and whispered something to Lily and handed her the keys. Lily smiled and then turned around to walk to the car.

"That felt like shit," she said. "But the thing is I knew it felt like shit to you too and you didn't try to pretend like it didn't happen. I could see that in you before we even saw Johnny and that Tammy person. I could see you tighten up." She reached up and put her hands on my shoulders. "Right here," she said, squeezing the muscle where it leads to the neck. "You were stiff like a corpse by the second Tesla. This may be your home, but you're not *at home* here. You don't have to apologize for something you're just figuring out."

I was quiet through three deep breaths, and when Mia stepped close to me, I could feel her breathing deep against me. "I know," I said. "You're right."

She put her head against my chest, and we stood very still, the redwoods shooting into the sky above us. I heard the music from the party fade when somebody shut the door, but I could still hear people talking on the lawn. The car next to us was so black I could hardly see it in the dark, but the blinking light on the dash had me worried that it was about to let loose with some night-shattering alarm because we'd stood to close to it.

"We should go," I said, taking her hand.

"Let's do that," she said.

16

Sleeping in your own bed is supposed to feel like, well, sleeping in your own bed. When it feels unfamiliar, strange, and just plain wrong, it's probably a sign that something has changed in your life. We'd moved around so much that you'd think that it totally wouldn't matter, but that night, back in my bedroom, with all the familiar clutter—the Foo Fighters poster, the stack of comic books, and two skateboards leaning against the closet door—I felt like I might as well have been in some other guy's bedroom in some other town. I was practically lonesome for the weird sloping-porch room back in Owl Harbor.

Of course, being on the run from weird treasure-hunting conspiracy dudes could have had something to do with my unease, but we didn't really feel like we had anywhere else to go. Two teens and a tween checking into a motel and paying cash was going to trigger a "Runaways!" call to 911. The fact that my maybe-almost-girlfriend was sleeping in my mom's bedroom on the other side of the wall might have had some influence on my slumber as well. I'd tried, awkwardly, to keep her from getting a peek at the disaster I'd left behind in my room in our panicky exodus half the summer before, but there is no way you can say "and you can sleep in my mom's room" without injecting a heavy shot of uncomfortable weirdness into the evening. Suggesting we share a bed had a *way too soon, dude* vibe to it.

Whatever it was, I only half-ass slept, but I still managed to wake up later than I'd expected. It was nearly 8:00 when I blinked awake and stepped into the hallway, remembering that the last time I'd opened my door I'd nearly tripped over my suitcase on a morning that felt like a year ago. The sound from the kitchen told me I wasn't the first person up, and I don't know why I was surprised that the earlier riser was Mia.

She had three cabinets open when I got to the kitchen, which was not unexpected. The refrigerator was bare but for some spoiled milk. We'd made a late-night dinner of canned soup the night before—the only thing we could find—but soup is hardly a breakfast food. She was wearing my mom's bathrobe, which was unexpected and maybe even weirder than her sleeping in my mother's bed the night before.

She turned to me as I stepped into the doorway, noticing how oddly unfamiliar the kitchen felt. "Just how health nutty is your mom?" she asked. "I didn't know there were that many kinds of granola. Gimme some gluten, man. Gimme some high-fructose corn syrup!"

I leaned over the kitchen island, my elbows on the butcher block. "I know a guy who can score you a little hydrogenated fat, maybe some artificial sweeteners," I said, "if you've got the cash."

"Anything that begins with Pop and ends with Tart would work."

She smiled at me and stepped around the island, putting her hands on my shoulders and kissing me on the cheek. "I'm going to get ready. We should probably get going," she said. "Wake up your sister."

Lily was a gifted sleeper. At eleven, I had still been one of those kids that was up with the TV on before Mom had even made her coffee. But Lily slept like she'd been drugged. I got her to acknowledge the existence of the conscious world only on the promise of a drive-through breakfast, and I went to get ready, even though I'd slept in the shorts and T-shirt I'd put on almost twenty-four hours before and there was not a lot of getting ready to be done.

Mia was in the hall when I stepped out of Lily's room. She'd ditched the bathrobe for a Lululemon windbreaker from Mom's closet, significantly less weird but still a little weird. "Let's do another walkthrough," she said. "We might have missed something last night."

The "Mom must have left a clue" sweep had been brief the night before. Somewhere between soup and sleep, we'd dug around to see if there was any indication of where she'd gone or even why she left. Her laptops were still there, which didn't make sense if she thought somebody was after her or even if she had gone somewhere for a while. It's not like she was going to leave a note. We hadn't found anything, but Lily had trudged straight from the car to her bed, not even pretending to participate. Mia suggested another set of eyes would probably help.

She was right.

Lily was awake all of maybe two minutes when she pointed up on a shelf across from the folding table where Mom sat when she patrolled the cyber underworld. On the shelf, next to two trophies from Lily's abbreviated and unspectacular peewee soccer career, was one of those blue bottles. It's possible it was there when we left. They're small. But it seemed unlikely. We'd been tripping over little blue bottles for weeks, and it probably would have jogged our memory.

Mia squeezed around the table and stepped over a nest of assorted cables Mom had left on the floor. She snatched the bottle and held it to the light, peering through the glass at the note inside. "I can't make it out," she said, "but it's not like the other bottles."

I took it from her. "I think we can bust this one open. There are plenty where this came from."

I'd never looked closely inside one of the bottles before. I'd always been curious what the notes said, but none of them were really legible. So when I rapped it on the side of the sink to break it and then plucked the note out of the blue shards, I was surprised to see the paper was obviously new. It wasn't some old timey parchment, and if you think about it, there is no way paper floating in water was going to last one hundred seventy-whatever years anyway.

But it was the handwriting that was a giveaway:

A safe place

Mia was looking over my shoulder. I read it aloud to Lily.

"What does that mean?" Mia asked. "I thought they were supposed to be wishes."

"It's a Ludlow note," I said, "But Mom wrote it."

"What do you think it means?" Mia asked.

I laid the note flat on the counter. It made sense that Mom had left the note for us, but it also seemed obvious to me that she hadn't wanted to leave a note that somebody would see and think was anything but another one of the old Gold Rush–era artifacts, like the dozens of them that were all over the Owl Harbor house or the ones we sold in the gift shop. The only reason we'd opened it was because I was pretty sure it hadn't been there when she'd rushed us out of the apartment now more than a month before.

"I think I know what it means," Lily said.

We turned to her. "Remember," she said, "Mom told us that if something goes wrong, like an earthquake or a fire, and we can't go here, we should go to the park—the one on the hill—with the statue. She said that was our 'safe place'."

"That might not be what she means," I said.

"But it might!"

I looked at Mia, but all she had to offer was a shrug. "We can try it," I said. "But I doubt she's hanging out at the park. Get your backpack, Lily, and let's go."

Lily dashed back to her room, a little more eager than I'd expected, and I turned to Mia. "We should probably check up on the drone dudes. Open the app."

"I did that first thing," she said. "No signal. Battery's probably dead."

"That makes sense," I said. "But it also sucks."

"What sucks?" Lily asked, stepping back into the kitchen with her backpack.

"Your phone's not transmitting. We can't track those dudes."

"We don't need to if we can find Mom," she said, and I suddenly understood her enthusiasm, though I wasn't sure I shared it.

It wasn't until we opened the front door a few seconds later that I knew how little I understood.

Right there, on the middle of the mat just outside the door, was Lily's phone, sitting with the battery pulled out on top of a piece of paper that looked like a hotel receipt.

Nice try, it read.

IT WASN'T LIKE we could stay in the house, although that was a really tempting idea. We probably could have called the police, but in that moment, all I could think about was calling 911 and saying "somebody brought our phone back" and how stupid that was going to sound. So we left. We didn't see the SUV. There weren't a whole bunch of places to hide on the street. The idea was that we could get to the park, and we'd hopefully be able to tell if somebody was following us.

It was a shitty plan, but it was a shitty situation to begin with.

"Here we go," Mia said, turning the key.

"Yep," I said. "Hopefully this isn't your second car chase."

"For the record," she said, "I prefer to be the chaser."

It was only about two minutes to the park where Lily thought Mom's note was telling us to go. It was just a tiny park, but it was close enough to our house and, according to Mom's theory, not near anything that was likely to fall down in an earthquake or burn up in a wildfire: California's two most common—but not only!—disasters. And it was high enough that it wasn't going to flood either, though that was low on the list of probabilities most years.

I didn't see anybody following us, at least not in a Gray SUV with *LUDLOW* plates, but we looked through the car when we got there to make sure they hadn't tucked a phone or any other tracking device in the Aspire while they'd been dropping off Lily's phone. We found three dollars and seventy-five cents in loose change and an earring Mia had lost six months before, but none of the kind of tracking tech I'd assumed treasure-hunting conspiracy geeks would have closets crammed full of at home.

"I think it's clean," I said. "But now we can only wonder where they're off to."

"I know," Mia said. "We should call your uncle again in a few."

The statue at the top of the park was one of those ones that people hadn't gotten around to toppling yet—any white pioneer guy in 1800's California was probably on the shortlist for a spot in the county storage lot. The cool thing about the statue though—and the thing that made me hope it didn't get hauled off—was that somebody took the time to dress frontier statue guy for the seasons. During the winter break, he'd be wearing an ugly sweater. At graduation, he did the whole cap and gown thing. On that middle-of-summer morning, he was wearing a Hawaiian shirt and a hula skirt.

"'Lot going on with this guy," Mia said. "I'm glad he's being treated with the dignity he deserves."

"You should see him at Halloween," I said. "No small number of pumpkins have been sacrificed to his honor. A big orange gorefest every year."

"Who does it?"

"I'm sure it's somebody at the facility," I said, and I pointed a building on the other side of the park from where we parked. "It's a mental health rehab place."

As soon as I said the words, I froze in my steps.

What place was safer than a place with no sharp objects, a place with a padded room, a place where people were taking care of you every hour of every day? And where do people go when they think they're being followed? When they think the world is closing in?

I looked over at Lily, who was walking around the statue, staring and turning her head to see it from different angles, searching for a clue in an exaggerated almost mime-like way.

And it was pretty obvious she hadn't seen the biggest clue, the one right across the street.

I pulled Mia aside.

"I think I know where my mom is," I said.

"Where?" she said.

"Right over there," I said, pointing at the building. "Maybe she thought she was going crazy. She thought she was imagining that people were after her. She didn't know people actually *were* after her."

"Are you sure?"

"I guess there's one way to find out," I said. "You stay here with my sister."

I took a big breath and called out to Lily. "I'm going to ask the hospital place if they've seen anything. You stay here with Mia."

She nodded and went back to scrutinizing the statue.

It had been nearly twenty-four hours since I'd left for Splashtown with Mia the day before. We'd been droned. We'd driven a panicky trip into the city. We'd tailed conspiracy dudes across the Golden Gate Bridge and then been stalked by those same dudes. And don't forget stumbling into the culture shock of Johnny Kim's extreme social makeover.

But the walk across that grassy field made all of that seem like a blip. Somehow it felt longer than all of those hours put together.

And also, not long enough.

It probably only took me a minute to get to the front door, a big glass job that opened into an atrium with a small fountain and a lot of plants. Except for the carved redwood sign that said *North Bay Mental*

Care, it could have been an architect's office or maybe a fancy hotel. It sure as hell didn't look like a place for crazy people. I wasn't at all surprised when I heard that sort of soft ambient violin music they play at massage studios. On the other side of the atrium, a woman sat at an elevated desk. She was wearing a headset and could have been the hostess at a fancy restaurant.

I walked over to her, gulping three times on my way.

"Excuse me," I said, "I'm looking for somebody, and I think she might be here. Can you check if Rachel Cortland is here?"

"I'm sorry, sir," she said. "I can only divulge the names of our patients to direct family members. Can I ask your name?"

"Nathaniel Cortland," I said, using Nathaniel because it seemed like that kind of moment.

I knew as soon as I'd said it that it triggered something for her.

"Can you wait just a moment?" she said. She smiled, but her jaw remained stiff while she reached for a phone console on the desk. She paused and then spoke into the headset. "Hi, it's Kristy, up front. I have a Nathanial Cortland at the Sycamore entrance." I saw her nod. "Okay, I will have him wait here."

She looked back to me. "The attending psychiatrist will see you in just a moment."

. . .

If I thought the walk across the field had been long, the three or so minutes I waited felt like an absolute eternity. It wasn't like a normal waiting room where you can sit and read old magazines. It was this weird little entry atrium thing with a fountain and nowhere to even sit. I'm sure the whole setup was supposed to be all easy breezy and non-threatening, but it just felt surreal when I was waiting to find out if my mom was in a mental hospital, a luxurious loony bin, but still a mental hospital.

I heard the door open behind me and looked up to see a woman in a white lab coat approach with her arm extended for a handshake. "Nathaniel," she said, "I'm Dr. Brayden. Would you care to step inside?"

"I'd care to know what's going on." I said. "Is my mother here?"

"Again, I think it's best if we step inside."

I followed her to the door, and we waited while the woman at the desk buzzed us in. The doctor led me to an office with a long leather couch and a desk that sat in front of a floor-to-ceiling window looking out on a hillside. If we'd been at a different angle, I could have seen Lily and Mia in the park, probably fighting over the remaining Red Vines by that point.

"Nathaniel," she said, "I am sure this is all very disconcerting for you but let me assure you your mother is being very well cared for and is making impressive progress."

"So you're saying she's here."

"Of course," she said, and then she paused and glanced to the side for a moment. "Were you not aware?"

"No," I said. "I just figured it out a minute ago. We've been staying up on the Delta for the summer."

"Yes, your mother said she made arrangements. That's why we were surprised to see you this morning. You were in the care of a relative, correct? Has something happened?"

I was pretty damn sure I hadn't done anything wrong, but there's nothing like being in an office, getting asked questions by an adult in a lab coat to make you think you've not only done something wrong but there's actually something wrong with you. I decided I didn't need to tell her about drones and Lily's psychic shenanigans.

"Can you tell me why she's here?" I asked. "Can I see her?"

The doctor took a deep breath and looked down at a notepad on the desk. I could see that the pad was completely blank, but I guess it gave her something to look at that wasn't me. "Your mother," she said, "has become very fearful, and she has come to believe that her fears were not entirely reality driven. She became concerned that she could not properly care for you and your sister, and she sought help here."

"This was her idea?"

"Yes, her admission was self-directed."

"Can she leave? Today?"

"Do you believe she needs to?"

It was my turn to stare at something, and I settled on a bench in the garden beneath the window. I was suddenly imagining my mother sitting there in the afternoons, just inside the gate that separated the facility from the park she'd declared our safe place. I thought about the times she'd called us on the Delta and how artificial it seemed now. She might have been calling from the office where I was sitting. I thought of the morning she'd left us in Owl Harbor and the hushed talk she'd had with Uncle Kevin. I thought of how careful Uncle Kevin had been when he talked about her.

I thought about a lot of things, but I couldn't think of what I'd say if I could see her.

Dr. Brayden saw me lost in thought and asked again, "Do you believe she needs to leave the facility?"

"I don't know what she needs," I said, "but I guess I always knew she needed help. And I guess I'm glad she's getting it."

"Would you like me to ask if she wishes to see you?"

It was not a question I was ready for. She'd put us with Uncle Kevin for a reason. She'd had a plan, and that plan did not include me and Lily surprising her at a mental health center.

I wanted to keep staring at the bench in the garden, but I looked right at Dr. Brayden instead.

"I think so, yes," I said. "Do you think she's ready?"

"Do you think you're ready?"

"No," I said. "But I guess I need to be."

17

Mia looked anxious and Lily looked suspicious when I walked out to talk. I'd only been gone maybe ten minutes, but I knew how long ten minutes can seem when you're waiting for somebody, and you don't really know what's going on. I'd decided I wasn't ready to tell Lily that Mom was in a mental hospital. I made up a line about how they could connect us with somebody who would help us figure out what was going on and I was just going to check with them again. She wasn't buying it, but when I told her Mia would take her to her favorite bakery, Flour Child, for gooey rolls she decided she'd settle for that instead of digging for answers I would not be providing.

I didn't need to tell Mia that I'd found Mom. We said a lot to each other with only our eyes in that quick exchange.

I headed back to the facility, knowing more than I'd known when I'd made that walk the first time, but the main thing I knew was that I wasn't ready. I think the woman at the front desk understood that because her smile seemed more concerned than forced this time. A man in blue scrubs waited for me at the door and took me to a room with a beige couch and an armchair that almost but didn't match and was positioned in a way that made it obvious it was where the person in charge of the situation would sit. Dr. Brayden was already there when the nurse led me in.

Mom sat at the end of the couch, dressed in joggers and a loose-fitted top, both gray. Her eyes drifted in some middle distance, and several seconds passed before she looked up at me. When she finally did, she stayed seated, and I had to lean down to hug her. She held me there with her head on my shoulder for enough time that I started to think about Dr. Brayden watching us, and when she let go I sat close enough to reach out and hold her hand.

"Hi, Mom," I said.

"Hello, Nathan," she said, and I could tell she was ready to cry. "You look good."

Dr. Brayden looked at both of us and smiled. "It's very good to see you two together," she said. "I know this can feel awkward and quite difficult, but I really think it could be an important step for both of you. How does it feel for you, Rachel?"

Mom's grip on my hand loosened slightly and then tightened again. She raised her chin up from her chest as she spoke. "It feels like I'm not ready. I've been thinking, thinking about what I would say, how I'd explain myself to Nathan, and now it's like I forgot all of it."

"Do you feel like you need to explain yourself?" Dr. Brayden asked.

"Yes," Mom said, almost instantly.

Dr. Brayden turned to me. She had a notepad and a pen, and I wondered what she was going to write that wasn't *This is SO AWKWARD!* But then she said, "Nathan, does your mother need to explain herself?"

I know it wasn't meant as a trick question because yeah, obviously, she had a lot of things to explain, but it totally felt like a trick question because it's not like you show up at a mental hospital and start confronting people about whatever it was that got them there. So instead of asking any of the hundred or so questions that I'd been carrying around for the last few weeks, what I said was, "I just want to know if she's okay."

"Are you okay, Rachel?" Dr. Brayden asked.

Mom squeezed my hand pretty tight this time, and then she turned on the couch to face me. If felt like she was already impatient with Dr. Brayden playing emotional traffic cop. I sure as hell was. "I'm better," she said. "And I'm sorry."

She wasn't crying, but she was damn close to it, something we had in common at that moment. I was kind of glad she kept going and didn't wait for Dr. Brayden to negotiate the conversation. "I realize I sometimes get ahead of myself," she said. "I get an idea, and then I draw out that idea to an ending, and then the endings aren't always good."

Okay, so that was both good to hear and difficult to listen to. I could have told her she was doing that back when I'd been, like, ten and I'd first started to figure it out. It was good to hear her own up to it, but in that room with Dr. Brayden and her notepad watching us, I couldn't exactly start splashing current events all over her self-discovery. I couldn't say, "Well, you know what, Mom? There actually some weird people following us, and they're kind of after you, and it all goes back to Owl Harbor and some shadowy conspiracy stuff that your family invented. But it's great that you're confronting your paranoia."

All of that crossed my mind, but instead I said, "I'm glad you can see that, Mom. And I'm glad you're here. Lily and I are doing great in Owl Harbor. I'm making friends, and Lily is helping out around the attraction. Uncle Kevin is taking good care of us."

I probably played it up too hard. In the old days, she would have folded her arms over her chest, dipped her chin, and given me the *Okay, buddy, let's hear the real story* stare-down, but I had an advantage sitting across from me in an almost-matching armchair. When you've checked yourself into treatment for a paranoia disorder, accusing your son of lying and vowing to "get to the bottom of this" is probably not the best way to demonstrate how much progress you've made. I could see her running the calculations on whether I was telling the truth but also diagramming a different kind of emotional calculus on how much longer she wanted to stay there.

I think Dr. Brayden saw some of that going on too because she nudged her way back into the conversation. "Rachel, perhaps you could tell Nathan something you've learned here, something you'd like to take with you when you leave," she said, and then added, "when you're ready to leave," in case Mom thought this was an exit interview, I guess.

"I've learned," my mother said, "that I need to stop running from things that aren't chasing me."

Dr. Brayden gave Mom time to continue and, when she didn't, said, "There was something else we talked about. Do you want to share that?"

Mom let go of my hand and put her palms on her knees, pressing down but keeping her hand flat. She seemed to look through her outstretched fingers as if admiring the symmetry. When she spoke, it was as much to Dr. Brayden as to me.

"If I worry about something and then it happens, that doesn't mean I knew it was going to happen."

"That's right," Dr. Brayden said. "Taking an umbrella because you think it might rain doesn't make you a meteorologist. Nathan, what did that feel like to hear that?"

I actually fought here for a second not to say, "Yeah, duh! Of course," but instead I nodded and offered my best sympathetic grin. "Well, Mom," I said, "growing up in a house of illusion doesn't mean you can't fall for the occasional illusion."

She smiled for the first time since I entered the room, but it was a quick kind of jerking smile, like she wasn't sure she was supposed to be smiling.

Dr. Brayden put down her notepad on the arm of the chair in a way that felt like a declaration that we were done with our session, tapping it with the felt tip pen as it were a wand, and she was casting a spell. "That was very nice," she said. "It was so good to see the two of you so open and ready to share, but I think it's best if we just sat with that for right now. Thank you, Nathan, for coming."

Mom put her hand on my forearm. "Nate," she said. "Tell Lily I love her and I miss both of you so much. Can you tell her something else?"

"What?"

"Tell her to keep the illusions in the illusion house."

She leaned in close, her head on my shoulder again. "The bottles are the secret," she whispered. "They're looking for the bottles."

LILY AND MIA had spread out the beach towels on the grass when I got back, and Lily had sticky cinnamon goo all over her cheeks. Mia handed me a mocha latte. She'd guessed me for a coffee-as-candy guy, and she'd been correct. Mia looked at me with the softest eyes I'd ever seen. I had this urge to put my head between my knees and rock back and forth for an hour, but I also knew that probably wasn't the most reassuring thing for Lily to see.

Instead, I sat down on the towel with Mia and nodded to Lily. "Gooey or chewy?" I asked.

"Gooey *and* chewy," she replied.

"Good to know somethings don't change."

Mia scooted close and put her arm over my shoulder. "Any more culinary hot spots we need to hit this morning?' she said. "That Flour Child place is no Los Burgerritos, but it's not so bad."

"I think we can get going pretty soon," I said, and

then I took a deep breath because I needed to tell Lily that Mom was okay but that she wasn't "*okay*". I started simply. "Lily," I said. "I found out about Mom. She's safe. She's doing really well. But she wants us to go back to Owl Harbor. We need to stay with Uncle Kevin a little longer."

Lily was peeling sticky bits of the gooey bun wrapper into strips and used her head to nod toward the facility. "Is she in there? Can I see her?"

"Not today," I said, knowing that she wasn't really going to put up a fight. If somebody had given me a choice of walking into a mental-health hospital to see my mother or gargling sriracha, I might have asked if the sriracha was chilled or room temperature. "But she's getting help."

"Why?"

"Because she needs it," I said.

Lily seemed to accept that and went back to dismantling the gooey-bun wrapper. Mia tugged my arm, and we stood up together. Again, those soft eyes.

We walked about twenty feet, far enough to exchange whispers without Lily overhearing.

"Are you okay?" she asked.

"I think maybe I am," I said, half surprising myself. "I'm actually glad she's there. I think maybe I understand her a little more than I did. But really, I think she's trying to understand herself."

"That's good."

We were holding hands, and I was fully expecting something like "Get a room!" to come from Lily, but she was concentrating on licking the last of the cinnamon sugar off the wax paper gooey-bun wrapper.

"There's something else," Mia said. "I think I saw the other car—the older guy's car—down by the bakery. I don't think they followed us, but I don't know for sure."

I put my hand on my forehead and sighed. Seeing Mom had distracted me from the Ludlow stuff. "Let's get going," I said.

I was reaching down to grab one of the towels when I saw movement behind the statue. The drone bros walked toward us with a guy behind them that I instantly knew as the one from Vista Point because I also recognized him as the guy who'd taken the tour at the attraction and asked a bunch of obsessively detailed questions about the Ludlow stuff. That's probably why I'd been thinking *mustache* even when I couldn't see him the night before. I didn't have a plan that didn't involve the three of us scurrying around the park with the three of them chasing us, a situation that clearly cried out for wacky cartoon music. So we stood there and waited.

Lily saw them and darted behind me. Mia stood at my left shoulder.

"Now what?" she asked.

"Now we find out what these fuckers are after," I said.

By the time they reached us, I was thinking maybe the cartoon chase scene was a good idea after all, but they were right on top of us and I was pretty sure Lily would be tackled in the first twenty feet. The drone bros were still in their black-on-black polo shirt getups. Mustache guy, who was a lot older, looked like he was ready to sell us a timeshare. He had khaki slacks and one of those super-stiff windbreakers you see coaches wearing on the sidelines at football games.

The way he held his hand in the right pocket of that windbreaker looked like every stupid guy with a gun in every stupid action movie I've ever seen. It could have been a cell phone for all I knew, but even if he just wanted us to think he had a gun, it seemed like a smart move to assume he had a gun.

"Greetings, kids," he said, looking at each of us in turn. "I'm so glad we could get together." He spoke in this grandfatherly way like he was getting ready to tell us about a trip he'd planned for us. And that turned out to be more or less what he did.

"You see," he said, the drone bros standing just behind him, "all we really want to do is borrow your sister for a little bit. Maybe just for the day. But we have the sense that you two aren't going to let us do that."

He paused and again looked at each of us very deliberately and one at a time.

"So I guess we're all going to have to go together. We don't want to hurt you," he said. "But that's really up to you, isn't it?"

A few things here: These weren't real tough guys. They were conspiracy nerds who'd watched a bunch of tough guy movies. Real criminals wouldn't be confronting us in the middle of a park in the middle of the day. They were wannabe criminals, and they weren't even smart wannabe criminals because smart wannabe criminals would have grabbed us back in Owl Harbor and not waited till we were two hours away from the place I was guessing they meant to take us. But the fact that they were obvious amateurs didn't make them less dangerous. It might have made them more dangerous.

"Hold on here," Mia said. "You're kidnapping us because you believe in some crazy cult treasure legend? Why didn't you just ask us? The girl tells fortunes. She could have told yours."

The older guy looked at the drone bros with a smirk that the bushy mustache couldn't hide. "Oh, we've asked," he said. "We've asked, nicely, a bunch of times. We sent notes, we left messages. For years. Their mom can tell you that, wherever she is."

Lily hid behind me. Mia stepped a little closer. Mustache guy and the drone bros suddenly evolved from goofy conspiracy dudes to sinister conspiracy dudes who'd driven a woman to question whether what she was experiencing was real. These were not guys who "asked nicely". They'd snuck around like they'd done back in Owl Harbor. It could have been what pushed Mom off the edge.

The older guy smiled again. "But that was before we knew about this wonderful little girl," he said, leaning over to see Lily who was hiding behind me, "before we saw her on TV. She gave us new hope, a new hope that we can find our family's birthright, the treasure that was taken from the Ludlows so long ago. You see, I am Orson Ludlow and these are my grandsons, Lucas and Julian Ludlow. We are descended from Luther Ludlow. The gold he found is rightfully ours."

It was almost like he was waiting for us to acknowledge the wisdom of his plan.

But then the plan got weirder.

"She can lead us there," he said, pointing to Lily. "The message is in the bottle, but only she can read the message."

He stood there like he'd just said something that made perfect sense, something that wasn't scary-ass crazy, like he was trying to convince us that it was going to be a weird little field trip and not the outright abduction it was turning into. But the "our family's birthright" part was what really stood out. These people weren't crazy conspiracy theory treasure hunters planning a road trip to pick up zombie JFK on their way to Area 51. The *LUDLOW* license plates weren't fanboy B.S. It was worse than a cult. It was a cult *family*. I imagined a family Christmas card with everybody wearing loincloths and carrying assault rifles. It was a dark little level of weird I didn't even know existed.

All I could think of right then was that getting back to Owl Harbor with them might turn up better opportunities to escape than trying to outrun Orson Ludlow and his gun on an open field with an eleven-year-old in tow. It was the crazy cult family thing that sealed the deal on that. This family was a whole deck's worth of wild cards.

I reached back to where Lily was standing, and she took my hand. Mia wasn't flinching, but it seemed obvious that I was going to be the spokesman for our half of this outing. "So how is this going to work?" I said. "I assume we're carpooling. Will there be snacks? Who's in charge of the radio? Can we have a sing-along? Because I think a sing-along would help ease the tension."

Orson Ludlow used his hand in the windbreaker pocket to point toward the SUV. "This way," he said. I guess the grandfather act was over because he'd shifted to straight-up menace. We started walking, him behind us with his hand still in the maybe-it's-a-gun pocket, and Julian and Lucas Ludlow on either side of us. It was lucky for them the park was deserted because I can't imagine anybody would have seen it and thought it was anything but an abduction.

Just like that, we were in the SUV and leaving the park, the older Ludlow all cramped behind us in the way-back seat and Julian, who seemed like the dimmer of the two brothers, driving. Mia, Lily, and I sat on the bench seat in the middle, Lily between us and all of us as close together as the seatbelts would allow. The other drone bro, Lucas, was driving the rental car, I assumed.

To every other driver on the road, we were just another SUV with dark-tinted windows. Inside, it was the world's crappiest carpool.

18

THE LAST TIME WE'D BEEN IN A CAR DRIVING EAST ON I-80, Mom had been at the wheel, and we'd been airlifted out of our summer—and, really, our lives—without explanation. I'd ground my teeth for seventy of the seventy-five miles, unclenching my jaw only to snarl at Mom.

I was feeling suddenly nostalgic for that carefree road trip.

It wasn't like I was expecting a joyful journey with a smile around every bend, but you won't really understand how long seventy-five miles can feel until you've endured it at gunpoint, with a tweener quietly biting her lip and crying at your side. Mia and I had our arms linked over Lily's shoulders, forming a quivering support group of three.

But there was entertainment—or at least narration.

Lily had read up on the Ludlow history, and I'm sure she was silently critiquing the finer points in

Grandpa Orson's soliloquy on the Ludlows' heritage, but for me it was a chance to hear the full crazy all at once.

"I'm telling you this because you need to understand that the Ludlow name is both maligned and forgotten by historians," he intoned. I swear it was like he'd practiced a audiobook voice or he was auditioning for Lesser-Known Psychos of California podcast. "The mark of our family on the settling of California is indelible, and the debt Californians owe us is incalculable. What they took from us is criminal."

Okay. I must admit I was already thinking what parts of it I could steal to use giving tours, but the longer he went on, the weirder it got.

"Luther Ludlow was a genius. While thousands of forty-niners were scratching through the sand chasing flecks of gold, he found the path to the mother lode, the true and single source of all the gold branching out into all the veins in all the hills of the California Gold Country. But he'd found it by way of spirit, not of science, and the forty-niners hated him for that. They took everything from him just as he stood on the brink of the greatest riches."

I was starting to wonder if there was going to be a question-and-answer period when his odd little lecture was over, but Mia wasn't waiting. "But wait," she said, "if he found the gold why are you still looking for it? Wouldn't he have dug it up and done something with it?"

"You don't understand," he went on. "He did find it, but he wasn't ready to unveil his treasure just yet.

The family was planning to share the discovery when the mob descended upon them, scattering our ancestors across the west and killing Luther before he could share his discovery."

"Sounds kind of far-fetched, don't you think?" Mia said. It seemed pretty obvious she was trying to keep him off balance, but I wasn't sure where she wanted to go with that. "I mean, his followers—your ancestors, I guess—they didn't just come back when the ruckus died down and dig it up? He didn't leave a treasure map?"

Mia's strategy seemed to be working. The old guy was flustered. I got the idea it wasn't a theory he'd shared a lot outside the family, and he didn't get confronted with pesky facts very often. But it didn't stop him. "Ah, but you see, he did leave a map. Tucked in that crate of bottles are all the clues we need to find the lode. We only need this little girl to find the right bottles and read the clues. She has the gift."

I decided it was my turn to back up Mia in the debate. "You don't have anybody in your family with the gift? Luther Ludlow's genius isn't hereditary?"

Mia's prodding had unsettled him. My questions pissed him off.

"The gift was taken from us. *Stolen* from us," he said. I couldn't see him because he was behind us, but I pictured his nostrils flaring and his mustache ruffling with each exhale. "The bottles are the secret. Your family discovered that, but they never understood it. It is our time now to take back the power."

I wasn't sure I was ready to keep escalating the

argument with a guy who may or may not have been holding a gun behind us but definitely had his "grandminion" driving up front.

"Okay," I said. "Sorry, I guess. How do you know all of this?"

"Research," he said and then explained how he decided to dig past the family legend and go through old records and genealogical stuff. But then, he "made an acquaintance on the internet".

That told me all we needed to know. This wasn't a long-simmering family quest handed down through the generation. This was some bullshit he found online and could probably be traced back to somebody who took Uncle Kevin's tour. And it was worse than that. A Google alert had probably told him about Lily's fortune-telling fame, but there was no telling how long he'd been nosing around Mom's cyber hood.

Julian had been quiet through all of it until his grandfather brought up the internet. "We know all there is to know about you and your family," he informed us.

"Grandpa knows the history," he said. "We know the technology."

Apparently, that technology didn't include a program that would tell them their grandfather was insane, but I was starting to get the idea that the apple didn't fall too far from the meth lab.

I couldn't decide if I wanted the Ludlow family historian to continue. It was some seriously stupid shit, but there was a chance something he said was going to be useful. I was thinking we could maybe trick them into letting us go and abducting some other kids who had more psychic gifts than Lily.

And didn't need to pee as bad as she did.

This always happened. In fact, it had happened more or less in the same spot when Mom had been delivering us to our new Delta lifestyle a few weeks before. Lily couldn't be in a car much more than an hour before she was begging to stop somewhere and relieve her nanoscale bladder. We'd just left the interstate for the network of raised highways that snaked through the Delta following the levee lines. We were probably only fifteen minutes from Owl Harbor when she made the urgent announcement.

"Nate," she said. "I gotta go, real bad."

"Can you wait?"

"No, it's real bad."

The "can you wait?" idea was always worth trying but never resulted in Lily gritting it out to the destination. There probably wasn't a rest stop in the whole state that I hadn't been to at least once. Usually, I found it super annoying, but during an abduction, abductees should see every stop as a potential escape.

I turned around to look over the seat at Orson. "Hey," I said. "We need to stop."

"She can wait," he said.

"I don't think you understand," I said. "She can't. I've been on enough car trips with her. It doesn't end well."

He looked super annoyed, as though our abduction was inconveniencing him. I saw his mustache drooped in resignation, and then he called out to Julian to look for someplace to stop.

While I was still looking back at him, he patted the seat next to him and smiled.

He hadn't been lying about the gun.

There are not a ton of places to stop on the Delta. With the roads all raised up like levees there's not even anyplace to pull over. Once in a while though, there are spots where I guess they unload whatever swamp buggy tractors they use down in the rice fields. Julian slowed down when he spotted one with a big water tank that I guess he thought Lily could hide behind to pee.

"You two stay in the car," Orson barked when we stopped. "I'll oversee this."

Lily looked up at me, clearly terrified. I nodded at her and said, "It's going to be okay. Just pee and come back."

Julian also got out of the car. I wasn't sure why it took two men to keep a scared little girl from making a run for it, but it left Mia and me alone. She elbowed me, and I looked down to see her phone in her hand.

"What are we going to do?" I asked, keeping my voice low.

"A couple of things," she said, nodding to her lap. The Ludlow clan were clearly not geniuses. Despite knowing we'd used a phone to track them, they hadn't searched us when they put us in the car, as if every teenager in America didn't have a phone within grabbing distance at all times.

"Call nine-one-one," I whispered.

"Can't. They'd see us talking. Plus, they wouldn't know where we are. I have another idea."

I looked down and saw her click on an app that

opened to a *Gulf High Alert* screen banner. "Kids at school made this. It's supposed to be for school shootings and stuff, but it sends a text to every kid at the school. The teachers don't even know about it, but every kid on the Delta will see it."

Mia started texting, one-handed, without looking down in case one of the Ludlows saw us.

abducted gray suv hwy 82 LUDLOW plates

"I'll text my Mom," she said, but then she slipped the phone back under her leg. Julian was back.

"Your sister is a pain in the ass," he said, climbing into the driver's seat.

"Don't I know it," I said as I looked over to see Orson opening the door for Lily. She stepped up to the bench seat and squeezed past Mia, winking at me as she sat down. I knew immediately that she'd never needed to pee. The whole thing was to give us time to cook up a plan. I smiled back at her, thinking about how many times she'd faked the pee just because she wanted to make Mom stop the car, and wondering if she would be disappointed in the half-assed plan we'd come up with while she was pretending to pee.

Orson climbed past her to the third-row seat. It was kind of comical because it's not like even big-ass SUVs have much of a third-row seat. So the oldest and stockiest of us was all cramped back there, with a gun, of course.

"Your sister is a pain in the ass," he said.

"So I hear," I replied. Julian put the van in gear and pulled onto the road, Lucas right behind us in the rental.

19

One of the things about driving on the Delta is that you can see everything coming at you in two-mile segments. The roads are built on the levee embankments and go in a straight line for about that far and then turn at some angle. For a few minutes, you're looking south and seeing all the silos and far-off hills in that direction, and then you'll turn onto another super straight road and see everything coming at you from a new direction, a different set of hills and silos.

We were three turns into the drive when we saw the station wagon parked on one of those tractor-drop pullouts. I recognized it immediately. I didn't even need to see the side mirror wrapped in duct tape to know who it was.

Hann-attie was on patrol.

In some ways, I was encouraged that they were on the case. But in another way, a massively bigger way, I was maybe even more worried about the situation than I had been before. It was possible, I thought, that they were out there looking for us *and* had called 911, but it was also possible—probably even more possible—that they had decided they were going to handle it on their own. I was imagining a whole posse of Delta teens coming to the rescue.

A Delta dragnet.

As we passed the Hannawagon, I looked over my shoulder to see Hannah at the wheel pulling onto the road behind us. "Friends of yours?" the elder Ludlow asked, so close on the hunched-up seat he was practically in my ear.

"Nope," I said, turning back to face forward, glad he couldn't see my face. A glance told me Mia had seen the station wagon too.

We turned again and saw a whole new set of objects slowly approaching, one of them the Los Burgerritos sign.

It was midday—no neon, but the silhouette was unmistakable. I'd had an idea that maybe we could get somebody's attention as we passed through Lago Vista, but the tinted windows made that impossible. Instead, we passed by a half-empty Los Burgerritos, but I saw two pickups I thought I recognized from 17 Poles. They saw us too, watching the SUV as we passed.

The Delta dragnet was suddenly a very real thing. No cops, no highway patrol, just a bunch of Delta teenagers coming to the rescue. Either that or they didn't want to miss the show.

We made it through the one light in Lago Vista on green, which eliminated another opportunity for escape. On a red light, one of us could have opened the door and tried to leap out when we stopped, and maybe somebody would have done the smart thing and called 911. There was a cop going the other way as we passed through the intersection who took no note of the gray SUV with *LUDLOW* plates, confirming my suspicion that the 17 Poles squad was taking the law into their own hands.

We were only ten minutes from Owl Harbor, and I had no idea what Hannah and company had in mind, but when I looked forward, there she was in the lane ahead of us. I don't know how she did it, but I guessed the Delta kids know the Delta backroads really well. We passed by the dollar store and the metal-shed church. It's not like Lago Vista is a big town, but I'd hoped that somebody there would present a chance for a rescue or way for us to get out of the car.

That wasn't going to happen.

When we drove past the park, I knew for sure that whatever Hann-attie and crew were going to do was going to happen on the highway. I looked over at Mia. She looked as worried as I did. We both knew that whatever bad judgment Hannah was about to deploy could include a level of vehicular mayhem neither of us was excited to witness.

When Hannah slowed down a half mile outside of town it came as only a small relief. I'm sure you can get hurt plenty bad at 35 mph. Then one of the pickups I'd seen at Los Burgerritos pulled up on the left, matching Hannah's decreasing speed. The other pickup was tailgating behind. The strategy was pretty clear. It was a two-lane, but you could see for miles. Unless somebody showed up going the opposite direction, they had the SUV boxed in.

"Pass this bastard," Orson yelled.

"I can't," Julian called back. "That truck's got me blocked."

Hannah was slowing down. I still couldn't believe somebody hadn't called 911 yet, but I had to appreciate that they were doing a damn good job of pulling over an SUV without running right into it. It was the kind of thing that would probably only work on the Delta. You can't exactly swerve right and pass on the shoulder when there is no shoulder. That steep slope would take out a car almost instantaneously.

But apparently, Julian hadn't read the Delta driver's manual. Because that's exactly what he did.

It's not like he kind of got away with it for even a second. I saw what he was doing, and I anticipated he'd be able to hang onto the side of the road for at least a little bit, like maybe he'd gun it and roar around Hannah all fast and furious. I'd seen cooler stunts than that in movies. But real-life driving and real-life physics don't seem to have a lot in common with movie chase scenes because as soon as the wheels left the pavement Julian Ludlow was no longer driving. He could have been in one of those cars you pretend to drive at an amusement park, where it doesn't matter which way you turn the wheel. Because it didn't. He yanked the wheel left like he thought he could get back onto the pavement, and the traction simply did not exist.

We were probably going under 30 mph at that

point, but we were going 30 mph sideways, sliding toward a reed-choked ditch at the bottom of a steep embankment.

The rear end of the SUV hit the ditch first, and then physics had its way with two tons of metal and glass.

The SUV didn't actually roll all the way over, but it felt like we were inside a hamster ball that somebody had kicked across the playground, everything blurred and jerked and the tumbling insanity of it slammed us into one another hard. When the SUV finally sludged to a stop in the muck, it came to rest on its side. I was on the right side of the bench seat, and Lily and Mia were slammed down on top of me. Lily was screaming. Mia was groaning. I was getting stream of a guttural profanity in stereo from Orson and Julian Ludlow.

And water was seeping in around the door jamb.

I put my arms around Lily to calm her but also to keep her elbows from smacking me in the face as she flailed. "It's okay. Hold still," I said. "Mia, are you alright?"

She mumbled something that sounded like "yeah", but could have been "huh". Both of them were still tangled on top of me. I could feel Mia twisting around and knew she was digging for her seatbelt buckle. She found it about the same time I got to Lily's. Free of the belt, Mia was able to stand on one of the front-seat headrests and then push on the door, which was now overhead, opening it and letting more light in.

Behind me, Orson was moaning and trapped in

his cramped confines. He was wedged in pretty tight and had surrendered profanity for groaning. Up front, Julian was wrapped in the airbag and didn't look to be making sense of the situation. When I looked up, Mia was out of the car and reaching down for Lily.

With an eleven-year-old off my chest, I was able to take my first full breath since we'd come to a stop.

The water was coming in faster.

With Lily and Mia out, I stood up and reached for the door jamb, pulling myself up and out of the SUV. I could tell we were only about half underwater. But half underwater is enough to get some real panic going.

Not enough, however, to drown Orson Ludlow and his idiot grandson. I felt no guilt, none, about leaving those fuckers to find their way out of the mud and muck.

And I didn't want to wait around and figure out whether the elder Ludlow had lost his gun in the crash.

From one side, the SUV didn't even look banged up. It looked kind of like a toy that a kid had thrown in the mud, and it was only about halfway into the ditch. If Hannah hadn't gotten our speed down before Julian Ludlow had decided he was a stunt driver, we could have slid farther or ended up upside down in the ditch. The wreck could have been a *lot* worse.

Mia had lifted Lily down onto the embankment, and I slopped down next to them, my feet dropping ankle deep into the mud. "Are you guys hurt?"

"I don't think so," Mia said. "I'm shook up bad, but I don't think anything's broken."

Lily had given up crying for whimpering, but when I put my hands on her shoulders she stopped long enough to say, "I'm okay," before going back to whimpering at a softer pitch.

"Let's go," I said. "Before those assholes can get out."

I was still pretty dazed and had just remembered how the whole wreck had happened when I heard shouting from the top of the embankment. "Are you guys okay?" Hattie yelled.

Even in that weird moment, I had time to wonder why it wasn't Hannah asking.

I guess Saucer Dude from 17 Poles was driving one of the pickups because he was now climbing down the embankment. It was so steep he was on all fours so he wouldn't skid down on top of us.

"Nothin' broken?" he asked.

"I don't think so," I said. "We're just banged up."

"Good. Let me help you guys up."

The sound I heard next was nothing I expected, but I knew what it was the instant I heard it. Yes, I'd just climbed out of a car wreck and was appropriately disoriented, but a gunshot is still a gunshot.

I was standing about two feet from the SUV's back side window. I don't know if he was shooting at us or just breaking the window so he could climb out, but all four of us were instantly in motion as the glass rained all around us. Lily, Mia, Saucer Dude, and I were halfway up the embankment before the sound faded.

When we got to the road, I saw Lucas Ludlow getting out of the rental. He must have been some distance back at the time of the crash. "We've got to go NOW!" I shouted to Hattie and Saucer Dude, pointing to Lucas Ludlow. "He's with *them.*"

Hannah was still in her car. When we got there, I could see she was crying. She'd pulled off some extreme badassery in the blocking maneuver, but I guess causing an actual wreck was traumatic because she was upset, really upset.

Mia and I climbed into the back seat, putting Lily in between us.

"Let's go, Hannah," Mia said. "Pull it together."

As we pulled away—pretty tentatively given the circumstances—I leaned forward and asked Hattie for her phone. "We've got to call nine-one-one," I said. "Why didn't anybody call nine-one-one?"

"We thought it was a prank," Hattie said. "Thought Mia was getting back at Chloe and Evan."

Mia rolled her eyes, too busy to argue the stupidity of whatever thought process had put two and two together and gotten seven. We both had our arms around Lily, who was still whimpering, burying her head into my chest and reaching out with her free hand to hold onto Mia. When Hattie handed me the phone, I punched in 911 and hit the call button.

It rang right through.

"Solano County Emergency Dispatch, what is the nature of your emergency?"

I didn't really know where to start. "At the beginning" would be a long story at that point— the whole abduction/car crash/gun/vigilante vehicle stop seemed ludicrous to lay out all at once. So I started with the gun part and decided we'd keep it there.

"There's a guy with a gun on the Owl Harbor turnpike. There was a wreck," I said.

"Are there injuries?"

"I don't think so, but we got out of there pretty fast because of the gun."

"Is the man still at the scene?"

"I don't know. We left."

"Where is the wreck?"

"In a ditch on the side of Highway Sixty-One, about a mile west of Lago Vista."

"Were there other vehicles involved in the accident?"

I didn't make the call expecting to lie to a 911 dispatcher, but I didn't think Hannah's vehicle stop was going to be easy to explain. I mean, other vehicles were "involved", but they hadn't gotten hit so I said, "No."

"Please stay on the line. What is your location?" the dispatcher asked.

"Westbound," I said, and I hung up.

Hattie grabbed her phone back, and I looked down to Lily, who was recovering somewhat but still flinched when I put my arm back on her shoulder. "It's going to be okay," I said.

She blinked and said the first words I'd heard from her since we crawled out of the car. "Are you sure?"

I wasn't. But I said I was.

. . .

It's only ten minutes from Lago Vista to the turn-off for Owl Harbor and maybe two minutes from there to the attraction. But silence stretches time, especially when that silence is shared. It was shared among five on that drive.

Everybody was in shock, which was part of it, but there was another part of it too. I only made it about halfway before I had to say something. But Hannah cut me off.

"The *LUDLOW* plates thing made it seem like a prank, like something you'd make up a to pull a joke on the local kids," she announced. "Like we were stupid or something."

She just let that hang in the air for a few seconds, an uncomfortable statement to break an uncomfortable silence.

"Everybody thought it was more stupid shit like Madam Lilith here telling the future, like the old Ludlow story was supposed to scare us."

I wasn't sure what to say, but Mia spoke. "Why would you think that?"

"Because you think you're better than us," Hannah said. "Ever since you came back."

Mia didn't answer at first, and her voice quavered just slightly when she did speak. "I didn't come back thinking I was better than you. I came back with my dad dead and my mom broken by it."

The silence was back, but this time it was the kind of silence that you know isn't going to last, and you wonder if it would be better if it did.

It didn't. Mia had more to say.

"I came back to a place Mom thought she'd

escaped and I still thought was home. I came back to everybody whispering and pointing and nobody caring. I came back not knowing if I was going to hold it together and people like you, who used to be my friends, too cool or too whatever to help me try."

I wasn't sure if Hannah was going to have an answer, but she just took a while to get to it. When you're a kid, you hear a lot of bullshit apologies, the "I'm sorry" somebody's parents force them to make when that somebody isn't sorry at all. Or the "I'm sorry" you hear when somebody just wants the situation to be over and they really aren't interested in seeing it resolved.

Hannah's wasn't like that. It started with the standard "I'm sorry", but then it went on to stories. She talked about stuff they'd done together when they'd been little and how much she'd liked Mia's dad. She talked about being upset when Mia had moved away when they'd been eight and all of a sudden, she didn't have any friends. She talked about not knowing what to say when Mia had moved back five years later. She talked about Mia coming back "so much more beautiful than me, so much more grown up than me" and how awkward that had felt "because it was like I'd been left behind again".

She was crying again, which is not really what you want the driver to do a few minutes after the car you were riding in skidded into a ditch. And then her tone changed. "While you were gone," she said, stopping to take two deep breaths before she went on. "While you were gone, the other kids teased me. They teased me about being friends with 'the half-brown girl'. I got mad. I got in fights. But then I stopped getting mad. I stopped fighting. When you got back, I didn't feel good about that. I didn't want to go through that again."

She bit her lip. "Maybe I should have told you that," she said, "a long time ago."

I saw their eyes meet in the rearview mirror, and I remembered how Hannah and Hattie had exchanged coded glances in that same mirror what felt like a week ago but had only been the night before last.

What went on between Hannah and Mia right then was not like that at all.

There wasn't a code, but there was a meaning. It got quiet again, but it was a different quiet, an easier quiet.

20

I WAS SURPRISED AT HOW RELIEVED I FELT WHEN I SAW the sign for the attraction, how much Owl Harbor in all its shithole glory was starting to feel like "home" —or at least like a familiar refuge. A mile later when we saw Professor Mysterio waving from the water tank mural, I let my breath out audibly. I could feel Lily's shoulders relax.

Mia and Hannah had ended their conversation with those glances in the rearview mirror, but Mia had reached over the seat to put her hand on Hannah's shoulder. It's not like Hannah and Mia were going to suddenly be BFFs again, but it also seemed like maybe they weren't going to be glaring at each other across the lunchroom anymore. I didn't expect them to hug in the parking lot, and I was right.

I don't know why I expected to see the attraction open, but the sign at the road flipped to *Closed* made perfect sense. We'd checked in with Uncle Kevin in the morning, pre-abduction, but he hadn't heard from us in hours. He'd probably been camped out by the phone since we'd left almost twenty-four hours before.

Lily practically sprinted to the house, and Uncle Kevin was already on the porch when she got there, catching her in his arms. I wasn't really sure Lily had accepted Uncle Kevin as close family, but right then she was looking for a grownup and he was the only available option. She was still clinging to him when I got to the porch.

"We're back," I said. "In one piece, just barely."

"Come inside," he said. "I want to hear everything."

I looked back at the parking lot. Mia and Hannah weren't hugging, but they were talking, with Hattie hovering farther back than she usually did. I waved at Mia that we were going inside and beckoned for her to join us.

Uncle Kevin had moved an armchair closer to where the phone hung on the wall, and we had to step around it to get to the kitchen. Mia was coming through the front door by the time we settled around the kitchen table, which he'd cleared of the blue bottles. They'd been gradually disappearing from the house over the last week or so, and only a few remained on the windowsill.

Lily scooted her chair closer to Uncle Kevin's before she sat down. He looked down at her and put his arm over her shoulders.

"Well, there may be some of this we'll need to talk about later," I said, my eyes quickly darting from Uncle Kevin to Lily and back. In normal circumstances, Lily would have thrown a fuss about being left out of any discussion and explained to us at high volume how she was grown-up enough to be included. But these weren't normal circumstances, and I think she accepted that because all she did was hang on to Uncle Kevin's arm as I explained the chain of events.

"We told you last night about the drone guys and the other guy who showed up at the bridge. The same guys showed up again at the park where Mom's note in the bottle told us to go," I said. I paused here because it wasn't like I was ready to tell Uncle Kevin that Mom was in the mental health place across the street from the park. That was definitely in the "talk about later" category. "The older guy told us they needed Lily because they think she's psychic. It turns out their great-great-grandwhatever was Luther Ludlow and they think Lily can help them find some mother lode treasure. They had a gun, and they told us to get in their SUV."

Uncle Kevin brought his left hand up to his forehead and kneaded his eyebrows between his thumb and forefinger. "How'd you get away? Did they let you go?"

"Not exactly," I said. "Mia has a Gulf High alert thing on her phone. She sent a message out, and some Delta kids tried to stop them with their cars, except the SUV went off the road. It ended up in the ditch on its side, and we got away."

"Are you hurt?" Uncle Kevin asked. "Do we need to get you guys to the ER?"

"I think we're okay—just some bruises," Mia said.

She'd joined us in the kitchen after using the house phone to call her mom.

"Yeah," I said. "We didn't hit anything, just kind of slid into the muck. But here's the thing, they got away. One of the younger guys was following in the older guy's car. We took off, but they probably got out of there before the cops came."

"Did you call nine-one-one?"

"Yes," I said. "We only told them about the wreck and the guy with the gun. We didn't tell them all the rest. We just came here."

Uncle Kevin took a big breath and closed his eyes for a second. "I'm glad you guys are okay, but we need to get the cops in on this, especially since they might still be out there."

Lily looked at me and kept her eyes glued on mine while Uncle Kevin stood up and walked to the phone. I reached across the table and put my hand on top of Lily's. Mia put her hand on top of mine, and the three of us sat there, listening while Uncle Kevin talked to the 911 operator. He answered a few questions and gave them the address. "Yes," he said. "Okay. We'll be right here."

When he rejoined us in the kitchen, he leaned over the table with one hand gripping the edge of the tabletop and the other on Lily's shoulder again. "Look," he said. "They want us to stay inside. We can get Mia home later, but right now they think it's best if we stay in here with the door locked. They got a couple of deputies out where you went off the road. One of them is on his way."

"Good thing we didn't have any plans tonight," I said.

IF THE LUDLOWS or anybody else had been able to see through the drapes Uncle Kevin pulled closed, they might have thought they'd stumbled onto the world's most boring family. We sat around the living room, while Uncle Kevin told us more about the whole Ludlow saga. It's not like we were barricading the doors or loading guns and figuring out how to defend ourselves from marauding gang like in a movie where they have a pile of rifles and everybody finds a window where they can pick off the bad guys before they can get close.

Really, it was just us sitting there while Uncle Kevin talked.

But we learned a lot.

Luther Ludlow's descendants had never given up on the cult leader's dream. There had been quiet periods, Uncle Kevin explained, but every few years another Ludlow would get it in his head that they could finally track down the treasure. Mostly that had nothing to do with Owl Harbor or the House of Illusion, Uncle Kevin explained, but sometimes one of them would connect the family saga to the attraction with the spiel about the dumped crate of blue bottles. Mostly they'd just show up at Owl Harbor and ask some questions, but Uncle Kevin said that one time somebody had broken into the House of Illusion and ransacked a storage room without taking anything.

"They're mostly just weirdos," Uncle Kevin said.

"I always figured it was harmless. This is the first time there's been anything violent."

He was about to tell us something else about the Ludlows when we heard a car in the parking lot. Lily gave me that same urgent look, her eyes wide but unsteady. "It's probably the cops," I said. "It's okay."

Uncle Kevin had already crossed the room and looked through a break in the curtains. "Yeah," he said. "The deputy's here."

THE DEPUTY WAS YOUNGER than I expected. I had this picture in my head that county sheriffs had to have southern accents and wear cowboy hats, but this guy looked as much like a Costco security guard as anything. He took notes in a little notebook.

"Did you hear anybody use a name?" he asked us after we'd given him the basics of the abduction.

"One of them was named Grandpa!" Lily said, and I felt some instant relief that she'd recovered her sarcastic streak. She'd had less than an hour since the wreck to pull herself back together, and the smartass interjection was reassuring.

"Thank you, miss," said the deputy, who'd introduced himself as Deputy Tim. I was almost surprised that Lily hadn't also pointed out that Tim was not a very deputy sheriff name and that he should change it to something like Clint or Butch.

"They actually introduced themselves," I said. "It was part of their whole Ludlow heritage thing. They weren't hiding who they were."

"Yeah, these are not criminal geniuses," Mia cut in.

Deputy Tim nodded and smiled. He explained to us that the SUV was registered to Lucas Ludlow and that Lucas and Julian lived on the west side of Stockton. Orson Ludlow was from the eastern part of Amador County in the foothills of the Sierra, not far from Luther Ludlow's old haunts, but he'd moved to Idaho, as far as the cops could tell.

"Did either of you see plates on the second car?"

"No," I said. "But it was a rental car, a Ford, white."

He scribbled in his notebook again and then looked at me and then Mia. "We'd like to contact the other drivers who were at the scene of the crash."

There was an instant here where I wasn't sure we were supposed to be ratting out Hannah and company for their vigilante *Mad Max* antics, but Mia had no such reservations. "Hannah Terling and Bart Patterson," she said. "Local kids."

It's not like Deputy Tim sighed at the mention of Hannah and Bart, but it felt a bit like he was fighting to keep from rolling his eyes, a kind of "oh, *them*" moment. "We're aware of them," Deputy Tim said, folding his notebook and standing up.

"We believe the suspects have retreated to the mountains or Stockton," he said. "It wouldn't make sense for them to remain in the area, but we can't be sure. I need everybody here to be careful. Stay vigilant. If you see any of them, or if anything feels out of place, we need you to call nine-one-one immediately."

Uncle Kevin had already stood up to walk Deputy Tim to the door, and he followed him out to the parking leaving Lily, Mia, and me in the living room.

"Stockton," I said. "I knew it."

"Don't be a place-ist," Mia said.

"Well, it ain't no Delta," I replied.

21

Mia's mom showed up not long after Deputy Tim had left. Mia hadn't told her much on the phone, and I was sure they were up for an interesting conversation on the drive back to the marina. Mia had given Lily a long hug before she left but seemed self-conscious with me in front of her mom, which I thought was kind of cute and also maybe proof that the 17 Pole-sters' description of me as her boyfriend was not that far off.

She smiled as she climbed into her mom's Toyota pickup and waved again as they left the parking lot.

"I like her. She's my favorite of your girlfriends so far," Lily said. "Oh wait, she's your only girlfriend so far."

What I said was, "Shut up," but what I thought was *There's the Lily I know.*

"Go upstairs, and lie down for a while," I told her. "You don't need to sleep, but you do need to chill out for a bit. I've got to talk to Uncle Kevin for a minute."

I'd expected more protest, but I got off with an exaggerated huff as she marched to the house, her arms folded over her chest. The smirk she threw me as she stepped onto the porch told me even that it was mostly an act. I think she was appreciating having a big brother right then.

I found Uncle Kevin up at the attraction. There were only three doors leading in and out and only two that we used: the door into the gift shop where people bought tickets and the fake wall door that led out of the Room of No Return where the guests had to turn the candlestick to get out. A third door in the back went into a storeroom. Uncle Kevin had told me the projector for the video loop delay trick was back there.

That's the door I found Uncle Kevin checking. It had a deadbolt, and it was a door he almost never used—I'd never actually been in the storeroom—so there was little chance it was going to be unlocked. That didn't stop him from checking it though. He kept a set of keys on a clip that attached to his belt loop, which I always thought was weird because it wasn't like he needed a whole bunch of keys: the house, his car, and two doors to the attraction. He turned the lock and stepped inside, and I followed him.

"What do you keep in here?" I asked.

He answered my question when he turned on the light. There were some tools on one shelf, but the rest of the room, which was maybe eight feet across in both directions, was packed with shelf after shelf of blue bottles. The light wasn't very good, but I could see each had a note inside.

And then I saw something else. In the corner, an open box brimmed with more blue bottles, and they were new. To the left of the boxes, a workbench was covered in ink stains, and a fountain tip sprouted from a glass jar next to a stick of that thick paper people use when they print invitations to parties.

Uncle Kevin didn't need to say a thing. He just stood there like he was waiting for questions.

"How long have you been making these?" I asked. "Were there ever any real ones?"

"A few," he said. "Your grandma found them on the banks where the river cuts through behind the house. A few dozen, that's all."

I felt a wave of *Boy, am I dumb!* sweeping over me. It would have to have been a big crate of bottles in the boat when the cult guy had capsized one hundred-whatever years ago if Uncle Kevin had enough to be selling them in the gift shop, but that's not even all of what suddenly became clear in my head. If you had put strips of parchment in a bottle of water back in the 1800s, it's not like that paper was going to last even a few years. It would have dissolved into nothing in probably a few months.

Even if it were magic spring water like the Ludlow legend said.

"Wow," I said. "Just...wow. Does Mom know?"

"Of course," he said. "A couple of times a year, your grandma would have us down there snipping out little strips of paper and writing on them with that special ink. We'd end up with our hands covered in black. And it's waterproof, so for the next week we'd look like we'd worked in a printing plant."

Uncle Kevin explained to me that it wasn't just the ink that was waterproof. He used a special paper that would last for a few years. To get the notes to look old, he'd rough them up with a pumice stone and then soak the strips in lemon juice to get the paper to yellow. He'd set them out on the windowsill in the kitchen to make the ink fade faster. He scuffed up the outside of the bottles with sandpaper. His theory was that by the time the paper dissolved, "whoever bought it probably threw it away". They were only seven dollars a bottle so it's not like they were selling in auctions or destined for a museum. I'm sure everybody who bought one probably had a "hey, wait a minute" revelation at some point if they ever even believed the bottles were genuine in the first place.

"Good racket," I said. "I'm impressed."

"Keeps The attraction going; every little bit helps. Follow me around here."

He locked the door behind us, and we stepped through some weeds to the end of the building where the tour ended when the guests figured out the fake wall. That door wasn't marked from the outside. The wall was all wood planks with peeling red paint like an old barn. Because it was hidden, you couldn't really put a lock on it. I'd never thought of that before. It's not like there's a big crime problem in Owl Harbor, unless you counted underage drinking and doing doughnuts in the Gulf High parking lot. The light was dimming when we got there, and I couldn't quite see what Uncle Kevin was doing when he bent down to the wooden deck. He slid a little peg that was notched into the wall where it met the deck. When he stood up, he shoved the wall where it would otherwise turn and reveal the hidden door. It flexed a little bit, but it didn't move.

"I don't even bother a lot of nights, but tonight feels different," he said. "I want to show you one more thing."

When we got to the main door, with the gift shop and the ticket desk, he unclipped his keys and swung the door open. He turned on the lights as we stepped in and pointed to a glass case on the wall to the left of the cash register. We sold the little blue bottles from a different display case over by the coloring books and the rack of cheap sunglasses that kids for some reason always begged their parents to buy.

The glass case on the wall was locked, and it was the spot where we would explain the legend of Luther Ludlow and the blue bottles. I'd never noticed, really, that these bottles looked different from all the other ones. They were blue, but they were more scratched up than the others. The paper was gone.

Like they'd been sitting in the Delta mud for one hundred fifty years.

"These are the originals," he said. "I guess they still have the original spring water in them. When I was little, you could still see some flecks of paper in there, but it's all gone now. I've shown 'em to a few of the Ludlow treasure hunters. Maybe if these new guys show up, we can explain that the whole bottles thing is a dead end. No treasure maps in there."

"I'm not sure they'd listen," I said. "These guys think they've got the whole mess figured out."

He nodded.

"But now it's my turn to share a secret," I said.

Uncle Kevin squinted and looked down before saying, "What are you talking about?" It was one of those moments when you both know what the other is thinking and you're almost daring the other person to talk first.

"Let's go over to the picnic table," I said.

The sun was behind a tall row of trees when we sat down across from each other at the table, and a bank of fog had broken over the hills west of Fairfield which softened it even more. The wind was at about half of the usual Delta velocity. It wasn't like I was going to have to shout to be heard over it, but I glanced over to make sure Lily wasn't out on the porch.

"I went to see Mom," I said.

Uncle Kevin picked at a splinter of wood that was coming loose from the table, peeling it off and then flicking it back toward the parking lot. "How is she?" he asked, making eye contact for the first time since we'd sat down.

"You could have told me," I said. "Our whole lives got turned upside down. We deserved to know."

"You're right," he said, keeping his eyes on mine. "You did deserve to know. But your mom deserved to be the one who would tell you. She asked me for that, as her brother, and I promised I'd keep that secret."

"Is this the first time? Can you tell me that?"

He took a big breath and let it out slowly, like a sigh but longer. "No," he said. "It's not the first time. I told you a couple of weeks ago about how she left the Delta and why she left. I'll just say she made a stop on the way out."

"For what?" I said. "I mean, I guess I know for what, but *why?*"

"She started imagining things, I guess is how you'd describe it. She started thinking that people were against her, that it was her fault that her friends died in the wreck and that somehow, she was going to suffer for it. People noticed her acting, I don't know, *different*, and that just made it worse because she noticed they were noticing it."

"Was she still telling fortunes?"

"Your grandma told her to stop," he said. "She told her again it was all made up, but I think that made it worse. It got bad, and then it was just best for everybody that she went away for a while. She got better. She really did. And she went on with things until, you know, this year."

It was my turn to look away. I wasn't sure how "better" she'd ever been. It wasn't how I would have described her all the times we'd suddenly moved from one town to another, the times when she'd crawl into her work and leave me to look after Lily. "What changed? What did she tell you? It seemed kind of all at once to me."

"She called a few times," he said. "She said she was noticing things, internet things. That somebody was nosing around in her stuff. She was afraid it was coming back—the dark stuff, the paranoia."

"It could have been real this time," I said.

"It could have," he said.

We sat there for another fifteen minutes or so. I told him about some of the times we'd moved, about how I worried about her. I talked, for one of the first times, about how Dad had left and what that had been like. He nodded and told me how hard that had been to watch from the outside. It was the first time I really got to see Uncle Kevin as a big brother to Mom, as somebody who cared about people and felt the hurt in that caring. I got the idea it was maybe the first time he'd talked about it too.

The fog had reached Owl Harbor by the time we finished talking. He put his hand on my shoulder as we walked back across the parking lot to the house.

I'll always remember those months with Uncle Kevin as the Summer of Pizza and Pop-Tarts and the summer when I was struck by the idea that there must have been a reason that Pop-Tart never made a pizza flavor because it made total sense to me. We were living it up at first because it was the kind of stuff that Mom never allowed us to have, but the truth was that a week into July I was getting pretty tired of frozen pizza two nights out of three.

But I didn't complain that night.

We hadn't really eaten since the gooey buns in the morning and by 7:00, with the sun behind the fog, I was ravenously hungry. I was almost surprised I could fit two frozen pizzas in the tiny old-timey oven, but I knew that one between three people wasn't going to be nearly enough, not when two of them were kids and hadn't eaten since morning.

"I bought some of those bitsy carrots," Uncle Kevin said, poking his head into the kitchen. "I don't want you to get scurvy."

Lily was sitting at the kitchen table, watching me and likely hoping to stare the oven into cooking faster. Lily is best avoided when she hasn't eaten for a while, but she was quiet that night. She'd brought a book from the stack of the books in the living room, and when she was done supervising my culinary enterprise, she opened it and flipped it around so I could see.

"Family resemblance, huh?" she said.

She'd opened the page to a photo of Luther Ludlow. It was one of those old photos where the people look all grim, and it was grainy and washed, but it was almost like we were looking at Orson Ludlow, our gun-toting abductor. "Spooky, right?"

"Oh yeah," I said. "Are Julian and Lucas in there too?"

"Nope," she said. "They're probably in the sequel. Know what else I found?"

"What? They're vampires?"

"Shut up," she said, thumbing through pages. "It says here that Luther Ludlow's grave has never been found and he supposedly had some magic rocks buried with him that they all thought would lead them to the treasure; *stones of power* from his bullshit ceremonies."

"Where's he buried now?" I asked, a little concerned that she was going to say something like "right where you're standing!" or maybe just "Owl Harbor" because the last thing we needed was even more gun-toting weirdos sniffing around. I was starting to think we needed a sign on the gift shop door that said, *Relax, we made all this shit up.*

"They think it's up in the foothills somewhere."

"Good to know," I said. "Perhaps we can send flowers."

"Shut up," she said. "Is the pizza ready?"

"Not yet," I said in my best hillbilly voice, giving the stove a knock. "This ain't one or your newfangled microwaves like you got back in the city."

She rolled her eyes at me.

We almost never used the TV, but that night Uncle Kevin told us he wanted to watch the news. There was a station out of Sacramento he could get if he twisted the antenna just right, a source of amusement for Lily who had not been aware there was TV that didn't come through a cable or the internet until we'd moved to the Delta. We'd watched the "Tween Psychic" segment that way.

Uncle Kevin thought the nine o'clock news might have something about our abduction. I was kind of surprised that we hadn't had news trucks out front, but I guess the fact that we weren't missing made us less interesting, even though there was a family of cult conspiracy theorists with guns who could've been anywhere at that point. We weren't expecting to make the lead story—it turned out to be something about a serial killer coyote that was attacking dogs on the west side of Vacaville—but we never learned where we fell in the lineup. A knock at the door cut our evening viewing short.

Uncle Kevin peeked through the curtains first and then opened the door. Mia stood outside. "You guys weren't answering," she said. "I was worried."

Uncle Kevin took the three steps to the wall phone, picking the receiver up and holding it to his ear while he clicked the hook thing a few times. I didn't really have a good idea of how landlines worked, but the look on his face told me something was wrong. "It's dead," he said. "It was working this afternoon, but it's dead now."

"Use your phone and see if there's a service outage or something," I said to Mia.

"I don't have a phone," she said. "Remember? I lost it in the wreck."

Okay, so normally your phone goes out and it's no big deal. It's usually just broken or services is down or maybe a squirrel chewed through the wire. But when you've been abducted and your abductors are crazy cult guys and they're still at large, it's probably one of those rare times when it's smart to jump to conclusions.

"Shit," I said. "Do you think it's them?"

22

"I DIDN'T SEE ANY CARS," MIA SAID, "NOT IN THE parking lot."

Uncle Kevin put the phone back on the wall. "You guys grab your stuff. I don't know if it's them," he said. "But we're not going to wait around to find out."

Mia looked at me. "I probably should have told my mom I was coming over here," she said. "But she probably wouldn't have let me if she'd known."

I didn't really have any "stuff" to get together, but Lily ran upstairs to get her backpack. Waiting at the front door with Uncle Kevin and Mia, I peeked through the curtains.

"I don't see anybody," I said.

Uncle Kevin reached for the knob and swung the door open really slow, stopping to listen. "We're heading straight for the car, quick as rabbits," he said, grabbing Lily by the forearm. "Ready?"

He didn't wait for an answer. A half second later

we were all sprinting down the white gravel path toward Uncle Kevin's Wagoneer.

The one with four flat tires.

We all kind of skidded to a stop, and if somebody had taken video it probably looked pretty funny. But there was nothing funny about your getaway car slumped into the gravel on four slashed tires. We were all turning to run for Mia's mom's pickup when we heard a voice that was becoming all too familiar.

"Goin' somewhere?" said Orson Ludlow, stepping out from the shadows on the front porch of the attraction. "We just need a little of your time, if you don't mind."

Uncle Kevin stepped forward, and Lily hid behind him. "We've called the cops," he said. "They're on their way."

"Kinda hard to call the cops without a phone line."

"We used the girl's phone."

"This one?" he said, holding what I recognized even in the dark as Mia's hot-pink phone case. "The one she left behind in the crash?"

My eyes had adjusted enough to the darkness that I could see two, Julian and Lucas on either side of the gift shop door, about a dozen feet behind their grandfather.

"All we need is the little girl," Orson said. "You're going to show us the bottles—the real ones—and then we're going to take the girl on a field trip. That's all. Let's continue our conversation inside."

He gestured with his gun toward the attraction, and we walked over, the four of us pretty tight together and Lily with one arm around Uncle Kevin's waist and the other holding onto me. Julian or Lucas had already broken the lock on the gift shop door because all the older one had to do was push on it and it swung open. Lucas stepped inside, and the lights came on a few seconds later.

It's not like the gift shop was particularly tight quarters. I'd given the "may not be appropriate for pregnant women blah blah blah" speech to as many as a dozen people in there at once. But it can feel pretty crowded with just seven people if two of them had guns. Lucas must have had a gun in the rental car because he was waving it around to make sure we noticed it.

"Here's how this is going to work," Orson announced, gesturing with his hands the way some people do except one of his hands had a gun in it. "You're going to show us the real bottles, and she's going to read the messages."

"The real bottles don't have messages in them," I said, surprising myself by taking part in the conversation. "They're super old. The paper's long gone."

Orson nodded his head to one side. "She don't need no paper. She has the gift," he said. "Put the bottle in her hands, and she will know the way. The water. The intentions. And the power of all that. It's the way it worked for Luther Ludlow, and it's the way it's going to work for your Madam Lilith here."

Okay, so this is stupid because we were in full-on crisis situation, but my thought in that moment was how stupid the name Madam Lilith sounded when a guy who really believed that "Madam Lilith" had powers said it. And I found myself hoping that Lily would see how stupid it sounded and drop the whole thing too when it was all over.

If any of us made it through the night with the Lunatic Ludlows.

"These bottles," he said, and he pointed to the glass cases on the wall before walking over and using the gun like a hammer to break through the glass. With most of the glass shattered all over the carpet, he knocked aside the remaining shards with the barrel of his gun before reaching into the case and handing bottles to Julian, who was lining them up on the counter next to the cash register.

Lucas kept his gun on us the whole time, though more than once he looked out the window and toward the road.

"Come here, little missy," the elder Ludlow said to Lily. "I want you to hold these bottles in your hand, feel the power of the water, and tell us what message you feel in that power."

Lily was having none of it. She'd been hiding behind Uncle Kevin since the Ludlows had showed up.

"Come on," he said again, still in that kindly but creepy granddad voice and then, "Come on," but with a tone of menace this time that wasn't grandfatherly at all.

I don't think he was really aiming at anything, but when the window behind us exploded into a cloud of tiny crystals, it struck me that it was the second gunshot I'd heard that day. I guess Lily wasn't anxious to hear a third because she stepped forward saying, "Okay, okay."

She stepped across the room slowly. She tried to bring Uncle Kevin with her, pulling him by one hand, but Lucas put one hand up, the other hand still holding the gun. "Just you," he said. "He needs to stay back there."

I could see Lily's knees shaking. I stepped forward, instinctively, but Lucas raised his gun and Mia drew me back with her arm on my shoulder.

"So," Lily said, when she was standing in front of the bottles, "am I supposed to guess the favorite? Pick a favorite? Tell me this isn't spin the bottle."

The Orson patriarch looked impatient, which was understandable when you have a gun and the eleven-year-old is still giving you attitude, but I'd never been more proud.

"You hold the bottle. You feel the power. You tell us where to find the Ludlow fortune. Whatever you see in your head, whatever vision comes to you, tell us what you see."

"I'll try," she said. "But the whole gun thing is throwing me off."

"Don't worry, my child," Orson said. "We wouldn't hurt you. You alone can lead us to our rightful inheritance."

She got quiet for a moment and then reached up for the first bottle. Holding it in her hands, feeling the weight of it, watching the water swirl inside. There was something in her posture, the way she held her shoulders, that gave me the feeling she had an idea. You take care of a kid for a long enough time and you know when they're up to something. It's like the way moms always know when you're lying.

"I see," she said, and I knew she was lying with just those two syllables. "I see a small town, in the mountains. It's near a canyon, and at the mouth of the canyon there is a graveyard. I see a grave. It's marked, but it's marked wrong." Orson leaned over her. His eyes wide. I almost felt like telling him, "Look, dude, she's taking you for a ride." Lucas and Julian kept looking over at her, Lucas's hand tight on the gun.

"That's all I see," Lily announced, placing the bottle back up on the counter. "The vision is complete."

"That's not enough," the elder Ludlow said. "We need more. Tell us more."

He handed her another bottle.

This time she took longer. Lily could spin up a pretty good bullshit story when she needed, but this one had to be really good. It had to be enough to make them think they'd figure it out, that they would know whatever town she was making up.

"There is a hotel," she said. "An old hotel. And a town square with clock."

Mom had dragged us all over California, staying in state park campgrounds and visiting all the historic stuff. I swear she could close her eyes and point to the nearest visitors' center. It was like we couldn't just have a vacation. She had to go all "homeschool mom". That meant we were visiting every quaint little town from one end of California to the other, and let me tell you, there are *a lot* of quaint little towns.

And *every one of them* had a hotel and a town square, and there was almost always a clock on some stone building. And there was always a church, which is the next thing she mentioned. It was almost like she was describing a movie set for a movie about a small California town.

"There's a small restaurant that serves breakfast," she said.

I worried that she was laying it on too quaint, but it looked like Orson Ludlow's gears were turning, like he was thinking of a particular town, or had already been thinking of it, and everything Lily said fit because every little town in California had all of that stuff.

But then he saw a problem.

"If the grave is mismarked," he said, "how will we know which one to search?"

Lily's shoulders tensed. She was no longer coaxing them along on her liar's journey. She was no longer feeding them plates full of B.S. that they were spooning down and asking for more.

She'd screwed up.

There was no way they didn't know the story about the lost grave of Luther Ludlow. Lily had said it was in several of the books Uncle Kevin had. It was basic Ludlow lore. They were looking for the magic rocks. I was certain.

She could have said something about it being under a cliff that was next to a waterfall or something, and they might have gone looking for it on their own. But it's not like they were going to go to some graveyard in a town that matched the bullshit description she'd given them and start digging up graves until they found old man Ludlow.

No, they'd need Lily to either spit out a name, or go with them to point out the grave.

The moment kind of hung there, on that sticking point, for a minute. I'd already figured out that she could just make up a name, Jebediah Standish maybe, but I think Orson asking for a specific name had thrown her off.

She panicked.

"I cannot see a name," she said. "The vision has not shown me that."

And then she added, "Sorry," in this squeaky little voice that she used when she really wasn't sorry but she wanted to fool Mom or somebody into maybe questioning her sincerity instead of questioning the bigger lie she'd come up with to get out of whatever she was trying to get out of.

Orson wasn't worried about whether she'd meant it or not. He was chasing a mystery, and an eleven-year-old girl had suddenly laid out a solution.

"We'll just need to take you with us," he said.

There are moments in life that give you a kind of freeze-frame memory, like you'll be able to look back fifty years later and recall specific details: what time it was, where everybody was standing, maybe what you were wearing. I have a memory like that when Mom told us Dad had left.

And I knew as soon as Orson Ludlow said those words that I had another.

"Wait a minute—no way, no fucking way," I said, as if the fact that they had guns didn't matter. Because it didn't. There was no way I was going to allow them to take Lily anywhere.

I'd crossed the room before Lucas could even raise his gun, and I hit the elder Ludlow in the chest with my shoulder, a full tackle that sent him sprawling into a novelty license plate display rack. He crashed to the floor just as the lights went out, a reflex move by Uncle Kevin that turned out to be the best move he could have made. I'd been working in that room all summer, ringing up ticket sales and starting the tours. I knew it a whole better than the Ludlows.

I'm sure Lucas was waving his gun all over the place, but he didn't have a target. When he did fire the gun, he shot a hole through the ceiling. I didn't wait around to assess damages. I pulled Lily behind me under the turnstile, dragging her through when I saw a second form right behind her and knew immediately it was Mia.

I knew Uncle Kevin was back in the gift shop with the Ludlow trio, but I also knew he'd want us to get out if we could. I kicked the door shut between the gift shop and the hallway where the tour started and stood up, lifting Lily to her feet while Mia shoved a chair in front of the door. Lily seemed more in shock than anything, and I was glad she wasn't screaming, even though she would have been totally justified in screaming her little lungs out.

"Let's go," I said.

There are two light switches at the start of the tour. One turned on the lights in the hallway; the one we always switched off when we started our spooky speech about the parallel universes. The other turned on everything in the rest of the tour. I flipped that up but left the hallway dark.

"This way," I said.

We sprinted past the first stop, the room with the peepholes and the distorted floor, but when we got to the mirrored hallway, I stopped. We could see the delayed video loop of ourselves at the end of the hall. One of the things Uncle Kevin had shown me when he was teaching me the routine was a button low on the wall we could toggle with our foot to set the video on endless loop. I told Lily to stand in the center of the hall, and Mia and I stood back while I reached down to hit the switch.

"What are you doing?" Mia asked. Lily remained silent.

"We need to slow them down," I said. We'd heard the crash through the door from the gift shop a few seconds before. "They'll think they found Lily."

The next stop was a bigger part of my plan, a plan I was making up as we sprinted through. Our best chance, I'd decided, was to trap them in the attraction. We couldn't know for sure if they'd slashed Mia's tires. I didn't want to get outside and not have a getaway car waiting for us. Getaway cars can be crucial when the guys you're getting away from have guns.

We slipped into the Well of Worlds room, and I shut the door behind us. "You two go over to the other side," I said. "Lily, show her the way."

The Well of Worlds was a square room with a big

hole in the middle and a glass edge. The edge was easier to see if it was dark, and the rings of light made it look like it dropped into infinity, but with the lights turned to blinding—and the glass edge extended halfway over the pit—there was a good chance at least one Ludlow would blunder over the edge and go right into the water.

It wasn't until we were in the room with the lights out and the glow of the infinity rings as the only point of reference that I realized I didn't really have a backup plan. If all three guys came barging in, the odds weren't good that all three of them would fall in. I could hope that at least one was back in the gift shop dealing with Uncle Kevin. We hadn't heard any shots since Lucas Ludlow had blown a hole in the ceiling, so there was a good chance Uncle Kevin was either holding his own or one of the Ludlows was holding a gun on him. Probably Orson, who would have sent the younger Ludlows into the attraction.

It was quiet in the Well of Worlds, but we could hear shouting out in the hall. "Come out, come out, wherever you are!" came one voice, echoed a moment later by a different voice.

"Lucas, there she is."

I heard glass crashing and guessed they'd taken out video-loop Lily. I was relieved that I didn't hear a gunshot, but I guess they needed the world's cutest psychic alive.

"You guys stay right there," I whispered to Mia and Lily. "I'm going to blind them with the light, and they'll walk right into the pit. Keep your eyes shut when he comes in."

The attraction wasn't built to any high standard of structural integrity. Like the farmhouse, it would creak when a mouse walked across the floor. I heard one of them outside the door, and I kept my hand on the switch. "I'll check this one," I heard him shout.

The door opened, and I let him take two steps into the room before I slammed the door shut and pulled the big industrial switch that turned on the lights.

I never asked Uncle Kevin where he got the lights or whether it was safe to have that kind of voltage in a rickety wooden building, but I sometimes wondered if he'd stolen them from a football stadium. They were that kind of bright.

And that kind of blinding.

Even through my eyelids, the glare hurt.

The drone bro, I couldn't see which one, didn't wait for his eyes to adjust. "There you are!" he shouted, and I could hear him step onto the glass.

The next thing I heard was a cracking followed by "Whoa!" followed by a splash. I yanked the switch to *Off* and opened my eyes. Mia and Lily were already coming toward me, sticking to the wall to avoid the yawning hole in the middle of the room and the splashing stream of profanity that came echoing out of it.

There were about three places in the attraction that the other Ludlow brother could be, four if you counted the Haunted Pendulum, but he had to have heard his brother fall, and he'd still be hearing the volcano of expletives coming out of the Well of

Worlds. That meant he was coming our way and probably coming fast.

"This way," I yelled as Mia and Lily followed me through the door. The next stretch of the hallway had a dozen chromed plastic mannequins hanging from the rafters and a strobe light I hit with my left hand as we passed through. I don't think Uncle Kevin had ever even named it as a stop on the tour. I always wondered if he'd come up with the idea or if somebody's truck had broken down on the way back from Burning Man.

Whatever it was, I was hoping it would be harder for the remaining Ludlow brother to see us with mannequins swinging all over the place and the lights flashing. The fog machine on the same circuit with the strobe lights might help too.

When we heard, "Julian! Where are you? Julian!" on the other side of the mannequin dance party, it gave me at least some confidence that we had a chance to get away. Maybe brothers don't leave each other behind.

Our best bet was the last stop on the tour: the Room of No Return.

It was the Room of No Return because the tour was over, but to get people into the room and not be trapped with them, the trick was to have them all to step in ahead of you. There was actually a sliding panel in the hallway right before you got there that hid a closet-size space. They'd be strolling down the hall looking at the weird paintings and stuff and turn around to find you'd vanished. They'd keep going, and then you'd trigger the sliding wall that would trap them in the room.

A lot of people told us it was their favorite part of the whole tour because they kind of had to figure it out for themselves, although, really, twisting a candlestick to trigger a fake wall to open was some pretty standard horror movie stuff.

And it was a perfect place to trap a guy who was trying to grab you.

The hidey spot wasn't really perfect for three people though, even if one of them was pretty dinky even for an eleven-year-old.

"In here!" I said and slid open the hidden panel. Lily stepped in first. Mia squeezed in with her, and then I had to really wedge myself in to get the door shut.

"Ouch," Lily said. She was jammed pretty hard into a corner. I felt bad saying "Shush," but we had to be quiet for it to work.

I was practically on top of Mia. We were facing each other, and the only way we could all squeeze into the space was for me to put my arms around her shoulders. She snaked her hands down around my waist. We'd shared a couple of quick kisses, and now we were pressed up against each other in the dark, practically entangled. Her head was against my shoulder. I could feel her breath on my chest.

The closed space grew warm with our body heat, making the cramped space seem even more cramped. My breath fell into rhythm with Mia's, and it helped me stay calm even as I could sense Lily boiling toward panic. You don't have to be an actual claustrophobe to start freaking out when you're squeezed into a couple of square feet of sweaty darkness so tight that you can barely breathe and somebody with a gun is hunting you down.

"We need to be super quiet," I whispered. "He's going to be right on the other side of this wall in a minute."

That minute seemed to last an eternity. I became conscious of every sound. The brothers were yelling to each other from a couple of rooms away, but up close every sound was exaggerated: the creak of the floor under our feet, the three of us breathing, Mia's heart beating against mine. On the other side of the hidden door, the yelling started to quiet down. There really wasn't a way out of the Well of Worlds pit without a rope or a ladder. The most a rescuer could do without one or the other would be to fall in there with you.

It took them several minutes for them to figure that out. Several minutes during which Mia's face was against my neck and my arms were holding her bare shoulders.

Several minutes during which we all tried to breathe as quietly as possible.

Finally, I heard his footsteps in the hall and the sound of a mannequins bumping up against the wall as he pushed through. A second later he was just inches away from us.

To pull the lever that pushed the false wall into place required me to get up on my toes and reach over Mia's head with my right hand. It took a pretty good shove, and I wasn't sure how easy that was going to be, squeezed into such a small space.

Plus, I had to time it just right. He had to be all the way into the Room of No Return before I shoved the fake wall into place, or he'd just grab it and stop it. And if that happened, he'd know right where we were.

We all held our breath, listening to the footsteps. There was a floorboard that made a particular creak near the fake fireplace on the side of the room across from the wall that I was about to slide closed. When I was giving tours, I always waited until I heard that creak to push the wall into place.

We waited. I heard footsteps, but I didn't hear the telltale squeak.

I wasn't sure how much longer we could wait without Lily exploding.

It wouldn't have taken him long to figure out that we weren't in the room. There were a couple of overstuffed chairs we could have hidden behind and a curtain hung on one wall to make it look like there might be a window. It was basically a dead end for hide-and-seek.

But he seemed to be taking his time. I let myself take a half breath.

And then the floorboard creaked.

I shoved the lever as hard as I could, and I heard the wall move on the rollers, sliding into place and clicking the latch.

I knew we'd trapped him when he started pounding on the wall.

The moving wall was a one-way affair. Nobody on the tours ever tried to open it because they knew it just opened into the hallway they'd just come through, but Uncle Kevin had still built a latch into it so that they'd give up on moving it if they did try.

It turned out to be a solid latch. The wall shook, but it didn't move.

The other wall, the one that customers usually took about three minutes to figure out, wouldn't move either, not with the peg Uncle Kevin had shoved into place a couple of hours ago on the outside.

"Two points for Owl Harbor, zilch for the visiting team," Mia whispered as we pulled ourselves out of the steamy little hidey hole.

But two Ludlows neutralized meant we still had Orson Ludlow to deal with. I wasn't ready to declare him the brains of the operation, not when they had so little brains to spare, but I still thought he was the most dangerous, even if he was probably just the meanest and certainly the most unbalanced.

I didn't want to go walking back into the gift shop and the line of fire without a good look first. We gave the tours as a straight-shot path from the gift shop to the Room of No Return, and there really wasn't a way to break off that path. If you weren't taking the turn-the-candlestick exit, the only other way out was to retrace your steps and end up back at the gift shop.

I stood there for a few seconds trying to come up with a strategy, standing under one of those Edison bulbs which probably made me look super mysterious because Mia and Lily tugged on my arm almost simultaneously, saying, "Nathan?" practically in harmony.

"I've got an idea," I said. "This way."

The video-loop mirror trick was accomplished with lights, a sheet of glass, and a video projector. The projector had to be tucked out of sight or it would ruin the whole gag. Uncle Kevin had built a box into the storeroom wall so that it wouldn't protrude into the hallway and mess up the effect, and I'd seen it two hours before when he'd been showing me the bottles. It looked like a wooden crate, and it could slide back so that he could change the light bulbs and do whatever it was you have to do to keep projectors working.

If I was right, it was just big enough for us to squeeze through.

When we got to the hallway, glass was everywhere. It must have been pretty obvious when they got close that Lily wasn't really standing at the end of the hallway watching them approach, but they'd charged through anyway. I hadn't heard a gunshot, but I imagined them using the gun to smash through the glass the way Orson had smashed open the glass case with the bottles.

Without the glass, the projection of Lily standing there and looking sad beamed up across the wood-paneled walls, all distorted and stretched out. I had to kick the big chunks of glass aside before I could bend down and shove on the box that held the projector. It slid far enough in so there was just enough room for us to squeeze through into the storeroom.

"After you, ladies," I said. "Watch out for the glass."

Mia and Lily were standing in the dark storeroom when I crawled through the hole. I reached over, feeling for the light switch. "This next part is top secret," I said. "Do you swear to tell no one?"

I have to admit it was a weird time to get playful, but I couldn't resist the drama. Still, I didn't wait for an answer before I flipped the switch and opened the door to the back of the attraction.

There we were, standing in a room full of blue bottles, blue bottles that obviously hadn't floated down the river in the back of a fleeing Ludlow's rowboat.

"I knew it!" Lily exclaimed.

Mia smiled at me. "Duh," she said.

I was glad the storeroom was locked with a deadbolt. If Uncle Kevin had put a padlock on the outside, we would have had no choice but to go back into the gift shop and whatever Orson Ludlow had waiting for us.

I turned the light back off before I opened the door. It was dark as hell outside. One of the things you learn when you live in the country is that there are no streetlights. Most of the world is pretty damned dark, and Owl Harbor is no exception. The lights in the house were off, but from the way the lights reflected off the gravel, I could tell the gift shop lights were on.

"Mia," I whispered, "take Lily. Follow the ditch to the high school. I'll find you there. I'm going to check on Uncle Kevin."

"Nate," Lily whispered, fiercely, "come with us. Uncle Kevin would want you to get away."

"She's right," Mia said.

I looked at Mia, ignoring the insistent glare that I

couldn't see in the darkness but knew was coming from Lily.

"Look," I said. "I can't just leave Uncle Kevin there by himself. At some point the guy stuck in the room is going to kick through a wall or something. Then he'll have two Ludlows to deal with. Maybe I can distract Grandpa Ludlow, and Uncle Kevin can get away."

I could barely see Mia's face in the dark, but her body language told me she was unconvinced.

"The old guy doesn't look like a track star, and I doubt he has night vision. If I can get him to chase me outside, I'm sure I can get away and Uncle Kevin can get out of there. Just take Lily."

Mia pulled me close again. Put her head to my shoulder again. Her breath on my neck again. "Be careful," she whispered. "For your sister. And for me."

Lily was pulling on her to leave, and I watched the two disappear into the darkness of the brush.

I had no idea what to expect in the gift shop. For all I knew Grandpa Ludlow and Uncle Kevin would be playing cards. It was also possible that that Luther Ludlow's identical descendant had taken off when he'd figured out his grandsons were trapped.

I still didn't know where they'd parked, and I had a sinking feeling he'd left the rental car at the high school, which I wished I'd thought of before I sent Lily and Mia that direction.

I stepped carefully, sticking close to the walls so I'd stay in the shadows. When I got to the front of the attraction, the part of the building all done up in the haunted-mansion façade, I was near the end with the gift shop. I didn't hear anything from inside, and I knew that if just I stepped up onto the wood plank porch, the creak would be the equivalent of ringing the doorbell.

So I stepped as carefully and quietly as I could, transferring the weight onto the wood very slowly. Pulling myself up to where I could peek through the corner of the window, bracing myself on the frame to peer through a display of pewter shot glasses commemorating Gold Rush crap. When I could finally get into position, what I saw was Uncle Kevin zip-tied to the bench where people waited for tours, gagged with one of those dumb cowboy bandanas we sold. The bench was built into the wall. Otherwise, I'm sure Uncle Kevin would have dragged it halfway across the parking lot by now.

What I didn't see was Orson Ludlow.

It was possible he was hiding somewhere in the gift shop—behind the counter, maybe—but it was more likely he'd gone into the attraction to rescue his idiot grandsons. I could hear both of them yelling, and I wasn't even inside the building. I didn't stop to come up with a plan.

In a drawer next to the cash register, we kept a pair of scissors to cut out the tickets that Uncle Kevin printed on an old inkjet. I went straight for the zip ties, and we were outside ten seconds later, running.

"Get inside the house, and lock up," I said to Uncle Kevin. "I told Mia and Lily to go to the high school. We'll bang on somebody's door and call nine-one-one."

"I'll do more than lock up," Uncle Kevin said.

I didn't hang around to figure out what he meant. I was sprinting through the brush to get to the football field, ducking through a hole in the fence I used as a shortcut when I would walk to the marina. Coming out of the brush and onto the field, the light changed. It's not like the school was all lit up, but just a few lights over doorways and the glow of exit lights inside made it seem bright. I could see well enough to run, and I sprinted across the field.

I instantly recognized a car in the parking lot as the Ludlow rental. I was relieved that Lily and Mia were nowhere near it. Rounding the corner to the front of the school, I saw them sitting on the steps, Lily leaning into Mia and Mia holding her with both arms.

"They're still in the attraction," I said, rounding the corner by the flagpole. "Uncle Kevin is in the house."

"We need to call the police," Mia said.

"Let's go meet the neighbors," I said.

The closest houses were across the street and down about a block. Lily was reluctant to move at first, but I coaxed her into motion. The lights were on at the second house. A woman in a flannel bathrobe answered the door, and Lily and I sat just inside the doorway while Mia followed her into the kitchen to call 911.

"Are you okay?" I asked Lily, who had both her arms tight around my waist with her head pressed against my stomach. She nodded against me, and I patted her on the back. "We made it," I said. "We're going to be okay. I'll keep you safe."

She nodded again.

Mia was on the phone for a while. She called out to me, and I held Lily's hand as we joined her in a kitchen that was basically a museum of the 1970s in patterned linoleum and avocado-green appliances. Our host made us hot chocolate, which was a weird thing to drink in the summer but was probably a reflex for her and comforting in a way I didn't expect.

Mia covered the phone long enough to say, "They want us to stay put," and went back to giving descriptions of the Ludlow clan. The dispatcher already knew a lot of the story. I guess Deputy Tim had filed his report. I could only hear half the conversation, but I could tell it had moved into the "keep her on the line" phase when Mia started saying stuff like "Gulf High", "I live at the marina", and "they moved here from Kentfield".

There was obviously a lot going through my head, the main thing being whether Uncle Kevin was okay and whether he should have come with us. It's kind of weird to think about now, but the part that struck me in that moment, with everything else going on, was "they moved here from Kentfield".

I'd wanted to think we were just stuck in the Delta. At best, we were visiting. But Mia was right. We'd moved.

There were three cult conspiracy clan dudes with guns trapped in roadside attraction and bent on kidnapping my sister, and all I could think was, *I guess we're Delta kids.*

23

It was only ten minutes or so until we heard the sirens, but it was the longest ten minutes ever—enough time to finish a hot chocolate and start wondering if two hot chocolates would be some kind of *most hot chocolates consumed in July* record. Our host introduced herself as "Miss Carolyn" and told us she'd known Mom and Uncle Kevin when they were kids. She'd been the school secretary.

"Your mother wasn't one of those kids you forget," she said.

Lily had mostly calmed down. She wasn't clenched quite as tightly around my waist, though the pressure increased again when she heard the sirens. Mia had called her mom, who I'm sure *wasn't* getting used to weird calls from her daughter.

We didn't step outside until we were sure the cops were at the attraction, and even then, we stayed on the porch, listening while one of the cops—whom I imagined to be Deputy Tim even though I had no real idea—barked through a megaphone. I knew "Exit the building with your hands on your head" wasn't going to work for a guy who was stuck in a pit.

"I should go over there," I said to Mia before turning to our host and asking if it was okay if Mia and Lily stayed a bit longer.

"Of course it is," she said.

I TOOK the road this time. The last thing I wanted to do was to come crawling out of the brush with a bunch of cops holding guns on a spooky mystery-house attraction. That had me, once again, balancing on the white line at the edge of the road. I had to scramble down the embankment twice to let cop cars roar by. When I got to the attraction's parking lot, there were sheriff's deputies crouched behind their cars with guns drawn, spotlights so bright it made the attraction look like a movie set.

The one with the megaphone actually was Deputy Tim, which I found oddly reassuring. Uncle Kevin was with him, which was even more reassuring. I'd worried he was going to find an old shotgun and go after the Ludlows, but all he had was a baseball bat and he'd had enough sense to wait for the cops.

"Officers!" I yelled from two steps into the parking lot with my hands over my head.

"Nathan!" Uncle Kevin yelled. "Where's Lily and Mia?"

"They're safe," I said to him. Then I looked at Deputy Tim. "I got info."

He waved me over. "Are they still in there?"

"At least one of them, I bet," I said and then told him about the Well of Worlds and the Room of No Return. "But their car is gone. So at least one of them got away too."

Deputy Tim pulled a radio off his belt and called in an alert for a white Ford sedan with rental plates, and then turned back to me. "If we go in there, what are we going to find?"

"It's complicated," I said. "Got a sheet of paper?"

It turns out police reports are all done on tablets now, but he found, of all things, a menu. I had no idea that Los Burgerritos had a location in Davis on the way to Sacramento, and I found myself wondering if that would have made it a "chain" for the 17 Poles gang.

I spread out the menu on the hood of Deputy Tim's squad car and did my best to keep from lapsing into tour speak while I sketched out a diagram of the attraction on the blank side. I had a hunch Deputy Tim didn't need to know how thin the membrane between universes was.

"He's probably still in that pit," I said, pointing to the Well of Worlds. "There's no way out without a rope or something. But the guy in that last room might have gotten out. It's just a latch, and he could have kicked the wall free, if his grandfather didn't unlatch it for him."

Two more sheriff's deputies pulled up while we were talking. I was wondering if the rest of the county was left unprotected because it was more cops than I'd seen all summer. I wasn't sure why they'd called in the crew from the Lago Vista Fire Department, but I'm sure it was the high point of their year.

It was lucky they were there though. The cops borrowed one of their ladders to get Julian Ludlow out of the pit.

In the end, the whole thing was kind of boring. They waited around a good forty-five minutes after I'd sketched up the layout before they went into the attraction, and it's not like they used a flash grenade or anything. They just kind of walked in, guns drawn and shouting warnings of course, but Deputy Tim had explained that "they're usually pretty settled down at this point, especially guys like these, from the way you described them".

Like I'd guessed, Lucas and Orson Ludlow had skipped out. I was trying to imagine the awkward conversation with Julian when they'd left him in the pit. That'd be a good story around the table at the Ludlow Thanksgiving, I was sure.

The cops did a really thorough sweep of the area around the attraction and past the high school. They even flew in a helicopter from I don't know where. It was 2:00 a.m. when they started to pack up. They'd declared "the suspects have left the area" around 12:30 and finally let me go check on Mia and Lily. They were out on the lawn at Miss Carolyn's house when I got there, along with Miss Carolyn and Mia's mom.

"Hi, Mrs. Romero," I said and got a surprisingly genuine smile in return.

"Most excitement we've had in Owl Harbor for a

while," she said. "Thanks for getting my daughter out."

"Glad I was there," I said. "Thanks for having such a great daughter. Can I borrow her for a few minutes? The cops want statements from everybody."

"I'll drive you guys over," Mia's mom said.

The pickup truck Mia had driven over was blocked in by cop cars when we got back to the attraction which was okay because one of the deputies wanted to get Mia's account of the story. Deputy Tim saw the blurry-eyed Lily and told me a detective would come by the next day.

I took her upstairs and tucked her in without protest. I sat on the end of the bed for about five minutes, holding her hand, before slipping out.

Uncle Kevin and Mia's mom were sitting on the porch when I got downstairs, talking about the "back in the day" times on the Delta. I saw the deputy finishing up with Mia and walked over. I closed my arms around her, and she looked up at me.

"Whatcha doin' next weekend?" she asked with a half grin. "It's going to be hard to top this one."

24

I WAS KIND OF SURPRISED THAT UNCLE KEVIN OPENED the attraction the next day. When I'd crawled into bed it had been past three, and he'd been up later than me. But there were a ton of cars in the parking lot when I finally stepped onto the front porch around eleven. News of "the most excitement we've had in Owl Harbor for a while" had spread quickly. Even locals who'd probably seen the attraction a dozen times wanted to walk through again and "ooh" and "ahh" at the scene of the crimes. Uncle Kevin probably knew most of them, but nearly all of them insisted on paying just the same.

It was a weird little community moment of Delta solidarity.

I was not surprised when he gave me the day off. I knew it would be at least a few days before I was ready to lead people into the Well of Worlds without tensing up about the drop off or feeling suffocated in the hidey-hole when I closed them into the Room of No Return.

Lily was on the couch reading a copy of *Teen Vogue* when I got up, something she must have picked up at a BART station. I thought it was weird in a kind of disturbing way, but I let her be.

For starters, it was nice to see her doing something normal, even if it wasn't exactly normal. I'd expected her to be staring into space or hiding under her bed when I got up. But she'd shrugged it off pretty well. Our crisis-to-crisis upbringing must have wired some resilience into both of us.

Also, she'd left me the last frosted Pop-Tart.

"I'm heading out," I said.

"Watch out for Gold Rush cultists," she said, not even glancing up.

"Will do."

The only way to reach Mia that day was to walk over and talk to her. The landline was dead, and I didn't know the number at the marina anyway. It was only a ten-minute walk, and hanging around the house didn't seem like a good idea anyway. I didn't want to fight Lily over what I had to assume was the only copy of *Teen Vogue* in the house.

I ducked through the hole in the fence, thinking about how different it had felt the night before, and was only half surprised when I saw movement on the other side of the bleachers. It was like staring through half-closed miniblinds, but the shape and motion was unmistakable.

I knew who it was before I stepped around.

She was wearing the same sports bra and running

shorts outfit she'd worn the first time I'd seen her and was slashing and stabbing at the same painting. She didn't have the phone for reference, but it didn't seem to stop her.

"I see you've rediscovered your artistic inspiration," I said, walking up from behind the easel. "Good to know." She'd seen me coming but remained focused on the work.

"It comes and goes," she said.

"Which do you prefer?" I asked, standing more or less even with the easel.

"Goes, I guess. It brings me peace to let it out. The painting gets heavier, and I get lighter."

I stepped around to look at the work forever-in-progress.

"'Heavy' is how I described it the first time I saw it," I said.

"And now?"

"Real."

"I like that too."

She dipped her brush in the jar of red paint clamped to the easel's frame. She applied one stroke and then turned to me, the brush still in hand.

"The painting is not a thing. It's a verb," she said. "It's the act itself. And yes, it's real, layers and layers of *real*."

She sounded both serious in the way she spoke and also very open. She pulled the brush across the canvas again, pressing the paint deep and dark. The sun glared over her shoulder, and I could see the sheen where the paint was still wet.

"What's beneath those layers of real?" I asked.

"Another act, another thing that happened. Do you remember that day on the Delta, out in the canoe?"

"Of course."

"We saw the magpie, remember?" she said. "I told you that the magpies can know their mortality. They can mourn. They mourn in song. I mourn in paint."

"Your father?"

"Yes, my father. He died. It was a moment. But I can't know that moment. All I can know is a place," she said. "Beneath all this paint, beneath all this... *heavy* is a map of that place."

She added a broad stroke up across the paint and then down again. "The layers are the days and weeks and years. It makes me conscious of the time that has passed, what I've forgotten, what I still remember, and all the layers in between."

"Heavy and real," I said. "I've never lost anyone like that."

"We've all lost something."

She placed the paint back into the jar and stood back, looking at a canvas now completely covered in wet paint, another layer, another week. She took my hand and laced her fingers through mine, leading me to the shade of a tree, another willow, like most of the trees. The wind was up, and the sun light coming through the leaves danced across the ground.

We sat facing each other with our legs crossed, and she took my hands. She leaned forward to brush her lips across my cheek and kept her head there on my shoulder, asking, "Do you remember what else we talked about when we saw the magpies?"

"You told me the Delta is a place and that being happy isn't all about place."

"Did I say *happy*, or did I say *satisfied*?"

"I don't know," I said. "Is there a difference?"

She sat up, moving her hands to my shoulders.

"There can be," she said. "Are you satisfied? Are you happy?"

"I'm trying to be both. You're making it easier."

"Good," she said, bringing her lips to mine. "Welcome to the Delta."

25

THERE WAS A CERTAIN PRACTICALITY IN DRIVING BACK to Kentfield and "the safe place". The fact that Mia's car was still there made it something we had to do. The fact that my mother was there made it something more daunting than practical though. That Mia was with me made it something I knew I could handle.

That she looked so effortlessly beautiful in her blue sundress made it feel like something more like an outing than an obligation. I found myself conscious of how I was dressed in a way that circumstances had not allowed on my first visit to North Bay Mental. After a ragtag summer on the Delta, I felt half ready for a job interview or a school event in my Gap shorts and button-down shirt.

It was almost like we'd dressed for a date, something that had never yet happened in all the weeks since we'd met.

We'd spent most of the four days since the night at the attraction together.

She'd come along on the first tour I'd guided, giggling—though not loudly—when I'd warned the guests that to descend into the Well of Worlds was to be "trapped and held in a reality you may find yourself unable to escape". I'd helped out at the marina snack bar two nights in a row, and we'd both spent an hour or so on "el barge de la fiesta". Hattie hadn't even seemed to mind when Hannah and Mia had sat off by themselves and shared stories from elementary school.

The time we'd spent alone was very different from the weeks when we'd hung out at the marina. The night at the attraction and the kisses under the willow tree had changed everything. We knew what it was to hold and to be held. I knew how her body quivered when my lips brushed her neck. We'd shared a physical urgency in those moments I'd never felt before.

I think the drive back to Kentfield would have been harder if not for those four days and that unknowable number of additional kisses. Driving the Wagoneer with its bench seat, she could sit close to me, and I could rest my arm across her bare shoulders.

It hadn't taken a lot of elbow twisting to convince Uncle Kevin to let me borrow the Wagoneer, even with just a learner's permit. "On the Delta, we learn to drive in grade school," he'd told us.

As we got closer to the park where we hoped Mia's car was still parked, I started pointing out places I remembered: a school we'd attended for a half a year when I'd been in sixth grade, the pool where I'd learned to swim, and no less than three apartments we'd lived in. I must have sounded nervous, or maybe I was just talking too fast, because Mia put her hand on my shoulder. "They're just places," she said. "They're where you were, not who you are."

"I know," I said.

"Remember that," she said. "We're almost there."

When we got to the park, it was sunnier than it had been the morning the Ludlows grabbed us, and we were relieved to see Mia's car still there. I parked behind her, across the park from North Bay Mental. We'd been in the car for nearly two hours, and I still thought an extra two hundred yards would better prepare me.

"It's going to be okay," Mia said as she unlocked her car.

"Are you sure?"

"Of course not," she said with a playful smile, "but I thought you needed to hear that."

She leaned back against the car and pulled me toward her, her forehead meeting my chest.

"Call me when you're done."

"I will," I said and leaned down to kiss her.

She unlocked her car as I stepped away.

WALKING ACROSS THE PARK, I felt like I was in the real world and not the tunnel-vision blur I'd dragged myself through a few days before. I saw a couple staring at their phones while their kids climbed all over the playground. I noticed the way the wind tugged at the tops of the redwoods but left the lower branches still. I'm pretty sure the statue was wearing a different shirt than he'd had on a few days before.

The truth was I didn't need to do it. I could have gotten into the Wagoneer and been back in Owl Harbor in time to guide a tour or two and pocket the tips. But there were things I needed to tell my mother and things she needed to hear.

The same receptionist was working at the desk in the atrium. It was obvious she recognized me. I don't think a lot of teenagers show up on their own for visits. She called inside when she saw me, and Dr. Brayden met me at the door. She wore a business suit, blue, and looked more like a real estate agent this time. She'd probably been giving tours to prospective residents. I wondered what that had been like for Mom.

"I'm glad you called this time," the doctor told me. "Your mother is better prepared for your visit."

"Thanks," I said. "How prepared is she to leave?"

"That depends."

"On what?"

"In part, on what happens during your visit."

She took me to a different room with a big window that looked out onto the park. Mom was already there, sitting on a love seat. She turned to me as soon I stepped into the room, her eyes brightening. "Nathan," she said, "you're back."

"Yeah, Mom. They couldn't keep me away."

She patted the cushion next to her, and I sat

down. Dr. Brayden took a seat by the window across from the loveseat but not directly facing it, like in the other room. She didn't bring a notepad, but she still had a pen and she rolled it between her thumb and forefinger. She seemed content to wait for us to speak.

"You look good, Mom," I said.

"I feel good," she said. "I've been feeling better since you came to see me. I feel like there are things we can talk about that were maybe harder before. I feel more *together*."

"That's nice, Mom," I said. "I'm glad."

Mom had her hair pulled back, which she almost never did at home, and tied with a black hair band. She looked at me when she spoke. "Tell me about Owl Harbor," she said. "Tell me what you've been doing. Tell me about life on the Delta."

Okay, so there were several directions I could have taken the conversation at that point, and I spent some time on the easiest of those. I told her how I'd learned the tour guide act and how "Uncle Kevin thinks I'm almost ready for a top hat". She smiled at that. I told her, "I've met a girl. I think you'll like her," and she laughed.

"Watch out for those Delta girls," she said.

"I know. They're nothing but trouble, especially when they grow up," I said, and I was happy to see her smile.

That went on for a while. She asked me if we'd been to Los Burgerritos, and I said, "Only about fifty times." She asked me about Mia, and I told her about

Mia's job at the marina. "Her bedroom is a boat!" I said.

I'm sure Dr. Brayden was bored by all of that, maybe regretting that she hadn't brought a notepad to doodle in. It was deeply ordinary stuff—"what I did on my summer vacation" stuff. But I liked the ordinary. With mom, ordinary had been in short supply for a long time.

I would have liked to stick with ordinary for even longer, but I knew that wasn't what I was there for.

I had to will myself not to find something in the park to stare at when I spoke. "Mom," I said, facing her, "we need to talk about things."

"We are talking about things," she said.

"I mean about important things—big things, family things."

She leaned back, just slightly, her hand still on mine.

"You've been worried," I said, "for as long as I can remember, that there were people after us, that bad things were going to happen, and that you could see what was coming."

"I know," she said. "That's why I'm here. I'm learning to let go of that, as much of it as I can. Your Uncle Kevin helped me decide to come here, you know?"

"What do you mean?" I asked.

"He gave me a bottle, one of the blue bottles from Owl Harbor. He wanted me to find a safe place. To write about what I needed, and what I needed was a safe place. He told me to put that message in the bottle."

I smiled. I'd thought that she'd written the note, a coded message to us. It wasn't a message *from* her. It was a message *for* her. It was a big brother taking care of his little sister. That was something I could understand.

I was so focused on her eyes, on her reaction that for a moment I forgot that Dr. Brayden was there. I thought about what Dad had seen in those eyes, whether he'd tried, whether he'd tried hard enough and how I knew that I couldn't stop trying, *wouldn't* stop trying. "Well, some bad things happened that nobody saw coming, and that's okay because everybody is all right now. Everybody's safe."

Her jaw tightened. "What do you mean?"

The last week was not a story that unspooled in thirty words or fewer, especially when you are choosing those words carefully. I started with "Madam Lilith" and saw Mom hold her breath as I described how her daughter became a viral hero. "Lily got to feel special," I said. "It was really cool."

And then the harder parts.

She sat very still while I told the whole story, as if she were saving her questions until I was done. I told her how we'd ended up in Kentfield the day I saw her. I told her about the Ludlows taking us back to the Delta, the wreck, and then the night at the Attraction.

I tried to be as honest as I could but also as quick and clear as possible. I had consigned Dr. Brayden to my peripheral vision, and I wasn't sure how long I could go on before she'd press some button and orderlies would show up. But she seemed as wrapped up in the story as Mom.

And Mom was calm but paying attention in a way I didn't think I'd seen a few days before.

"This isn't really easy to talk about, Mom," I said, after I'd assured her I was okay and Lily was okay and both Uncle Kevin and the greater Owl Harbor community had survived the excitement. "But there was something you said when I was here before that I think is important."

"What's that?" she asked. Her voice was soft—relaxed even, not the voice I'd grown up with, the one she used when she was sure that the end of the world would come thudding on the doorstep every morning.

"You said that just because you worry about something and it happens, it doesn't mean you knew it was going to happen."

"Yes," she said.

"And nobody could have known all this would happen, right?"

"Yes," she said again.

The words did not come easy to her, but they came. Her eyes drifted from mine, first to the window and the sun on the park, then to her hands. She held them clasped tight in her lap and studied them closely before releasing her grip to watch the blood return to her palms.

"I guess when I'm ready to come home," she said, "we need to get used to not knowing what's coming, huh?"

"Which home?" I asked, my voice turning soft.

"Owl Harbor, I think."

I leaned in to put my arm around her shoulder. "That sounds right," I said.

WALKING through the atrium on my way out, I felt the air in my lungs in a way I had not when I'd last taken those steps. The fog divided the sky, leaving part of the park in shadow and a larger and growing part in light. I was halfway across the street when I remembered that I'd promised to call Mia from the hospital phone when I was done.

I was about to turn around when I saw, all the way across the park, Mia's car still parked behind the Wagoneer. I heard her voice behind me.

"Heavy?" she asked.

I turned around. Our eyes met.

"It gets lighter," I said.

A LOOK AT: THE ATTRACTION: ILLUSION RUN

Rick Polito continues the story of Nate and Lily in this sequel to the hilarious mystery *The Attraction: House of Illusion*.

After a violent encounter with the descendants of a Gold Rush cult who believe his family's House of Illusion roadside attraction will lead them to their rightful treasure, Nate Caldwell is attempting to settle into life on the California Delta with his sister Lily and his girlfriend Mia.

But when a massive flood forces them to flee their small town, they soon find themselves back in the hands of the same depraved family and forced to outwit their captors in the Sierra foothills.

"An engaging and moving blend of comedy, suspense, and a well-defined male teen voice."—*Kirkus Reviews* on *The Attraction: House of Illusion*

AVAILABLE JANUARY 2022

ACKNOWLEDGMENTS

I'd like to thank every teacher, newspaper editor and reader who supported me as I learned my way around the keyboard, and especially Carol Dow and Kristin Tully at Sahuaro High School. And, of course, thank you to the team at Wise Wolf Books for believing in this story.

ABOUT THE AUTHOR

As a career journalist and a former newspaper reporter, Rick Polito has covered everything from political scandals and natural disasters to taking his dog to a pet psychic seminar. Polito attended the University of Missouri School of Journalism and worked at newspapers in Arizona and California. Along the way, he won multiple state and national feature and news writing awards and fit in a stretch as a syndicated humor columnist. Jokes from that column have been quoted in places as varied as The Tonight Show and The New Yorker, with his viral Wizard of Ozsynopsis tweeted, posted and shared hundreds of millions of times. Polito prides himself on "thinking three jokes ahead," a skill he has taken on stage as an occasional standup comic.

Polito writes in the young adult genre because he appreciates the "urgency" of the teen years and believes it takes readers to a place that is both dramatic and familiar to everyone. A father of two and a native of Arizona, Polito now lives in Denver, with his girlfriend Angela and Rocket, the insane Jack Russell Terrier.

CPSIA information can be obtained
at www.ICGtesting.com
Printed in the USA
LVHW030329301221
707525LV00006B/653

9 781953 944160